Emeline

Finding Strength

During the Panic of 1893

Emeline

Finding Strength

During the Panic of 1893

KATHY J PERRY

Finding Strength (During the Panic of 1893)
Copyright © 2024 by Kathy J Perry

Manufactured in the United States of America. All rights reserved. No other part of
this book may be reproduced in any form or by any electronic or mechanical means,
including information storage and retrieval systems, without permission in writing from
the publisher, except by a reviewer, who may quote brief passages in a review.
Published by Chickadee Words, LLC, Kansas City, MO, first edition

For more by this author, visit KathyJPerry.com. Printed in the United States of America
Finding Strength Softcover ISBN: 978-1-7357338-4-5
Finding Strength Hardcover ISBN: 978-1-7357338-3-8
Finding Strength E-book ISBN: 978-1-7357338-5-2
Finding Strength Audiobook ISBN: 978-1-7357338-6-9

Library of Congress Control Number: 2024900007

Bible verses were taken from
The Ryrie Study Bible, King James Version, 1986, 1994 Published
by the Moody Bible Institute of Chicago, IL

References to songs from the 1800s
Lavender Blue (partially sung)
Many others mentioned

References to books from the 1800s
The Adventures of Huckleberry Finn
Little Women
Oliver Twist

Illustrations by Claudia Gadotti
Narration by Ceci Garcia
Edited by Fija Callaghan
Cover & Interior Design by Design for Writers @ designforwriters.com
Copyright © 2024 Kathy J Perry All rights reserved.

This book is dedicated to my daughters
Cassidy Anne and Emily Danielle

May you always have the joy of the Lord in your hearts,
strength from His promises,
and find happiness in your lives.

Contents

The Letter

In the parlor of my Indianapolis home, I stood, speechless, the news dangling from my hand.

"My goodness, child, what does it say?" Clara Witherspoon asked. She smoothed her apron and put her hands on her hips.

Her husband fetched his pipe and carefully packed it with fresh tobacco, a sign of stress in the middle of the day, while Jonathan leaned against the doorway, a sliver of hickory protruding from his mouth.

I read the letter I received in the morning mail aloud.

April 5, 1893

Dear Emeline,

I'm sorry to write to you with bad news, but Mr. Pickwick has taken ill and can no longer manage your farm. Please come

to Kearney as soon as possible to speak with him and your caretakers, the Coopers, about its future.

We miss you and hope you'll come soon.

Sincerely,

Miss Ambrose

My arms dropped to my sides, the paper quivering, as I stared through the front window of the house. To the three, I said, "And this took six days to arrive. What's happened since then? Will you excuse me, please? I need time alone to think." I donned my wool coat, folded and tucked the news into its pocket, and left them as I slipped across the yard. My voice cracked as I called my Morgan. "Dakota! Here, boy." I climbed over the fence rails as he clip-clopped toward me. Dropping into the pasture, I used his black mane to pull myself onto his bare back.

Salty tears fell, but dried in the crisp breeze as we trotted around the pasture. What about the people and the place I cherished? We slowed to a stop and Dakota munched on new grass. The scent of lilacs wafted in the breeze, calming me. Memories of my old life in Kearney bubbled to the surface. Losing Ma and the baby to a tragic childbirth had turned me from a ten-year-old child to a motherly figure, as I took care of Pa before and after school. Three years later, Pa's heart failed, and I'd found myself alone in the world. Oh, I had friends, but no close family. Now the farm belonged to me, but what would I do with it? My eyes squeezed shut. Falling over Dakota's neck, I sobbed for a long while, clutching a fistful of the horse's black mane.

Then I dismounted and rested on the soft spring grass mixed with fragrant clover, dried my eyes with my sleeve, and breathed in the cool spring air. I picked long clover stems and wove them together to keep my hands busy. I'd always believed things in Kearney would stay the same until I married, but now I was worried about Mr. Pickwick and the O'Connor Farm I'd inherited. How long could I expect others to manage my property?

I'd chosen to fulfill my promise to Pa and had journeyed to Boston to meet his pa: Grandfather Silas. I recalled Pa's last words three years ago: "Promise me. Let him get to know you — love you, as I do. Family's important." But on the way, the Witherspoons had found me unconscious in the woods near their home and had cared for me until I recovered enough to continue, and I loved them dearly.

My thoughts stilled as I faced the blue sky replete with fluffy white clouds. "Lord, please show me the way. I know you work all things together for good to those who love you, so there must be a purpose I can't see right now." I stood, took a deep breath, and placed the clover necklace over my head. "At least the decision is obvious, Dakota." He nickered, as I resigned myself to meet this forced challenge and returned to the porch where everyone sat, waiting for me.

Jonathan spoke first. "Well? What have you decided?"

I smoothed wisps of windblown hair and said, "Thank you for giving me a moment to clear my head. I've decided I *must* go to Kearney. It's my legal responsibility. Hopefully, Mr. Pickwick will recover, and things will return to normal." With red, puffy eyes and a stuffy nose, I turned to Mr. Witherspoon. "It's Tuesday and I'm sorry I might not complete the order of spindles, sir." Tears welled up again as I searched for a sign of approval from him.

Samuel smiled and nodded. "I knew you'd do the right thing, Emeline."

Jonathan tried to lighten the mood. "Don't worry. We'll finish them, though I will miss you sharpening my tools."

"Thanks, Jon." I gave him a feeble grin.

"Seriously, I hope everything works out for you." His piercing, ice-blue eyes met my hazel ones. They peered into my soul, but after all these years, I doubted his true feelings for me. Yes, he was a little older, but hadn't we been close friends for years? Jon remained a beautiful, pleasant mystery.

"Works out…" I repeated the words as I gazed into his handsome face. "Jon, you *know* I abhor change. I prefer everything tidy and in its place. The unknown scares me to pieces."

Samuel motioned with his pipe to Clara, and they excused themselves and moved to the kitchen.

"But change is healthy, like the growth of a tree." Jon continued, as he leaned against the jamb of the front door and gazed outside. "It's essential to growth, in fact. If nothing changed, wouldn't life be dull?"

"I suppose. I *love* the change of seasons, but spring and fall are my favorites."

He laughed. "That's ironic, because those are the seasons when things change the most."

Embarrassed, I smiled and stared at my shoes. "But I prefer a comfortable pair of old shoes to a shiny new pair that needs breaking-in."

Then the Witherspoons returned. "We have a thought," said Samuel. "Jonathan and I will manage here while Mrs. Witherspoon accompanies you to Kearney. You shouldn't travel that distance alone as you did years ago when we found you — honestly. We love you too much, Emeline."

"I'll accompany Emeline on the train, if you like," Jonathan McFarland said. He shuffled over to a chair, sat down, and leaned forward with his muscular forearms crossed over his knees.

"No, Jon. That would appear improper and besides, I need you here in the shop," Samuel said.

Shocked, I said, "Goodness, thank you. Are you sure?"

"Yes," they said together. They reached out to me, and we embraced each other like it was the last time.

"I love you, too."

After dinner, Clara planned our trip. "First, we'll drive the carriage down to the train station and purchase tickets," she said. "I believe the train runs from Indianapolis to St. Louis and then on to Kearney, but I'm not sure. Get ole Applejack ready, will you please, Emeline?"

Orders given, Jonathan and Mr. Witherspoon went back to the wood shop. I, with carrots and a bridle in hand, approached the Witherspoon's chestnut horse, who grazed in the pasture with my Morgan. "Applejack, we're going out today. Hello, Dakota! Here's a carrot for you, too."

I stroked Dakota's face and pressed my cheek against his velvety nose as he nuzzled the carrot from my open hand. "I must leave you for a while, but I'll be back soon. Be good, boy."

Applejack was easy to bridle, thanks to his love of carrots. I led him to the tack room, strapped him into his harness, and hitched him to the wooden carriage. He shook his head and stamped his front foot. "Do you have something caught in your foot, Applejack?" I checked them all — I found no stones caught in his feet.

Alone with the horse, questions rippled through my mind. Would Peter Pickwick recover? Would the farm be in good shape? How was Harriet? Miss Ambrose? Would I be able to come back? Would I still want to? Would Jon find a girlfriend? What would I do? Since losing my parents, change had equaled uncertainty, risk — and challenge. How would I handle it?

I drove the horse and carriage up to the house, hopped out, and tied Applejack off at the hitching post. "We're ready, Mrs. Witherspoon," I called as I climbed the steps, crossed the front porch, and opened the front door.

"Fine," She picked up her pocketbook. "Hope the tickets aren't too expensive. Prices have gone sky high lately. Have you read the news?"

"No, not much. Should I?"

"All I'll say is, I'm glad we own our property and still have plenty of work. So many have lost their jobs… oh, don't get me started."

"Let me buy my ticket, at least, with the money I've saved. Hold on." I ran into the house, pulled a box from under my bed, and tucked several paper bills from it into the pocket of my dress — a black and white pinstripe I'd made. I would always be thankful for Ma's sewing lessons and hoped her Singer machine would still be at our farmhouse in Kearney. Pinning my hair up into a high bun, I tied a white scarf around it, pulled a swoop of hair down over my forehead, and walked outside, my head held high, though I trembled.

We climbed into the carriage seat. "My, that hairstyle favors you," Mrs. Witherspoon said.

Like Ma, she encouraged me. I gave her a wide smile and felt older, attractive, and empowered. "Thank you."

She returned my smile and clicked to Applejack, "Gid-up!" The gentle, dapple-gray horse ambled down the road toward downtown Indianapolis, Indiana.

Applejack's long silvery mane and tail drifted in the light breeze as we traveled over the bumpy, dusty road to town. Our seat springs made the bumps tolerable. Fresh green leaves adorned the trees and bright yellow forsythia bushes were harbingers of spring. I opened an oversized parasol to protect our skin from the sun, while Mrs. Witherspoon held the reins.

"We're sure going to miss you, Emeline. You've been like a daughter to us. But don't despair about leaving us. You're practically seventeen now and old enough to make your own decisions."

"Oh, Mrs. Witherspoon, I'll miss you too, and I'm thankful for you both. You've been the parents I've needed since I lost mine. I hope to return soon."

"No matter what happens or where you are, remember, the Lord will be with you. You'll always have friends who love you in Indianapolis." She turned her face away from me for a moment. "I suspect the same will be true in Kearney, but don't forget, our door will always be open to you."

The train depot remained as spectacular as ever: a stunning silver-white edifice with soaring arched doors and windows. Built entirely of hewn granite stones, the tracks ran straight through the interior belly of the building, giving easy access to oncoming passengers on one side and outbound passengers on the other.

A slender man in a black uniform with brass buttons, complete with a billed cap, met us at the ticket counter. "May I help you?"

"Yes, please," said Clara. "We are traveling to Kearney, Missouri. What is the best route?"

"Normally, passengers either travel through Chicago or St. Louis first, switch trains for Kansas City, and then again for Kearney. You'll need three tickets: one for each leg of the trip."

Pulling money from my pocket, I asked, "Which way is least expensive, sir?"

"St. Louis, miss. Hold on, let me check the availability and pricing."

"Thank you." Clara opened her purse.

"One moment, please, ma'am." His fingers flew over the timetables and prices. "A train departs for St. Louis in three days — on Friday at seven o'clock in the morning. But they've paused the Wabash railroad line to Kansas City. It will cost $15.00 for the ticket to St. Louis."

"What about through Chicago?" she asked.

"Checking… no, I'm sorry, they've paused the line from Chicago to Kansas City, as well."

"Oh, dear. Why?"

He explained. "Some lines are bankrupt, while others fight union strikes. It's a sad state of affairs, which I hope settles soon."

"We must get back to you. Thank you for your help, sir." We sat down on a bench in the station. To me, she said, "Well, Emeline, *that* won't do."

"Hmm, let's give this some thought," I said. "I'm comfortable riding Dakota across Missouri, if there's a way for him to travel with me to St. Louis."

"What about me?" she asked.

"You would stay here. I was fine when you sent me on the train to Boston, right?"

"Yes. Partially because I asked the conductor to look after you."

"And he did. I even met the nice man, Mr. McCarthy, who helped me find Grandfather. I believe the train is a safe way to travel."

"I don't know… It's probably safer than traveling by horse for days. Let's consult Mr. Witherspoon."

"I should at least ask about Dakota and buy a ticket to St. Louis before they're gone."

"Ask about Dakota, but don't buy any tickets yet. You'll need to pay more for him, too, no doubt."

"Alright." I went back to the ticket counter while Clara stayed on the bench. After a brief wait, I made my request. "Hello, again. Will you please tell me if the train to St. Louis has a livestock car? I'd like to take my horse with me."

"Your horse will have to travel on a freight train, miss. We have protective pads for him, and he'll be free to move in one of the four stalls in the car. The only difficulty we sometimes have is getting the horse into the car. Loading spooks some horses," he said.

"Do these trains depart at the same time?" I asked.

He checked his timetables again. "We have a freight train departing an hour after the passenger train. I have tickets available for both on Friday morning."

"Fine. How much will a ticket for him cost, please?"

"More than yours, I'm afraid. It's $20.00, miss."

"Thank you. I'll return soon."

I updated Clara, and we scurried through the depot and hopped back into our carriage. Applejack nickered as we turned toward home, while my adopted ma reminded me to make a list of things to take. "Three days isn't long. We'll have to get your clothes washed up and dried first thing. And on Thursday, I'll pack a sack of food for you to take along. And don't forget your canteen."

I laughed, "Thank you! You remind me of ma — organizing me. I'm an excellent packer." A pang hit my stomach as I thought of how much I'd miss her. Tears stung my eyes, but dried quickly in the wind.

Back at the house, Jonathan McFarland had returned home for the night. Clara Witherspoon lit the lanterns as daylight waned after supper, and we settled into our respective chairs to discuss the matter.

"How will you ensure your safety traveling alone, young lady?" Samuel Witherspoon asked.

"I've made two safe trips alone by train before: to and from Boston. I know to befriend the conductor." I smiled.

"Hmm." He puffed his pipe. The tobacco scented the room with a sweet bakery odor — like cookies baking. "Mrs. Witherspoon, what are your thoughts?"

"I believe she will make it on the train fine, but it's such a long trip on horseback after St. Louis. I'd rest easier if she could stay with friends along the way or have a companion rider."

"I know to be wary of strangers. I'll travel near the railroad lines and look for schools or churches to spend the night. And I'll get supplies from the teachers themselves, or in town with their help. Missouri's full of small towns. I promise not to spend the night alone in the woods again."

"I suppose that's reasonable," Clara said. "Mr. Witherspoon?"

He tapped his fingers together in thought. "We must let her go. Alright. We'll keep you in our prayers, Emeline. Send us a postcard whenever you can to apprise us," Samuel said.

"I will. And I'll write Miss Ambrose tonight. Since the Coopers are living in my farmhouse, I'll ask if I can stay with her for a while."

"Very good," Samuel said. "Come back whenever you can, young lady. We love having you here and you're a terrific help in the shop."

"I shall. Oh! I'll have Wednesday and Thursday to finish your spindles," I said, grateful for the respite of time.

Samuel switched pipes, filled a new one, lit it, and walked outside to sit on the front porch swing. Two pipes? If I smoked, I would join him. Instead, Clara and I brought out a blanket and sat on either side of him on the swing to watch the wildlife at dusk. "I'll be careful," I reassured him. He put one arm around my shoulders and the other around Clara's. I leaned against his side and pulled a blanket up around my neck. I memorized the scent of his tobacco, as two deer grazed by the tree line.

Thursday morning, I rode Dakota to town to purchase the tickets for our travel on Friday morning, missing two hours of Wednesday's work in the shop.

When I returned, Jon made his usual request. "Emeline, will you pleased sharpen this curved chisel for me?" With a broad, white smile, he handed me the tool, handle first, as he waved a fly away from his face. "It's spring!" he said.

I nodded and said, "One of my favorite seasons." Holding it at the proper angle, I sharpened it with three sharpening stones: coarse, medium, and fine. After a few minutes, I returned it to his workbench. "Tell me if it needs more, Jon." I caught his eyes for a moment and giggled.

"Thank you." He held the chisel, lightly checked the edge with his thumb, and carved a new groove on one face of a hickory post with ease, with his broad shoulders and muscular arms. "It's perfect." He grinned and continued slicing perfect grooves into the square piece of hardwood. "I'll miss you while you're away, and not just because of your work."

"I'll miss you, too," I said. He examined his workmanship after each score. After three years of working with Jon in the woodwork shop, I learned he was a passionate artisan who took pride in his craft. With steady, skillful hands, and a keen eye for detail, he aimed for perfection in every piece. He chiseled several deep furrows on the newel post: all straight and parallel to each other. "Finished," he said, a wood chip sticking out from his mouth's corner.

"You're a true craftsman, Jon," I said.

"Thank you, Emeline." Proud of himself, he flashed a perfect smile and turned the newel post to expose its blank side, ready for embellishment.

"Jon?" I asked.

"Yes?" He stopped and turned toward me.

Time grew short, and I considered professing my true feelings for him right then, but I stopped myself. What's the use of it now when I'm leaving? I smiled, but my stomach churned. "Oh, nothing. I'd better get back to work."

At the lathe, I secured a three-foot long stick of hickory, set the wheel for a medium speed, and pressed the foot treadle to start it turning. Within thirty minutes, I'd turned the stick into a shaped spindle with multiple curves using various chisels. Loosely holding a flat chisel against the contours, I swept them lightly to check for smoothness. Any bouncing would reveal flat spots. *Smooth and round.* I smiled with pride and stacked it with the other finished work.

Clang, clang, clang. Clara rang the bell on the farmhouse porch.

I echoed, "Jonathan — Mr. Witherspoon — time for dinner!"

Samuel placed his tools and apron on the workbench and mopped his brow with a kerchief, as did Jon and I. We approached the sprawling white farmhouse with its wraparound porch, ornate with its homemade gingerbread trim, eager for dinner.

"I love crisp bacon," I said.

"Hot coffee," Samuel said.

"Warm cornbread," Jon said. "With sweet honey butter. My mouth's watering."

Clara served these, plus scrambled eggs and fresh milk. After a thankful prayer, we devoured our dinners.

"How's the Johansson job coming along? Will we finish it by tomorrow?" she asked.

Samuel paused and sipped his coffee. "Yes, I believe so. Jonathan, Emeline, what do you say? I'm about finished with the hand and bottom rails."

"Yes, sir," I said with confidence. "Only eight spindles left."

"Of course," Jonathan said. "I'm working on the last post." He winked and grinned at me from across the table and I returned it. "Emeline's an expert with the lathe now, too." Turning toward me, he asked, "Do you ever get bored with making the same shape repeatedly?"

"Honestly, I don't, because each piece of wood is unique, even if its shape's the same," I answered. "Someday, I hope you'll teach me how to carve the newel posts and broaden my skills, but I doubt I'm the artisan you are." I smiled and continued. "And I'm not as strong."

After lunch, Jonathan whispered, "Let's surprise Mrs. Witherspoon and wash up the dishes for her. What do you say?"

"Great idea — I'll wash while you dry and put away." We chatted as we worked side by side at the sink, thankful for the inside water pump which filled the washtub.

"I'm nervous about what the future holds," I said.

I handed him a plate to dry, and he asked, "What do you want?"

Wistful for a moment, I said, "My big dream is to have a husband and children someday." My face flushed. "What about you, Jon?"

Either my answer or his secretive nature prevented him from answering immediately. "Oh, I don't have a big dream yet. I'll have to think about it. I may have one when you return to us."

It felt natural and comfortable working next to Jon, and to me, it was a special feeling that I never wanted to end. But why didn't he use the word "me" instead of "us"? I ignored the slight.

Train Travel

Wednesday morning, I would turn the last of the Johansson spindles. I donned my work apron, tied my hair back, and strode toward the shop. Hitched before the entrance to the shop stood a new customer's horse and cart. Inside, an attractive young woman, about Jon's age, stood near the men. "Hello," I said.

"Oh! Hi, Emeline. Come meet Ruth. She's ordering a porch railing for the Wilmington School," Jon said. "She's a new teacher."

"Hello, Emeline." Ruth greeted me with a sincere smile, extended her gloved hand, and shook mine.

Without further ado, Samuel continued. "Your railing will include carved newel posts, handrails, bottom rails, and turned spindles." He motioned toward a display wall. "We have a variety of shapes to choose from."

I interrupted with a timid smile. "Normally, I would turn your spindles, Ruth, but I'll be out of town for a while. It's been a pleasure meeting you." With a mature, business-like air, I excused myself. "Mr. Witherspoon, I'll be at the lathe if you need me."

The lathe and smoothness of hickory centered my thoughts. The whir of the wheel, the methodical precision of different chisel placement, and the fresh-cut woody fragrance pulled me away. Conversations in the background blurred and soon Ruth departed, but thoughts of her bubbled up in my mind. Attractive, well-dressed, auburn hair piled atop her head, talkative, friendly… I forced myself to concentrate on my work and created five perfect spindles before the dinner bell rang.

After eating, Jonathan and I offered to clean up again. "Jon, have you given any more thought about what your big dream is, or must I wait?" I passed him the bowls of wood ash, sand, and vinegar for washing while I pulled a clean tea-towel from the drawer.

"Yes, I have. I couldn't sleep for thinking about it last night." He placed some of the cleaning agents in the skillet to soak. "My dream is to own and manage a millwork shop someday. But, if I'm honest with myself, that's not all."

"There's more?" I asked. "Please… continue."

He stopped washing and stared straight ahead. "I'd rather not say."

"Why not?"

"It's personal, and I'm not ready to share."

"I'm sorry. I didn't mean to pry."

He shrugged and grinned. "That's alright."

"Do you *believe* you'll get it? Your own shop, I mean."

"Yes, I do. But I need to learn more, particularly about the business end."

"As long as you believe, I'm sure you will. Don't give up."

"Not likely." He smiled as he emptied the tub of rinse water outside and headed back to the shop.

We continued working, and I finished all but a few spindles. I planned to start early Thursday morning to turn them before dinner and packing for the trip. Leaning against the closed workshop door, I glanced uphill at their white farmhouse, in peaceful contrast with the warm glow of the sinking sun and surrounding trees.

Jon climbed into the saddle of his bay horse, Big Ben, wished us well with a smile and a wave, to return home for the evening. "See you tomorrow."

No difference. Every day the same. *Who am I to him, honestly?* My brow furrowed.

I took my seat at the supper table.

"Are you all right, Emeline?" Clara asked as she read my expression.

"Yes, I'm fine," I said, as I passed the peas.

"Hmm." She passed the chicken. "Will you assist me in the garden after supper, please, Emeline?"

"Of course." *She knows.*

"You worked hard this afternoon, Emeline," Samuel said. "I've examined your spindles and they're all first-rate. You've learned well and have a genuine talent. I hope you're not away long."

My eyes watered. "Me too, Mr. Witherspoon. Me too."

In the garden, Clara brought up the subject of Jonathan first. "I sensed something amiss when you said goodbye to Jonathan today. Did you expect something different from him?"

"You know I've always liked Jon. Yes, I thought he might be a little more attentive to me somehow, as he's well aware I'm leaving for who knows how long."

"Jonathan's a private person, especially concerning his emotions. He's hard to figure sometimes. But, Emeline, remember, he's about three years older than you."

"I know, I know. But the difference means less with time. Doesn't it?"

"Jon trusts you and enjoys teasing you. He considers you a close companion, or perhaps, like a sister. When you first met, you were but a young girl. It would've been inappropriate for him to take you seriously then." She dug a long row and planted it with green bean seeds.

"But now I'm a young woman. Wouldn't the years change his feelings for me?"

Clara continued. "Other than playful conversation, he's given no sign of further interest. He's never thought of you romantically. You don't want to hear this, Emeline, but it's true, dear."

"Do you think he's interested in that new teacher, Ruth?" I asked.

Mrs. Witherspoon stopped and leaned on her hoe, the purple, pink, and orange sunset behind her. "Mr. Witherspoon told me he's asked her to accompany him to the Spring Festival next month. Yes, I believe he is at least interested in knowing her better."

So, that's it. Raking the soft dirt over the seeds, I buried them — with my hopes.

She sensed my despair. "During your Bible time tonight, why don't you read Proverbs 3? It helps me whenever I'm disappointed. At your age, I found a young man attractive, but our personalities clashed. I reached twenty-three before I met Mr. Witherspoon. We're different, but share the same values and beliefs. Our strengths and weaknesses strengthen us as individuals. Have faith — and patience."

"Thank you, Mrs. Witherspoon." We hugged and went back into the house.

That evening, I pulled my rucksack from under the bed, stiff from disuse, and piled my clothes together with personal items and money. I stuffed the money in a linen pouch, which would hang from a button inside my riding skirt. It represented all the money I owned in the world, all the money I'd earned here, most of which I'd saved. The Witherspoons paid me a little, outside of room and board. Having such a sum on my person, not quite $700.00, made me nervous — and cautious.

Tomorrow would pass, and I'd be on the road again. I prayed and lay in bed to sleep, but it eluded me. As I considered Jonathan, my pride smarted. I snuggled into the quilt and read the comforting chapter Clara suggested.

"Trust in the LORD with all thine heart; and
lean not unto thine own understanding.
In all thy ways acknowledge him, and he shall direct thy paths.
Be not wise in thine own eyes: fear the
LORD, and depart from evil.
It shall be health to thy navel, and marrow to thy bones."
(Proverbs 3: 5-8)

With a sigh, I repeated, "Marrow to thy bones," closed the Bible, and prayed. "Dear Lord, thank you for these words. You alone understand me, down to my bones. You're in control and I trust You will be with me through it all."

Sleep came over me like a warm blanket. Thursday morning passed, and I completed the required spindles for Friday's order. After dinner, it didn't take long to finish packing all my belongings. The last time I'd done this was three years ago — another lifetime.

Friday morning, we ate an early breakfast to make the seven o'clock train. I dressed for the trip with a crisp white blouse, my black split riding skirt, and my western-style hat.

Though the unknown frightened me, it held excitement, too. I hadn't been to my family's farm for ages. Would it be in disrepair? Would Peter Pickwick recover? How long would I be away? I reassured myself with God's promise about all things working together for good. *They must.*

I yawned and stretched when a gentle tap on the door signaled Clara's presence. "Come in."

"Are you ready?" She stood in the doorway, dabbed her eyes with an apron corner to soak up fresh tears, and with resolve, smoothed it down. "We need to load Dakota's tack in the cart next."

My eyes caught hers. I cried. "Oh, my." We fell into each other's arms. "Don't worry Mrs. Witherspoon. Everything will work out." It was my turn to blot away tears.

She sniffed. "I *hope* so." We left the house for the barn.

The familiar smells there soothed me. I took a deep breath and collected Dakota's tack and the burlap sack of supplies. I hoped he'd have energy enough to ride outside of downtown St. Louis after his arrival around four o'clock.

Samuel approached, hefted the saddle into the cart for me, and placed a bag next to it. "He'll want some carrots for the trip," he said with a smile. "And he'll enjoy a grooming before he travels."

I grabbed the burlap sack. "I'll get to it." Mr. Witherspoon tacked up Applejack and hooked the cart up, while I ran over to the Morgan's stall. "Are you ready, Dakota?"

He scraped the ground with his hoof.

I used the currycomb and brush to clean off the dust from his coat. "You're going to travel on the train, Dakota, and then you and I will ride across Missouri to Kearney, just like we did long ago." With care, I lifted each foot and cleaned out his shoed hooves and checked for problems. "Good. You're in perfect shape." With sweaty palms, I attached his halter and lead rope and walked him over to the cart as Samuel checked Applejack's harness.

"Shall I tie him to the back?"

"Yes. Tie it with a cow hitch to the loop in the center," he said as he finished loading the cart. "Be sure to leave a length of rope to give him some leeway." We led Applejack and the cart up the hill to the house, where I collected my rucksack.

With trembling hands, Clara added a flour sack to it. "Here's some food for your trip."

I smiled. "Thank you." Just like Ma, so thoughtful.

There was still no sight of Jonathan. Had he forgotten I was leaving this morning? Or did he not mind as much as I, that this trip would part us for what might be months? My heart sank, but I tried not to let it show.

"Ready?" Samuel asked as he assisted Clara onto the seat in front. But before it was my turn, Jonathan's horse cantered up the drive as he arrived for the workday. I stood on tiptoes to find him.

"**WAIT!**" He shouted. His arms swung as he climbed the hill with long strides. "I'm glad I made it in time. You wouldn't leave without saying goodbye, would you?"

His broad smile and ice-blue eyes still took my breath away. "I thought you forgot I was leaving today." We hugged, and he gave me a familial kiss on my forehead. "Will you write to me, Jonathan? I want to keep in touch." I reminded myself to buy stationery for letters.

"I promise. Make sure Mrs. Witherspoon has your address. Please stay safe, Emeline."

"I will. And take care of these folks and yourself." As we drove away, Jonathan waved goodbye, and I turned around and waved back until I could no longer see him.

On the way, I memorized the beauty of springtime with the majestic trees and scented flowers of Indianapolis as we drove past neighboring farmhouses, then city homes, and businesses.

Frost on the depot's cold stone facade glistened as it melted with the morning sun. Inside, the steam train waited; an oily odor and heavy humidity permeated the air. The Witherspoons offloaded the cart as I loosened my Morgan and led him through the freight entrance of the depot. His ears pricked forward and back as he surveyed the unfamiliar surroundings, so I reassured him by patting his neck. "It's okay, you'll be fine."

A boy directed me to the holding stall for Dakota, his tack, and supplies. "I'll meet you soon." I gave him two carrots and rubbed his soft muzzle as he pawed the straw-covered earth and nickered softly. "Good boy."

As I marched to meet the Witherspoons in front of the train's first passenger car, I observed workers tending to the engine. They filled the steam train's reservoir with water and added more coal for the fire. Four conductors in sharp uniforms assisted passengers as they boarded each of four cars, loaded luggage, and punched tickets. Mrs. Witherspoon rubbed the back of her neck and was wide-eyed as I approached. "Goodness, I'm excited for you. I wish I was going along."

I smiled and hugged her. "Goodbye. I'll be as quick as I can and won't forget to write." I took the heavy rucksack and bag of food from her.

"Take care." Samuel held his head high as he gave me a slender object. "It's a pocketknife. You shouldn't get lost because you have a compass, but you should pick up a Missouri map in St. Louis. And here." He fiddled with his pants pocket. "I want you to have my pocket watch." He handed me a round brass timepiece on a chain with a raised oak tree on one side and an engraving on the back: Tempus Fugit. "It was a gift from Mrs. Witherspoon, but we'd like you to have it." I held my breath as my heart fluttered and my eyes watered. They loved me.

"You remembered!" I said. I'd worn my pa's pocket watch when I first met them, but I'd left it with Grandfather Silas and have missed it ever since. My heart ached. "These are precious gifts I'll always treasure. Thank you."

He grinned and held up one hand in a prolonged wave.

"Be safe, dear." Clara blew me a kiss and clasped her hands as in prayer.

I climbed the steps of the coach as the conductor punched my ticket, took a window seat, and stuffed my rucksack and sack of food underneath. The seat next to me was empty, for now. That would likely change, as we would have several stops for ongoing and departing passengers, as well as for refilling the engine with water and fuel. The Witherspoons left the depot.

My stomach tightened. I loved them, Jonathan, and woodworking. They'd become my new family. Now I was forced to return to Kearney. Home. Wasn't home supposed to be with the people you love?

Two notes, one low and one high, blended in the train's whistle. My heart pounded as I gripped the armrests. *Here we go, Lord.* The train hissed long hisses of steam first and then, "**CHUFF**, chuff, chuff, chuff." The engine choked, then smoothed out as we pulled out of the station. Like a huge dog panting, it gasped and sputtered, but with speed, it breathed as regular as clockwork. The sound of the accented first chuff was rhythmic.

The city flew by as buildings dwindled in size and frequency until there were none. Whenever we rounded a curve, the car's metal wheels squealed along the rails, and clouds of steam rose in the crisp, cool morning air above the train. *Beautiful!* In a few hours, I'd arrive in St. Louis and wait for Dakota.

Discovering Options

The pulsing noise and rocking of the train lulled me to sleep during the first leg of the trip. At the first stop, with time to stretch my legs, I used the privy, and ate one of Clara's sandwiches: ham and cheese on her homemade wheat bread. Soon we had crossed Indiana and most of Illinois. I chatted with the conductor about my plans to ride Dakota west to Kansas City if trains remained unavailable.

At the next-to-last stop, a girl about my age approached me. "Hello. Mind if I sit here?"

"No, not at all. Please do," I said. "Are you traveling far?"

"Just to St. Louis. I'm Charlotte. What's your name?"

"Emeline. It's nice to meet you." We exchanged pleasantries for a short time and then gazed out of our window at the passing scenery, which was mostly cropland, woods, and an occasional farmhouse.

I considered my plan of action, once in Kearney. Peter Pickwick had managed my family's farm for the last several years, along with the caretakers, the Coopers. I would simply meet with him and the Coopers, possibly sell the farm to them, and then return to Indianapolis, where I belonged. I wouldn't consider any other options, yet.

I located our position on my map, and said to my companion, "Soon, we should see the widest and longest river in the United States: the Mississippi. Once, my horse and I crossed it on a ferry."

"I've never been on a ferry, though I live here," Charlotte said.

About thirty minutes later, the waterway appeared, and I said, "Look! Isn't it amazing?" Several steamboats ferried passengers, goods, and livestock across, while others navigated around them as they traveled north or south. "Imagine: some passengers on the southbound boats have traveled down the Ohio or Missouri rivers to join this big ole river, bound for parts before this or to the end at New Orleans and the ocean."

"Yep, that's right, that's somethin' isn't it?" Charlotte said. "Around here, we call it Ole Miss, or Old Man River." We both stared at its expanse as we traversed the bridge.

The bridge spanned its breadth, a thousand feet in three arched sections. The St. Paul Union Depot loomed ahead, where the tracks lay outside between the river and the enormous building of red brick with contrasting white stone accents. Tall arched windows and doorways and a few slender chimneys rose from the rooftop. Horses, carts, and carriages stood near the passenger entrance. "Why are people with signs walking back and forth on the sidewalk in front?" I asked.

"They're the reason there's no westbound trains. The union has been on strike against the Wabash Railroad since I've been away. It's too bad, too, because St. Louis has more railroads connectin' here than Chicago." Charlotte gathered her belongings from under her seat.

"Inconvenient, isn't it?" I collected my things. "It was a pleasure traveling with you, Charlotte."

The train's low, melodic whistle blew as we came to a slow stop and the locomotive released its steam with a loud hiss.

The conductor rose and announced, "Arrived. St. Louis!" He opened the doors at the front of the car and assisted us down the steps.

"Mind yourself on your horseback ride west, Emeline," the conductor said.

"Thank you, I will." I stopped and turned to him for directions. "Can you tell me where the freight train will stop?"

"I don't rightly know, offhand, miss. You might ask the fella over at the ticket counter. I jest sticks to this train," the conductor said.

"Thank you, sir." I headed straight to the ticket counter and asked my question. A postcard rack stood at the end of the counter, and I chose one picturing the rail bridge over the Mississippi to send to the Witherspoons.

After a brief wait, it was my turn. "I'm expecting my horse on the next freight train from Indianapolis. Please, where should I wait to meet him?"

He smiled, peered over his wire-rimmed glasses, and gestured to a distant sign. "Wait in the area with the white sign hanging from the ceiling: PASSENGER WAITING."

"Oh, of course, sir, thank you. Is it on schedule?"

He checked his log. "Yes. The freight train should arrive around four o'clock, miss. It unloads up the line northward: about a ten-minute walk from the waiting area." He pointed to a corridor east of the waiting area. "Go up there when it's time. Would you like to purchase the postcard?"

"Yes, sir, and thank you again. Also, I need a Missouri map. Have you any idea when trains might resume service to Kansas City?"

He pulled the map from a rack behind him and handed it to me. "Ten cents, please. Regarding the strike, it happens the stationmaster is talking with the union steward right now. Let me check for any fresh developments."

"I appreciate it." We exchanged money for goods, and I waited while he spoke to the stationmaster.

He returned and said, "Sorry, miss. No settlement yet, unfortunately."

With my rucksack and flour sack in hand, I cut across the bustling lobby to the waiting area and found a safe, empty place next to a family of five. I opened my food sack and snacked on an apple. Delicious! Afterward, I wrote my postcard and mailed it:

April 14, 1893

Dear Mr. & Mrs. Witherspoon, & Jon,

We arrived safely in St. Louis, thank goodness. Still no train to Kansas City. I've bought a map and will write again in the next town.

Love,

Emeline

Thankfully, he did fine on the trip, and soon enough, Dakota and I found the road out of town, thanks to my map and compass. Without them, there's no telling where I'd end up. I set a bearing for St. Charles, about twenty-five miles northwest of St. Louis, and away from the bustle of the expansive city. Riders, buggies, and carts frequented our route, but no one bothered me and there was safety in numbers.

My horse, thrilled to stretch his legs, gave me a few miles of cantering, on and off again. Rain had softened the dirt road, muffling the sound of his hooves. I loved riding him. We alternated gaits as usual: the walk, the trot, the walk again, the canter for a mile or two, and then a brief stop to rest and check my bearings once more. I sang to him, to the rest of the world, and to God, as anticipation grew inside me. I checked the time on my new pocket watch. Six o'clock. We should arrive in about another hour.

The steeple of a tall church building rose in the distance. "That's where we'll go, Dakota, to the church. Hopefully, there'll be someone around this evening." Shortly, we pulled up to St. Peter Catholic Church in St. Charles, Missouri. What a magnificent building! Made of bricks, it stood with reverence, a tower in front of it reaching toward the heavens.

After securing Dakota to a nearby hitching post, I climbed the few steps to the massive front door and knocked. Soon, a man dressed in a black cassock and white clerical collar opened the door. "May I help you, child?"

Unsure of how to address him, I said, "Yes, sir. I mean Father." I fumbled over my words, more than a little weary from traveling. "I'm on my way to Kearney, my home in Western Missouri, and need someplace safe to spend the night. Would I be able to stable my horse and sleep here somewhere?"

"Of course, we'd be happy to help. You may stay in the school building to the east, which now houses our nuns. I'll introduce you to Sister Margaret Vogel. Leave your horse for now." As we walked, he asked, "What is your name?"

"Emeline O'Connor. Thank you, Father." The setting sun cast its warm glow over us as we walked the short distance to the old school building. Dogwood and redbud trees were in full bloom. Colorful tulips and jonquils popped their heads up around the trees and in the gardens around the buildings.

After the priest knocked, a mature woman, a nun, answered. "Good evening, Father Wilmes."

"Sister Margaret Vogel. This is Miss Emeline O'Connor who's seeking refuge for the night. She's making a long trip. Would you assist her in stabling her horse, giving her a tasty, hot meal, and a bed for the night?"

"Yes, Father Wilmes. I'd love to."

"Fine. I'll leave you then." And he did.

"First things first, Emeline O'Connor. Let's get your horse settled," she said. We walked back across the lawn, where I untied Dakota and then followed her to the stables. "Here's an empty one. I assume you'll need some time to ready him for the night. He'll enjoy the hay in the rack on the far wall, plus you can give him some oats from the bin out front. You'll need to fill his bucket with water and set it back in its stand, so it won't tip. The pump is out front, along with some clean towels. I'll check on you in about thirty minutes."

"Thank you, Sister Margaret Vogel." After she'd gone, I gathered the oats and water and began taking off Dakota's tack. His blanket would dry overnight as it hung over a rail. With a towel, I wiped the sweat from his back and brushed him with his currycomb. His foot, already in resting position, showed he was tired, even though he was still eating. He neighed in response to the other horses, snorted with pleasure, and after I finished, he laid down and rolled in the soft bedding of straw. "Good night, Dakota. Wasn't this a grand idea?" He snorted again, and I left him comfortably stabled.

Sister Margaret Vogel headed toward me. "Oh, finished, are you? Do you need to use the privy first? It's behind the building, around the back corner." She pointed.

"Yes, please." Long ago, I'd enjoyed Boston's indoor plumbing. Would it become commonplace everywhere, someday? Afterwards, I rejoined her in the yard.

"I've heated a bowl of vegetable beef soup for you, with biscuits and a tall glass of fresh milk. Come inside." She sat me at a long wooden table in the sparse dining room where she'd placed my meal and then sat across from me.

"Thank you, Sister Margaret Vogel." I prayed silently over the meal, truly grateful for this provision.

As I ate, the nun said, "You may address me as Sister Margaret while you're here, Emeline. Are you planning to ride your horse all the way across the state, then?"

"It wasn't my first choice, but the railroad strike has forced me to that conclusion."

"St. Charles lies by the Missouri River and train tracks run right alongside of it for quite a distance, although I'm not sure how far. But that train isn't running, presently. Have you considered traveling by steamboat upriver? The Big Muddy, as we call it, goes west all the way to Kansas City and then turns north."

"No, I hadn't thought of that. I'll check with them in the morning."

"It wouldn't hurt. You might also stop at the train station here. I don't believe the workers for the line that travels north to Hannibal, then west to St. Joseph, are on strike. You might prefer that transportation."

"Yes, Sister Margaret. Thank you for these suggestions, this delicious food, and for allowing me to stay the night. I'm exhausted."

"You look it, child." I had seen no other nuns milling about, but surely there were.

"Where's everyone else?" I asked.

"Oh, they're in the period of prayer and solitude until after the same period in the morning."

"Oh, I'm sorry to interrupt that for you. I'll finish in a moment."

"It's my pleasure. I'm glad you stopped by."

Afterward, she led me to a small room with a single cot covered with a white sheet. Two folded blankets lay at the foot of the bed and a soft pillow at the top. "Thank you, Sister Margaret. Good night."

"Bless you, Emeline. When you're ready in the morning, return to the dining room for a healthy breakfast before you go."

"I will." So far, staying overnight here had proven to be one my wiser decisions. Snuggling between the sheets and blankets, I laid my head on the feather pillow, prayed, and slept like a rock.

After breakfast, I bid Sister Margaret and the others goodbye, filled my canteen, and saddled up Dakota for the day. The map showed the location of both the landing for the steamboats and the train depot. Though I leaned toward the train, I wanted to ask about the steamboat, anyway.

The city of St. Charles lay on both the north and south sides of the vast, brown river. Smaller than the Mississippi, it was still a force to cross. At the Landing, I dismounted and walked Dakota toward the office and spoke with an official. "I'm curious about traveling by steamboat to Kansas City with my horse. Would you give me some information, please?"

"The Big Muddy is a wide river, as you can see, and Kansas City is up-river. With many twists and turns, this old river changes with the rains and seasons. It takes approximately two weeks' time to reach Kansas City from here. Delays due to sand bars or tree snags are common. Would you like a ticket for you and your horse?"

"No, thank you. I thought it might be quicker than riding. I can't wait so many days, but I appreciate your time."

"I understand. Farewell," he said.

The train depot stood only three blocks from the Landing, a quick walk. I tied up Dakota and went inside to speak with the stationmaster, a short, wiry man of about forty. "Hello, sir. I wonder, could you tell me: are any trains running west?"

"We have one that runs north to Hannibal and then west to St. Joseph. So far, we've been able to keep this line running with non-union workers. Need ticket information?"

"Yes, please. How long will the trip take? My horse and I are heading for Kearney, Missouri, south of Cameron."

"Hmm. One moment." His eyeglasses slipped, so he pushed them back to the top of his nose and opened a book with timetables and pricing. "If you're willing, you can purchase three tickets for you and your horse. Since we're a smaller line, we combine passenger cars and stock cars, too, so you and your horse will arrive together."

"Oh, that's perfect, thank you."

"Right. So, the first leg, to Hannibal, will be $17.50 for both of you. The second leg, to Cameron, will be $25.00. The last leg, to Kearney, will be $10.00. As far as time goes, you'll arrive in Kearney by this evening, if you take the next train, which departs in just an hour."

That sounded unbelievable. "Alright. Where's the nearest privy?"

"Go outside and turn to the right. Behind this building." He pushed his glasses up again and addressed the next customer.

Inside the privy, I pulled the required cash from the linen pouch hidden under my skirt and returned to the depot's counter. I waited behind another customer and then purchased the tickets. Postcards sat in a rack at the end of the counter, as well as an outgoing post box. "I'll purchase a postcard too, please."

April 15, 1893

Mr. & Mrs. Witherspoon, & Jon,

 We arrived in St. Charles, Missouri, and I spent a wonderful night with nuns. Fortunately, we can continue on a train and should arrive by tonight!

Love,

Emeline

Outside, I waited with Dakota. "Isn't it marvelous? We'll be home tonight. Won't I surprise Miss Ambrose? We might even beat the letter I sent her." I handed him a couple of carrots and rubbed his neck. *Home.* Did I say that out loud? Hmm. "I'm glad we're making this trip together, Dakota, even though we're riding the train rather than you for days. It'll be easier for us, won't it? And safer and quicker. Hopefully, the more direct route will have trains running when we return to Indianapolis."

With his reins in hand, I walked toward the loading area, and Dakota followed me without my urging. We waited and waited. He rested his head on my shoulder and relaxed. "Someone will guide us onto the train soon." I took out his curry comb and brushed his ink-black mane and tail, which complimented his nutmeg coloring. Such a pretty horse and the perfect size for me.

The conductor, sharp in his navy-blue uniform with brass buttons and cap, shouted for all the waiting passengers. "Now boarding for Hannibal. ALL ABOARD!"

A lanky young man in overalls marched toward me. "I'll take care of your horse, miss."

"Okay, Dakota, it's time to go." I handed the young man a couple of carrots.

"Thank you."

My horse turned his ears to listen for me, but he went along peacefully with the fellow, as I followed to observe. Hesitating before he boarded the stock car, he finally lurched forward. They secured him, along with his baggage. The handler skillfully removed his tack and hung it on the wall, wrapped his legs for protection, and tethered him with a length of rope, allowing the animal to move around. Also provided were bumper cushions on its sides and plenty of straw, hay, and water.

Satisfied with his treatment, I climbed aboard the passenger coach, just in front of the livestock car, where the conductor punched my ticket for Hannibal. I made myself comfortable near the front and ate a wheat bread and cheese sandwich from the flour sack. Confident that I would reach Kearney this evening, my mind muddled through scenarios once I arrived. Without more information, a decision would be impossible to make, but I determined to solve my problems in Kearney logically. *Just a temporary setback, that's what this is.*

Kearney, Missouri

Our train reached Hannibal in only three hours without changing trains, so I strolled about and stretched my legs for a few minutes, visited Dakota and fed him a carrot. I dared not take him out for a walk, though. The depot was near the Mississippi River, and I saw the steamboat crossing — the exact one we had used on our first journey. Pleased that we were riding the rails now instead of plodding along the roads and crossing rivers on boats, I took my seat and handed the conductor my tickets for Cameron. I asked him, "Sir, how long till we arrive?"

"Between four and five hours. We stop at several towns along the way to pick up and drop off passengers, as well as mail and other goods. And, of course, to fill up with fuel and water. Use any of these stops to walk about or visit the privy. They usually last about fifteen minutes." He smiled and tipped the bill of his cap.

The rhythm of the train's movement facilitated the closing of my eyes for a while. From my map, and my experience, I knew the way was straight and flat. In northern Missouri, trees grew along creeks and small rivers, but most of it was farmland.

Two stops came and went, as did several passengers. This trip, I didn't engage in conversation with anyone, except for friendly greetings or nods. Anxiousness grew inside me the closer we came to Cameron. At the third stop, Brookfield, I took the fifteen-minute break, visited Dakota in the stock car again, and returned to my seat. Our train proceeded along the rails, building up speed outside of town.

All at once, outside the moving train, men yelled, and gunshots sounded. I slid to the edge of my seat and peered out the window.

The train slowed, but I couldn't see why. "What's happening?" I asked.

The conductor answered. "Sounds like a hold-up to me. We'll find out soon enough." Louder, he said, "Stay in your seats, everyone, and hide any valuables you may have. Be silent. Don't look at them if they come in. Try to stay calm." Some women screamed. I froze. "Quiet, *please*," he said.

I noticed the conductor checked his gun and put it back in its holster, hidden from view. Would he use it against these armed bandits in this car loaded with people? Terrified and vulnerable, I wrapped my arms around myself and shrunk down into my seat, reducing my size as much as possible. My feet pushed my rucksack back under my seat even further. Did I have any kind of weapon? I dared not bring out a knife against a gun. Helpless, my stomach turned, and my head spun.

Outside my window, I saw four rugged men shouting at the engineers. I noticed three divided up and entered each passenger car and pulled every conductor outside and stood them together with the engineers. One bandit held this group at gunpoint. Then, one of them came into our coach, brandishing his gun wildly. **BANG!** He shot our conductor before he could pull his gun out. He wasn't killed, but the bandit took his gun. After he'd deposited him with the others, he came back in. "Gimme your jewelry and your money and no one'll get hurt. You first, girly," he said to me.

"Sorry, I have nothing." I held up my hands to show him I wore no rings or other jewelry.

"What's on that chain, missy?" He saw the silver chain which slid into my skirt pocket.

"Oh, nothing," I said weakly. *My new pocket watch.* I prayed he wouldn't press me further to discover the hidden money bag, which held my small fortune.

He tugged at it and pulled out the watch. "Nice." He ripped it from my skirt band and stuffed it into his bag.

Victimized and paralyzed, I didn't expect anyone in our coach to challenge this vile man. He shouted and held out his bag for the goods as he stomped down the aisle between us, shoving people with his gun for compliance, which worked.

Another bandit went into the stock car. I suppressed a shout. "Dakota!"

Another man from their group led him out of the train, pulled him along, tied him to his horse, and boasted. "Look what I got," he said.

BANG! A deafening shot rang through our coach again, followed by terrified screams, including mine. The bandit fell to the floor, dead and bleeding from his chest. Shrinking lower into my seat, I bent over, covered my head with my hands, and prayed, too frightened to do anything else. Two others rushed in, their guns drawn, but our gunman shot each one as they entered. Soon, the only bandit left was the man guarding the railroad workers. I peered out of my window as he jumped on his horse and rode away. He didn't get far, though. Soon, he, too, lay dead — shot by the one of the railroad crew outside.

"Dakota!" I shouted. He trailed along behind the horse they tied him to for quite a distance.

The conductors collected the horses and brought them back. Other staff members, except the wounded conductor, pulled the dead bodies out, strapped them over their horses' backs, and discussed their next steps.

Avoiding the blood on the floor, I bolted out of the coach and ran to my horse and looped my arms around his neck. "Oh, Dakota! I almost lost you." One conductor helped me load him back into the stock car, where I stayed for a few minutes and could overhear their conversation just outside.

"Let's tie the horses together and take them back to town, and report this to the sheriff," one engineer said. "It's not too far back to Brookfield. Thomas and Nicolas, we need you to move the rocks they've piled on the tracks ahead. Pry them off with a rock bar and roll them away."

One conductor volunteered. "I'll haul them back and speak with the sheriff and catch up with you on the return trip."

I found my seat. The gunman who had saved us all came up to me and asked, "Is this yours, miss?"

The pocket watch. "Yes, sir, it is. Thank you for what you did." I took the watch from his hand, studied his face, and smiled. About thirty, he was slender and attractive, with short brown hair under his bowler hat, a shaven face except for his long bushy mustache, and eyeglasses. A russet leather apron covered most of the front of him, which concealed the gun belt he wore around his waist. Who would have guessed at his courage and ability with a gun? "Thank you," I repeated.

"Just keeping others from getting hurt, that's all, miss. We've tamed the Wild West, haven't we?" He smirked and gave an eye roll.

I smiled at the irony as I sat again and rested my head against the seat's back and sobbed as anxiety waned. Was I wrong to take the train? The dramatic turn of events fortunately ended well, for us, although not for the bandits. While the conductor mopped up pools of blood as best as possible with rags, I prayed, giving thanks for our safety, and for the souls of the dead men.

On our way at last, the passengers gathered their wits and remained silent. An hour later, we reached Cameron. This was where I switched trains for the southbound route toward Kearney and, ultimately, Kansas City. With the conductor's help, we unloaded Dakota, let him walk around a bit, then re-loaded him on the other line's stock car. "Only a quick ride now, boy," I said. He groaned. "Be back in about an hour."

In my seat, I ate the rest of Clara's food. Thrilled to be on the last leg, I started making a list in my journal of things to do upon arrival and sorted them in order of importance. The sun dipped behind the tops of the trees and my eyelids grew heavy. At least the weather was fair and allowed us to have our windows down a bit. Without air flow, it would've been stifling.

Finally, the conductor announced, "Arrived, Kearney, Missouri."

My heart raced as the train came to a stop and vented its steam. I gathered my rucksack and said to no one in particular, "Coming, Dakota."

"Let me help you with your horse, miss," a conductor said.

I smiled and said, "I appreciate that. Thank you, sir."

We unloaded Dakota and tied him to a rail and then retrieved his equipment and tack. I switched his halter with his bit and laid his blanket over his back. "I'll help you with the saddle." The conductor lifted it up and over his back with ease.

"You're very kind. Thank you, again."

"My pleasure, miss. Have a pleasant stay, and sorry about the incident earlier. Doesn't happen much anymore, but it sure can."

Holding the reins, I turned to the conductor. "I'm grateful we all survived. Hopefully, you'll never experience another encounter like that again. Even after that terrible event, I believe the train is still safer than traveling on horseback alone. Don't you?"

"There's safety in numbers. That's a bottom fact. Take care now." He waved and headed back to the coach.

I cinched up Dakota's saddle, tied my rucksack and his grooming tote behind it, and mounted him. "Now, let's go see Miss Ambrose."

Ten minutes later, we arrived at the teacher's house near the school. I smoothed my hair and inhaled a familiar odor. Baking bread's scent filled the air at the moment. After dismounting and tying Dakota, I knocked on her screen door. My heartbeat quickened against my chest.

The door opened. "My stars! Miss Emeline." Maude Ambrose came out onto the porch and wrapped me in her arms. "Oh, I've missed you."

I held her tight and sniffed. "Chamomile soap, like always. I've missed you, too."

She put her hands on her hips. "You still have Dakota." Trembling, she took my hands and gave me a smile, which dimpled her cheeks. She looked different, somehow. "Tend to your horse first and then come in for supper: leftover chicken with noodles and fresh bread."

"Mm. I won't be long. I'm famished." As I was tending to Dakota, my mind wandered. I loved the Witherspoons and Jonathan, but I had forgotten how fond I was of Maude Ambrose, too. Tomorrow, I would visit the farmhouse I grew up in. Memories of my parents tugged at my heart and salty tears mingled with Dakota's oats. I shook my head. *Stay in the moment.* I hurried to the house.

I set my rucksack inside her front room. The front room's pale gray walls held a desk and chair in the far corner. Two wooden rockers with cushions sat atop an oval braided rug with side tables by each. Two bookshelves hung above an oak storage cabinet and two sash windows bordered by white linen curtains provided light during the day and a view to the front property. Simple and charming. "Your home is very inviting, Miss Ambrose."

"Thank you, dear. I'm just slicing the bread. Have a seat at the kitchen table. How was your trip?"

"May I help with anything?"

"No, thanks." She handed me a bowl of chicken with noodles, a generous slice of fresh, warm bread, and some cool water. "Enjoy, Emeline."

"This is delicious. Bread, cheese, and apples only go so far." I shared the details of the trip with her, and she gasped when I told her about the hold-up on the train.

"Goodness! I'm thankful you came out of that. How terrifying!"

"It was."

While I supped, she prepared a place for me to sleep on the floor in the front room. She would sleep in her bedroom: the only one in the house. "But I'm glad you came so quickly. I'm worried Mr. Pickwick doesn't have much time left. Perhaps I should have written sooner, though I doubt it would have changed anything." She plumped a pillow and set it at the end of the pallet of colorful quilts.

"What's wrong with him?"

"It might be his time. You'll visit in the morning?"

"Yes, ma'am. That's my plan." After today, I couldn't handle any more stress without rest. I cleaned up after supper and settled in for the night.

I headed to Pickwick Mercantile and entered the store. Andrew Pickwick, their son, stood behind the counter.

"Hello, Emeline. Happy you're here," he said. He waved and motioned for me to go upstairs.

I tiptoed up the steps to their apartment. At the door, I saw Peter Pickwick lying on his back in bed, while his wife sat in a chair next to him, her shoulders stooped, her spine bowed, as she held his hand. I was stunned! Her silver-gray hair strayed wildly from her bun, her worn blue apron, still as I remembered, tied around her neck. I didn't recognize him. He was pale, slightly bluish, and thin; his gray hair sparse, his empty eyes fixed on the ceiling. He labored to breathe through his open mouth in the warm, malodorous room.

I tapped on the open door and tiptoed softly toward the bed. "Mrs. Pickwick?" My stomach turned and I couldn't find the words to say. I knew he'd been ill, but I didn't expect death.

"Emeline O'Connor!" She stood and embraced me. "I'm glad you're here. I feared you might be too late." She crumpled into her chair, exhausted.

I sat on the edge of the bed opposite Audrey, held Peter's hand, and asked, "Mr. Pickwick?" I glanced her way when he offered no response. "What happened?"

"It started with a simple cold. *A simple cold!* He couldn't recover and it turned into bronchitis. His doctor says the disease has progressed to pneumonia. We have tried linseed oil poultices, medicines, water, and soft foods, but nothing has helped." Her voice trembled as she searched for her handkerchief in her pocket. "He's failing more with each passing hour."

"Oh, I'm so sorry." I knew only too well how she felt — exactly how I had felt when I lost Pa. "What can I say, except, would you like me to pray with you?"

"Yes, please. I've prayed continuously, but now I believe the Lord wants to take him." Tears welled up as we stood, clasped each other's hands, and closed our eyes.

I started: "Heavenly Father, we ask for your care for Mr. Pickwick, who may be with you soon. Bless him and give Mrs. Pickwick and their son, Andrew, peace and comfort, knowing he will be home with you when it's his time."

Audrey added, "Dear Lord, you know Peter's heart and how he loves you. Be with him now and forevermore. Thank you for your goodness toward us. Comfort us. In Jesus' name, Amen."

"Amen," I echoed.

We sat on either side of his bed again, each holding one of his once-strong hands, our tear-streaked faces staring at his fading countenance. The emotional scar of Pa's death ripped, re-opening the wound of that day long ago. But I reminded myself that God's in control, and He's always good. Death is but a part of life.

As Peter couldn't speak for himself, his wife did. "He wanted to tell you the Coopers have done well at your farm. He withdrew most of your money from your bank account and placed it in our store's safe next to ours. Andrew can explain it better than I. He thought it was in our best interest."

"I understand. Thank you." Money — I'd worry about that later. With heavy hearts, we waited. No need for idle chatter. I pulled a chair next to hers and we leaned against each other, holding hands in silence. My sympathetic tears fell onto her shoulder. Though moist, her eyes were drained, red, and swollen: cried out.

Peter's breathing became inconsistent. Audrey rose and called from the top of the stairs. "Andrew, please close the store now and come upstairs, son." It was late in the afternoon and the sun had set behind the building. She lit a lantern; its glow adding cheer and hope to the now dark room.

Together, we waited, prayed, and waited some more. His raspy regular breathing became more and more irregular with time. *Hours passed.* Then, finally, poor Mr. Pickwick did, too. For a time, we huddled together, held hands, hugged, and finally released restrained tears.

Moving On

My arm wrapped around Mrs. Pickwick's slumped shoulders. "After you've made the arrangements and rested, I'll return."

Despite her weary eyes and grief, she expressed concern for me. "Thank you, Emeline. Do you have a place to stay tonight?"

"Yes, ma'am, with Miss Ambrose."

"Excellent. Thank you for sitting with Andrew and me. It means a lot to us."

Andrew added, "This must have been difficult for you as well. Thank you." His dark eyes glinted in the lamplight — sad, but stoic.

"Of course." Bowing my head, I turned and descended the stairs. But before I opened the front door, I remembered: *I need to write to the Witherspoons and Jonathan.* I chose a couple of postcards from the rack on the wall and left my payment by the register.

Outside, the air was refreshing, though humid, as we hadn't received the promised rain after all. I took in three slow, deep breaths, clearing stale air from my lungs. It was dusk already and Dakota, who had waited patiently, held his back foot up to rest it. At least he could reach the water trough. "I'm sorry, boy. Let's get you to Miss Ambrose's barn."

Maude Ambrose stirred the potato soup on the stovetop and sliced more of the fresh bread. "Tell me what's happened at the Pickwicks', Emeline."

Exhausted from the emotional day, I sobbed. "He passed away this afternoon." I allowed my tears to fall at will. So far, this trip had met with tragedy, and I missed the happy rhythm of the Witherspoon's workshop.

"Oh, I'm sorry, Emeline. I expected that might happen." She put her arm around my shoulders and handed me a cloth napkin.

"Mrs. Pickwick, Andrew, and I were together for several hours today. He was deathly sick and suffered for a long time, unlike Pa and Ma, who each passed away within a few hours." At the table, I stared into the distance, my hands clasped together in my lap, recalling the stinging loss of each of them, years apart. I dabbed my eyes with the napkin.

She set two bowls of soup, grated cheese, and a plate with sliced bread on the table and held me again. "Shall we pray?" We held hands and bowed our heads. "Lord, you know the pain of the Pickwick family right now. Comfort them, knowing Mr. Pickwick knew you, and is with you now, without sickness, pain, or sadness. Please help Emeline find strength and comfort the Pickwick family. Thank you. In Jesus' name, Amen."

"Amen. Thank you, Miss Ambrose." I sniffed as we took our seats on either side of the oak table. She always focused on the spiritual side during a crisis. She prayed with me after I lost Pa, too. Losing him ached like it was yesterday. "May we change the subject now?"

"Of course. What shall we talk about?" she asked as she poured each of us a glass of fresh milk. She sat up straight in her chair. I noted her perfect posture, well-groomed appearance, and flawless complexion.

"How do you keep your skin so clear and your lips moist?" I asked.

"I use my chamomile soap in the evening to cleanse my face and then apply tallow to it afterward, and again in the morning. Tallow is good for lips too but sometimes I use beeswax."

"I'll have to try that." Rubbing my face with the cloth napkin, I removed the soil from today. "I'll see for myself tomorrow, but can you tell me what's happened at my farm?"

"The Coopers are friendly folks. The farm itself is well-kept, and they've acquired several more Jerseys. You're drinking their milk." She held up her cup.

We drank the sweet liquid. "Delicious. I'm thinking of selling the place and hope they'll buy it from me." I read her face for her reaction.

Her eyes caught mine. "You don't want it? That surprises me." She scoffed. "Why in the world wouldn't you want it?"

Obviously, I'd disappointed her. With resolve, I said, "My home is in Indiana now." I shared the important developments over the past three years with her.

"Well, I'm glad you've found happiness in Indianapolis and have learned a new skill, but have you forgotten your love of the farm and Kearney?" A playful smirk crossed her face.

How well she knew me. "Maybe I have, maybe I have." Had I forgotten on purpose? Did I create distance from it to protect myself from painful memories? Had distance erased the fondness of my birthplace, and the friends I'd made? "Have you heard from Harriet since she moved to Westport?"

"Not lately. We have communicated little since then, but they haven't sold their place. Hired hands plant and harvest their crops for them."

My stomach was full, my heart was confused, and my mind and body were exhausted. Since leaving Indianapolis, I hadn't read my Bible, so I opened it to the bookmarked page: Proverbs 3. Solomon shared the value of wisdom, correction, peaceful sleep, and helping others. I repeated the last verse out loud:

> *"The wise shall inherit glory: but shame shall*
> *be the promotion of fools." (Proverbs 3:35)*

"Please, Lord, give me wisdom. Thank you. In Jesus' name, Amen." Sleep eventually came, after troubling thoughts of loss subsided.

In the morning, we attended church, ate lunch, and rested throughout the day. I pulled out the postcard and the fountainpen

and wrote a quick note to the Witherspoons to inform them I'd
arrived safely.

April 16, 1893

Greetings to you all,

    **We arrived at Miss Ambrose's house. Sad news: Mr.
Pickwick died today. Tomorrow I'll visit the Coopers
at my farm.**

Miss you desperately,
Emeline

Early Monday morning, we ate a quick breakfast and got on with our
days: Maude to the school to ready it for the summer term from May
through August, and me to the farm. I gave Dakota his head, and he
galloped headlong toward the country home. "You know the way,
don't you, boy?"

A few minutes passed, and we were — home. The white farmhouse
remained the same: the water pump, fed by a spring, stood in front of
the porch with its familiar border of tulips. Dakota pulled toward the
pasture. "Wait a minute, boy. We need permission first." I dismounted
and tied him to the hitching post in front of the house. I skipped up

the steps and rapped on my old front door. Anticipation swept over me, my palms moistened, my heart pounded. *This was my house.*

Sarah Cooper opened it. She wore a starched white cotton apron over a blue gingham dress. A neat bun at the back of her head held most of her dark brown hair, though some shorter wisps encircled her round, ruddy-cheeked face. "Emeline! It's grand to see you, at last. Won't you please come in?"

"Thank you." The moment I entered, a flood of memories swept through my mind. Though different, it was the same layout, down to Ma's Singer sewing machine. They cared for the home as if it was their own, which pleased me. "I love how you've decorated the house. It's lovely."

"Thank you. Would you like a glass of lemonade? Mr. Cooper and William are working in the dairy barn and will be up soon. He'll be pleased to see you."

"Yes, thank you." I sat down on one of the four wooden chairs around the old oak table, now protected by a red and white checkered cloth. "Who's William?"

"Oh, he's a young man, about your age we hired to help. Our dairy farm has outgrown a one-man operation. Mr. Cooper will tell you all about that. Anyway, young William Kavanaugh is energetic, dependable, and ambitious: a hard worker. I care for the house and sell our dairy products to families who come by and to the Pickwick Mercantile. Getting acquainted with folks is my great pleasure."

We shared stories from the past as we drank lemonade. They had added a few more Jersey cows, as well as one bull, built a new dairy barn, a cattle barn for cold and stormy weather, a creamery, and even an icehouse!

The men came across the porch, but Mr. Cooper stopped in the doorway. "Ah, Emeline! I recognized Dakota and figured you must be here. Would he like to have a run in the pasture?"

"I'm *sure* he would," I said. "He hasn't run free for days."

Turning to a young man, Logan Cooper said, "William, will you please remove his tack and release Dakota in the south pasture?"

"Aye. Be back straight away," he said. But before he left, he glanced at me, nodded, and tipped his hat. What an attractive young man! A familiar flush heated my cheeks as I swept my hair behind my ears.

Sarah slipped a pan of cornbread she'd prepared into the oven and stirred the pot of navy bean and ham soup on the stovetop. "Dinner will be ready in a few minutes."

"Ahh. Let me sit down. Backbreaking work, it is — this dairy business, but I love it. I'll take some lemonade please, Mrs. Cooper." Logan wore a long-sleeved flannel shirt and denim bib overalls like Pa, but he was more barrel-chested.

"Here you are." She handed him a tall glass of lemonade.

"Ah, thank you, dear." He gulped half of the lemonade before turning to me. "First, have you visited Mr. Pickwick?"

"Yes, sir. I have." Our eyes met. "He passed away yesterday." I said. It still saddened me, and the memories of the loss were still raw.

"Oh, I *am* sorry. Mr. Pickwick was a fine man; God rest his soul. I'm glad you've come, though, as we have plans to discuss."

My back stiffened. "Plans?" I clutched my glass but kept eye contact.

"Yes. Times have changed in our home state of Wisconsin. A few years ago, the dairy business there was difficult: land was outrageously expensive. Most Wisconsin farmers grew crops: wheat, barley, oats, even cranberries. But now, dairy is booming. My best friend purchased an expansive acreage and has built his home, barns, and so forth. He's invited us to build our home on his property and work with him. We love Kearney, but we *dearly* miss our friends and family back home."

I picked up my glass of lemonade and drank — at a loss for words. *I can relate to feeling out of place*, I thought. My smile wavered. "I understand wanting to be back with your friends and family all too well. When will you move, then?"

Sitting next to him, Sarah picked up his hand, and said, "We haven't firm plans for the timing yet, Emeline."

"No, not yet, but sometime this year, for certain," Logan said. "My friend invited us to live with them until we build our house next year. We've saved up for travel by rail. We've built a thriving business here in Kearney and can teach you everything necessary to keep it going, but you'll likely need to hire another full-time hand."

My eyes, wide as saucers, stared at him in disbelief. I wiped sweat from my palms onto my skirt. "I had planned to ask if you wanted to buy the farm." My voice cracked. "Any chance you would consider buying instead of moving?"

Logan laughed heartily at my question. "And I was going to ask if you would buy my Jerseys and reimburse me for the improvements!" He laughed again.

His laugh reduced some of the tension, but I repeated the question. "If you'd consider buying, I'm sure we could work something out."

He glanced at Sarah. "I seriously doubt *we* can afford it." He shook his head. "No, even if we had the money, and as much as we love Kearney and its people, we love our family and friends back home more."

My mind reeled. I pulled in and released a slow, deep breath and re-evaluated my position. "This is quite a shock, I have to say. I scarcely have words at the moment. Will you show me around after we eat? I'll need to understand the improvements you've made. Possibly the banker can help."

He pulled his suspenders out with his thumbs and said, "Proud to give you a tour."

Then the young man entered. "Done!" He glanced at me and smiled. "Nice animal, Dakota."

I returned a demure smile.

"Take a seat, William. Dinner is ready," Mrs. Cooper said. "Oh! We haven't made introductions yet. William Kavanaugh, meet Emeline O'Connor, owner of this farm."

"It's a pleasure to be meetin' you." He smiled and took his seat.

"And you." His Irish accent reminded me of Grandfather Silas. William, with his broad shoulders and animated expressions, was charming: Jonathan's counterpart in Kearney. Oh, my.

Logan and William chatted about their afternoon tasks as dinner was served. Smells of cornbread and ham and bean soup wafted through the house. After giving thanks, they dug in with ravenous appetites, while I took my time.

Afterward, Logan said, "Thank you, my love, for the tasty meal. Emeline, join us in the dairy barn when you're ready."

I will." I hurried to finish and rose to help Sarah with clean-up.

Once the house gleamed once more, I started for the barn but stopped at the fence by the south pasture. Seven contented Jersey cows grazed with Dakota. I searched for Nellie, the cow I'd grown up with. I found her. "Nellie!" I climbed over the wooden fence rail and walked over to her. "Oh, I'm happy to see you again, girl." I patted her neck. Would she remember me after all this time? She mooed softly, while Dakota romped and kicked in the distance. A gentle spring breeze blew across my face. I chuckled and my body warmed at the sight of him running — free and joyful, once again. He deserved it after that terrible train ride.

I regarded my farm as I turned in a complete circle. *My farm.* I let it sink in. In Indianapolis, I was *like* a family member and an employee of the Witherspoon Trim Shop. Still, I owned this place, but nothing in Indiana. But wasn't home where your loved ones were, no matter the place? My ownership had interfered with my happy home with the Witherspoons.

The classic white farmhouse remained steadfast and simple. Pa and Ma had built it themselves along with the massive barn for horses, hay, and our one cow, Nellie. The Coopers had added more outbuildings and cows. Of the one hundred sixty-acres, the pasture represented but a small part. Acres of fertile fields for crops covered the rolling hills, while undeveloped woodland still occupied half of the tract. Several heaps of manure and straw stood piled in one corner of the pasture. Chickens roamed freely between the buildings and in the pastures, and, at night, they roosted in the roomy coop Pa had built. What would the banker say it was worth? Did I even *want* to sell? Or *could* I? I shuddered. *I'd think about it later.*

I followed a worn path toward the new dairy barn to where the open sliding door beckoned. "Hello," I said, as William spread clean straw on the floor in the milking areas while Logan was busy in the back.

"Hi." William set down the rake and faced me. "So, are you ready?"

His ginger hair accented his green eyes. It shone like a new copper penny in the sun. "Yes, please. Today, a quick look, but later, I might want to spend time alongside you both to learn what it takes to be in the dairy business."

"Aye, you've got to do your own growin', no matter how tall your grandfather was." Turning around, he shouted, "Mr. Cooper, Miss O'Connor's here."

What a curious young fellow William was! It took me a minute to understand what he meant by 'do my own growing'.

Mr. Cooper approached. "Let's start at the beginning: in the pasture."

The three of us walked outside. He continued, "The cows, calves, and steers rotate, grazing between this and two other pastures, and one bull lives in a smaller meadow nearby."

"Beautiful! I found and patted ole Nellie. It surprised me to find she's still here."

"She's yours. We wouldn't do anything with her without asking you first, of course."

She's mine. I'd always thought she and everything else belonged to my parents, but it belonged to me now, didn't it? Well, my farm might be someone else's soon, and I'd be unencumbered and on my way home to Indianapolis, where I belong.

Logan said, "We love Jerseys for dairy cows because of their high percentage of cream. William and I milk them at seven o'clock in the morning, don't we? And then a second time around five o'clock in the evening."

"We do," William said. "After mornin' chores, and then after the milkin' we eat a bit of breakfast. I love sunrises, don't you?"

"I do, William, and also the quietness of early morning, except for the twittering of birds," I said. His build reminded me of Jonathan, as did his quiet manner. But, unlike Jonathan, I found him often staring at me, waiting for his opportunity to speak. Did he find me as attractive as I found him? I clasped my hands behind my back.

"Aye." He shoved his hands in his pockets and focused on the budding trees, feigning disinterest.

Logan waved us onward. "Let me show you the new dairy parlor and creamery. We're mighty proud of it."

Inside the barn, he showed me where the milking took place: standing on opposite sides of the entry were two narrow stalls, with a railing on either side and, at the end, a bin for hay to feed and distract the two cows.

Memories of my milking days gnawed their way from the recesses of my mind to the forefront. The familiarity pleasured me. "It's been a long time since I've milked Nellie, or any cow. But I'm sure it has changed little."

Logan continued. "No, but certainly the icehouse has changed the handling of the milk. When we're finished milking, we take the pail over to this long table in the creamery." He walked us over to it. Covered in steel, the table housed three steel drawers below, which stored tools and supplies. Shelves hung on the wall above it and held clean, empty glass jars, turned upside-down to keep out dirt and dust.

"Spotless! What happens here?"

He laughed. "First, we cool it down as fast as we can, which we'll show you another day. Here's our newest addition. Come over quick, once, hey."

William and I followed him to the back of the barn and a narrow wooden door. His green eyes flashed as he said, "You're goin' to love this. Look."

Logan said with pride, "May I present — the icehouse."

Stacks of golden straw bales insulated the room on three sides to keep the ice frozen. They had placed filled bottles of milk in wooden crates on top of and between ice blocks. Crushed ice topped off the crates and fell between the bottles, surrounding each one with their coldness. Over that, sawdust insulated the whole crate.

"The cold must keep it fresh for a long time," I said. "Impressive!" I truly admired his prowess. "Where did you learn about this?"

"Oh, when you have friends in dairy, word gets around."

"This parlor, creamery, and icehouse must have cost a fortune," I said.

"The investment makes all the difference in quality and sales." Mr. Cooper puffed out his chest. "Sure, it keeps our meat cold, too."

Regardless of what happens, I feel blessed to have such a bright, enterprising caretaker. "It's amazing and I'm eager to learn as much as I can. Thank you, Mr. Cooper, and you, William, for showing me the remarkable things you've done here." Unsure of how to end this meeting, I shook hands with each of them.

"It's been my pleasure," said Mr. Cooper.

"Be seein' you," William said. "Let me help you saddle your horse."

I retrieved my Morgan from the pasture and met William in the barn, who hefted the saddle with ease. After thanking him, Dakota and I walked back to Miss Ambrose's house, as I reflected on the past week. Overwhelmed by powerful emotions, I'd experienced contentment, fear, disappointment, loss, and joy. Emotions aside, the facts included: my manager had passed away and my caretakers would leave. And why had my money been withdrawn from the bank?

My eyes searched the heavens, and I shouted, "Pa, this is a lot for a sixteen-year-old!" A small voice in my head whispered, '*Read your Bible and pray. He won't give you anything you can't handle unless he makes a way to escape.*' "Thanks, Pa."

Weighing Options

In the time before supper with Maude Ambrose, I wrote another postcard to the Witherspoons. *I mustn't forget to buy some stationery for writing longer letters.*

April 18, 1893

Greetings to all,

The Coopers, my caretakers, plan to leave for Wisconsin and can't buy the farm. I'll speak with Andrew Pickwick and the banker tomorrow. Keep me in your prayers.

Miss you,

Emeline

I tucked the card inside my rucksack to mail tomorrow, picked up my Bible, and turned the pages to the Book of James — one of my favorites. Though the whole of chapter one spoke to me, this verse, I repeated and wrote in my journal:

"But let him ask in faith, nothing wavering. For he that wavereth is like a wave of the sea driven with the wind and tossed." (James 1:6)

This verse described my current condition in a nutshell: a wave tossed by the wind. I prayed an earnest prayer for wisdom and direction.

I decided to surprise her and make cornbread to go with our supper later, just for fun. A few chunks of wood smoldered in the firebox before I added more dried, split wood from the stack outside. While the fire rekindled, I mixed the few ingredients in a bowl and poured it into a metal baking pan. In about ten minutes, the oven was hot enough.

During baking, I set the table, filled her porcelain pitcher with fresh water from the well's pump, and cut a few yellow jonquils to arrange in her red glass vase. "Oh, Ma, what should I do?" Though she couldn't answer, the house and its contents tugged at me to come back to our home. But home was in Indianapolis with the Witherspoons and Jonathan now, wasn't it? My heart ached and my mind swirled as the smell of cornbread filled the room, which signaled it was done. I pulled the pan out of the oven and placed it on the coolest part of the stove to keep it warm. I set a plate with butter and the honey pot on the table, too.

I considered Jonathan McFarland. Why did he have such a hold on my heart? If I'm honest, he had never returned my feelings. Was it only his appearance that attracted me? Yes, his eyes were crystal blue, like the sky. His hair, dark and wavy, accented those amazing eyes. His smile gleamed white across his face, and his teeth were perfect. Meticulous, he sometimes became frustrated if things didn't meet his expectations. He had a sense of humor, but also a quick temper. I must admit, he annoyed me by not sharing much personally. You'd think after three years of working together, we'd know each other well. *But we don't, in fact.*

Winnie clip-clopped toward the barn and soon Maude walked in and hung her shawl on a hook by the door. "Mm, cornbread's baking." She set a pot on the stove to reheat the leftover chicken and noodles. "Thank you, Emeline, what a delightful surprise, and the flowers are lovely. How was your visit?"

"It's thriving, but the Coopers can't buy it, and were you aware they plan to move back to Wisconsin sometime this year?"

"No, I wasn't. I knew they had built a new dairy barn last year and added the icehouse. People come from all around to buy their milk. That they would move away after all their work and expense astonishes me."

"They've certainly added value to the property, and they have an interesting farmhand named William, but this news shook me to my core — and my plans. I like to make a plan and stick to it." I sighed as I poured water into our glasses and then sat in the front room to wait for supper.

"Sounds like you have some important questions to answer for yourself," she said.

I picked up my journal from the side table and shared my last entry with her. "I'm like a wave of the sea driven with the wind and tossed."

"Ah, reading your Bible is always helpful." She smiled as she rocked her chair and unpinned her blonde hair, allowing it to cascade onto her shoulders and down her back. "What do you hope to do with your life? Who is Emeline O'Connor?"

"Oh, my, Give me a moment." After a minute or two I said, "I've tried to please others: Ma and Pa, of course; you, as a student; everyone I met in Boston; the Witherspoons; and even Jonathan, sort of." I winced at the last comment.

"Nothing wrong with pleasing others, to a degree — it's probably *part* of who you are."

"The only decision I've made for selfish reasons was to live with the Witherspoons because they took me in, as they resembled my parents." I added with a sigh, "And their apprentice, Jonathan, attracted me." I glanced up to check her reaction.

"You've no regrets about making that choice, I'm sure, as the Witherspoons obviously care for you, although I'm not sure about the young man." She spread butter on a chunk of cornbread and drizzled honey over it. After a bite, she said, "Mm. This is delicious."

I smiled, pleased. "I'm not sure about him either. In fact, when I left, a young teacher named Ruth had captured his interest." I pushed my shoulders back and changed the subject. With conviction, I said, "I have three choices: keep the farm and learn to run it, hire another caretaker and manager, or sell it." Selling the farm sounded like the final nail in the coffin for Pa and Ma. That was a bottom fact. My inheritance and their legacy would disappear forever. My mouth felt dry, like cotton. I *couldn't* do that, could I?

"Sounds reasonable." She smiled and rose to serve the soup. "Supper's ready."

I moved to the table and drank some water. "Tomorrow I'll visit the Pickwicks' and the banker. And I'll pray about your questions."

Morning dawned a cool, fresh April Tuesday and Dakota and I made our way to downtown Kearney, where I would visit Audrey Pickwick at their store. I tied Dakota to the rail in front and opened the door. The tinkling sound of a bell announced my arrival, along with the creaking of the door's hinges.

"Good day, Emeline." Audrey said. "How are you today?" Her eyes were still a little puffy and red, but she appeared rested.

"Fine, thank you. I'm sorry to intrude, but may we visit for a while?" I asked. "I'll treat us to some hot tea."

"Oh, don't be silly. You're like family. Take a seat at a table and I'll get us some tea." She pulled two mugs and a teapot from the cabinet, scooped some green tea leaves into the pot's strainer, and filled it with steaming water. Meanwhile, Andrew stocked tins of food onto deep shelves.

"Hello, Andrew," I said.

"Hello, Emeline." He continued stocking as Audrey brought the teapot and mugs to the table.

"Thank you, Mrs. Pickwick." I cupped my hands around the warm mug, and she sat across from me. "How are you doing?"

"Fairly well, but I miss Peter terribly. After forty-one years together, he'll always live in my heart, despite his absence now." After a pause, her voice wavered as she added, "Now it's just Andrew and me."

I reached across the table to hold her hand. "The folks in town will never forget him."

She sniffed and held her handkerchief to her nose. "Did I tell you he told Jesus he was ready to go the day before he passed? And he was smiling, too."

"No, you didn't. May I share something with you?"

"Please."

"Once I was near death from an incident on my trip to Boston. A man had hit me over the head, and I experienced an unfamiliar place. Beautiful music and a bright white light surrounded me, as well as an indescribable and overwhelming feeling of love, which enveloped my mind and heart. A hand and robed arm came down through the light and drew me upwards — and I rose. I thought I had died, and this must be Heaven, but then I woke up in the back of the Witherspoons' wagon. Do you think Mr. Pickwick might have had a similar vision?"

"What an incredible story, Emeline! Possibly. It's a comfort knowing he's with Jesus." She soaked a tear away with the tip of her apron and sipped her tea.

"I'm glad we're friends, Mrs. Pickwick. Remember, if you ever want to talk or need help, I'm here and will stop by whenever I'm in town. I'll never forget Mr. Pickwick, like I'll never forget Pa or Ma."

"Thank you, Emeline." She smoothed her apron and continued. "We've scheduled the service for ten o'clock in the morning this Friday. You'll attend, won't you?"

"Of course, along with most people in town, I expect. All of us will miss Mr. Pickwick's generosity and kindness."

"I believe you're right. I'm blessed with Andrew, who's the spitting image of him."

"He is." I hesitated, but forced myself to ask the question. "Apologies for the bad timing, Mrs. Pickwick, but I *need* to discuss the farm business. I'm hoping to settle things so I might return to my new home in Indianapolis."

She forced her shoulders back, stared at me, and said, "What's holding you in Indianapolis, Emeline?"

"I'm part of their family. The Witherspoons have included me in their lives, taught me to turn wood spindles, and much more."

"You'll have to sit with Andrew if you want to talk about business matters. Mr. Pickwick and he were the managers. I have nothing to do with decisions about your finances."

"May I speak with him today, or should I wait until next week?"

"I can manage the counter for a short time." She stood and gave me a hug, picked up her mug of tea, and walked to the counter to speak with Andrew, who then approached the table with a clean mug for himself.

"I understand you have a few questions about your business. How can I help?" He poured himself some tea, faced me, and pushed his thick, dark brown hair back from his forehead.

"I'm sorry to bother you with this now, Andrew, but I'll be brief. First, will you explain why my money was withdrawn from my bank account?"

He sighed. "I don't know how much you understand about our economy. Do you realize just what the economy is?"

"Is it about people's ability to buy and sell?"

"Exactly right, Emeline." His voice took on a teaching tone. "Let me explain. Currently, our money is based on the 'gold standard', which means we can turn our bank notes into gold anytime. Gold supplies increased with the California Gold Rush. Then, America began producing a lot of silver for coins. Stimulated by railroad bankruptcies and strikes, and the closing of the National Cordage Company, many people have panicked and exchanged their bank notes for gold. This year, gold reserves in the US Treasury have fallen dramatically. Pa expected this might happen a few months ago."

"Oh, please go on."

"Even worse, smaller banks have been forced to sell assets to stay open and others have closed their doors."

"How's *our* bank doing?" I asked.

"Ours is still open, but Mr. Kingston is barely managing. He hopes things will turn around later this year and *I* hope he's right."

I paused. "About our money?"

"Just before Pa got sick, we exchanged *most* of your balance for gold, which is in our vault. I'll show you." He rose from the table and said, "Follow me, please." We walked to the store's back room where a heavy, black safe, standing as tall as me, was wedged inside a wall. "We left a little in the bank to keep the accounts open." After dialing in the combination, he opened the thick door and pulled out a metal container with my name written on it. "No one else but Ma knows about this. You *must* keep it between us."

"Of course." I clasped my trembling hands to my chest.

He opened the box.

I gasped, startled by stacks of shiny gold coins inside, and whispered, "Oh, my stars and garters! How many coins are here and what are they worth?"

"Your pa deposited quite a lot before he passed and, thanks to Pa's management of the farm's finances, and the Cooper's caretaking, the value of your account has grown. This currently holds $2,300.00, or sixty-five Liberty Double Eagle gold coins. Each coin is worth $20.00."

"Oh, goodness!" I covered my mouth with my shaking hand. "Pa always scrimped and saved. As a child, I thought we were poor." I collapsed on a nearby stool as I tried to comprehend what this fortune meant. I faced him, agog. And I still hid $650.00 in my linen pouch, too. "I've cash saved from my work in Indianapolis. Should I put it in here, or deposit it at the bank?"

"It's safe to leave it here, but you can deposit it, if you wish."

I slipped the bag from underneath my waistband. "Here. I'd like to keep it all together. Thank you." I pulled most of the money out and set it inside the box, keeping a little on me.

"That's a great deal of currency for a young lady. More unencumbered wealth than most families in Kearney have ever seen. Most people pay rent or a mortgage. At your tender age, you own a farm, without debt, and have a healthy nest-egg besides." He smiled as he returned it to the safe and locked the door. "Let's return to our table."

Clearly, Andrew was proud of his pa's management. "Thank you for taking care of me." I took a deep breath and released it. With wealth, I could afford most anything I desired. I couldn't sell the property in good conscience, I'd decided. But what would I do with it if I didn't?

At the table, I sipped my tea and asked, "Have you heard of anyone, possibly someone new to town, who might have an interest in the position of caretaker? With a pleasant house, a barn, and now a dairy barn with creamery, and an icehouse, it's a great opportunity for the right people. The Coopers are moving to Wisconsin later this year, and I hope to return to Indianapolis as soon as possible."

Elbow on the table, Andrew leaned his jaw against his closed hand. "No, I'm afraid not. I suppose I could continue managing if you find one, but why not reconsider and stay in Kearney? We'd sure love it if you did." His kind brown eyes were sincere and held my hazel ones. "If you're set on it, you might speak to Mr. Kingston at the bank. He might have an idea or two."

"I *will* stay until I figure things out. I appreciate you, Andrew, and thank you for spending time with me today." We stood, shook hands, and he held mine a little longer. "I'll see you Friday morning at the church." Turning toward the counter, I added, "Goodbye for now, Mrs. Pickwick, and thank you."

"You're welcome, Emeline, come back anytime, dear."

"Oh! I almost forgot. I need stationery for writing letters. Please excuse me, Andrew." He busied himself by cleaning off the tables and sweeping the floor.

I walked to Audrey and said, "I'd like to write longer letters than a postcard will allow. Do you have any stationery in stock?"

"We do." She pulled three boxes with twenty-five sheets of paper and foldable envelopes in each from the display case under the counter.

"Oh, this one is perfect." The paper was ivory, thick, and a perfect size with matching envelope papers.

She asked, "Do you have a fountain pen, ink, sealing stamp, and wax?"

"I don't, and I'll need those, too. May I see some?"

She chose three metal fountain pens, from which I chose one with a barrel with a comfortable grip which narrowed and flared at the tip. I smiled at her. "I'll have to practice my penmanship, won't I?" I selected a bottle of indigo blue ink, too.

"Here are a few sealing stamps and waxes to choose from."

Of the stamps, I chose a circular one with a maple leaf design and a stick of dark green wax. "Thank you, Mrs. Pickwick. I can't wait to use them."

She packed my purchases into a small bag, and I reached into my pocket for the money and felt the two postcards I'd written.

"Oh!" I handed her the postcards. "Will you send these, please?"

"Certainly. Let's put them in the outgoing mailbox. Follow me, please." Mrs. Pickwick shuffled to the corner of the store, which was dedicated to the post. A wooden counter held a box out front. "Here's where outgoing mail goes. But to pick up mail, you'll need to ask one of us to help you. Patrons must pay postage on letters received without stamps, but more and more senders are pre-paying with stamps these days. Alphabetized slots in the back sort incoming letters. Carl Frick, our rural carrier, rides by on his mule each afternoon, except Sunday, around three o'clock to drop off and pick up mail."

"A mule?"

"He can't afford a horse and says the mule gives a more comfortable ride, anyway. He's a fine, dependable older man. The postal service brings folks into the mercantile regularly. If you want to send or receive letters, this is the place."

"Thank you, Mrs. Pickwick. I'll see you both Friday at the service."

Waving from the counter to which he had returned, Andrew said, "See you later, Emeline." I smiled and returned his wave.

With hope, I marched across the dirt road toward the sturdy bank.

The bank, fortified with hewn stone walls, possessed a heavy door laden with no less than three locks, and the windows were tall and protected by steel bars. One other customer stood at the teller's window. I waited my turn and then asked if I may speak with the manager, Mr. Kingston.

"I'll check, but may I tell him who's inquiring?" the teller asked.

"Emeline O'Connor, if you please."

"Yes, miss, one moment," he said as he left and momentarily returned to unlock a gate next to the teller area. "Follow me, Miss O'Connor."

"Thank you."

Mr. Kingston, a bald, rotund man with a long, springy beard and mustache, sat in a wooden chair behind an imposing desk with a black leather top, gold filigree border, and matching carved legs. Puffing on his pipe, he said, "Come in, Miss O'Connor. How may I help you today?"

Tobacco smoke hung in a cloud at the tall ceiling and scented the room with a fruity odor reminiscent of warm blackberries. I stifled a cough, though the aroma was pleasant enough, and took a seat in a leather cushioned chair in front of his desk. "Hello. I'm Tavis O'Connor's daughter, remember? I withdrew a little money from Pa's account after he passed, to make a trip to Boston to find my grandfather: Pa's last request."

"I recall. That was several years ago. And your manager, Peter Pickwick, has exchanged most of the balance of your account for gold coins. Are you aware of this?"

"Yes, sir. Andrew Pickwick has explained this, thank you. Since Mr. Pickwick has passed, I must make important decisions about my farm. I've decided to hold on to it, but I need to find a new caretaker, with Andrew Pickwick as manager. My current caretakers, the Coopers, are leaving sometime this year, and I need someone in place before I return to Indianapolis."

He faced me and took his pipe out of his mouth to speak. "Why not sell it? I can offer you $25.00 per acre as an investor. That's a right fair proposition in today's economy."

"You mean, you'd buy it? What would you do with it? Oh, no, sir. I appreciate it, but I can't, not yet." Whew! I'm glad I came to this decision earlier or I might have sold the farm for too little to a man whose interest in it was merely to make a profit. Ma and Pa must be smiling down at me right now.

Twiddling a wisp of hair around my finger, I continued. "I don't mean to offend you, sir. I'm sure it's fair. But I'm only looking for a temporary solution: a caretaker." I pushed stray hairs behind my ear.

He set the pipe in an ashtray. "Have you given thought about living on your farm and managing it yourself with some hired help? Currently, no one qualified for the caretaking of a dairy farm is available."

I lowered my head. With little conviction, I said, "Indianapolis is my new home." But, somehow, my thoughts about home had become snarled.

His brown eyes narrowed with a sense of urgency and seriousness about them as he leaned forward. "To be frank, Miss O'Connor, everyone in the country, including Indianapolis, is hunkered down and waiting for better times." He pulled at his springy beard and added, "The bank has a few people remiss in their mortgage payments. We might find someone who would be a suitable caretaker with some training. I'll arrange for you to meet a few of them at the bank, if you wish."

As it was his business to have the pulse of the town, the banker would hear of any prospects. "I would consider it if they have some experience. But wouldn't they stand to lose their investment in their home altogether if they made that move?"

He sat back in his leather chair and laced his fingers together. "They might lose it anyway, if they can't make their payments. Most experienced people are busy with their own farms. No, the folks I have in mind are laborers, not specifically dairy-related: mostly plowing, collecting hay, and so on. Employers have laid many people off and those folks are having trouble meeting expenses."

Resigned for now, I said, "Alright, thank you. I'll consider it. What is the balance of Pa's account?" I straightened up in the chair, held my shoulders back, and smiled, despite the disappointment.

"Of course, but you understand, it's *your* account now. Let's check." He pulled a leather-bound ledger toward him and turned the pages.

I admired three gold-framed paintings of Kearney landscapes on Mr. Kingston's office walls during the silence.

"You still have $50.00 here. I believe the economy should improve later this year. I wouldn't rush to withdraw it unless you need it, absolutely. You shouldn't, given your savings in gold. And, speaking of that, as soon as the economy recovers, I recommend you re-deposit that money."

I smiled. "Thank you for speaking with me, Mr. Kingston. I'll be in touch."

He rose and accompanied me to the locked gate and let me out into the lobby. "I'll look forward to our next visit. Thank you for coming and have an enjoyable afternoon, Miss O'Connor."

"You, as well."

Dakota and I rode back to Maude's. Alone on the country road, I allowed tears of disappointment, gratitude, and confusion to stream down my cheeks and dry in the wind as we cantered. I would contact the banker if I needed to hire help, but I wasn't sure about re-depositing the gold — not for a long while.

We slowed to an amble as I thought about Miss Ambrose's questions. Am I trying too hard to do things *my* way, with *my* timing? Is determination ever an undesirable trait? I decided to relax and take things slower, more prayerfully.

I decided to relax and take things slower, more prayerfully.

Dairy Days

The next couple of days I would spend at the farm. Tonight, before bed, I read again from the first chapter of the Book of James. I never tired of how verses could strike me differently. Each time I read, it was like a new book. Today, this familiar verse spoke to me:

> *"And we know that all things work together*
> *for good to them that love God, to them who*
> *are the called according to his purpose."*
> (Romans 8:28)

I thought more about Miss Ambrose's questions. Who is Emeline O'Connor and what does she want to do with her life? Grabbing my journal, I wrote a few ideas, beginning with the big dream I shared with Jonathan: my heart's desire to marry my best friend and start a family.

Running through names of friends in my life, few stood out, truthfully. Adults have been my supervisors and caregivers: Pa and Ma, Maude Ambrose, Peter and Audrey Pickwick, the adults in Boston, and Samuel and Clara Witherspoon. Harriet Steiner used to be my best friend growing up, but we had not been in contact for years, and she had moved to Westport. Jonathan McFarland, whom I considered a close friend in Indianapolis, was a far-flung fantasy. I prayed: "Lord, you made me perfect for your purpose. Lead me and mold me for it, not by my will, but by yours. Amen."

Thursday morning. I awoke refreshed after a sound night's sleep on the pallet. Dressed for work, I wore my khaki riding split skirt and dark red blouse. I rolled up a full-front apron with pockets to wear later. To keep stray hairs from falling into the milk, I drew my long, wavy brown hair up into a high ponytail, wound it into a bun, pinned it, and tied it off with a red scarf. As I stepped into the kitchen, I said, "Morning, Miss Ambrose."

Dressed in a lovely sage green dress, she had already set the table and was ladling oatmeal with raisins into our bowls. "Good morning. You're just in time for breakfast. Sleep well?"

"Oh, yes, I did, and I'm prayerfully considering the answers to your earlier questions. All I can say now is I'm open to whatever the Lord has planned for me." The thought of working at the farm today made me both nervous and excited. Was fear of the unknown the source of my basic insecurity, which had plagued me all of my life? I thought I'd have outgrown it by now.

"Hmm, a positive attitude should improve your day. I find it gets me through some mighty rough days. But I love teaching the children of

Kearney, even then." She smiled. "I'm looking forward to resuming a full class in June. While some younger children continued through March, I haven't seen the older ones, especially the boys, since February."

"You know something? I miss school sometimes — I miss the learning." I'd never felt insecure at school; it had always been safe and fun.

"You're welcome to visit anytime and try teaching. Witnessing the flash in a child's eyes when he understands something new, after struggling, is amazing." Her eyes fixed on mine. "There's nothing more satisfying. All the labor and sacrifice are worth it."

"That's food for thought, and I might try it sometime, thank you."

We cleaned up our dishes and departed for our respective workplaces. Filled with energizing food and hope, I expected a beautiful day.

Dakota and I arrived by nine o'clock and they had already milked the cows. The Coopers and William enjoyed their breakfast while I set Dakota free in the pasture. Afterward, we all sat and enjoyed each other's company on the front porch before morning chores.

"Since you weren't here at six o'clock this morning, we held off one cow for you to milk, Emeline, so you can experience the entire process." Logan Cooper said. "But we've a busy day ahead and can't hold your hand all day."

"Thank you. No need for handholding. I'll follow along or help Mrs. Cooper."

William played a tune on his harmonica, an instrument which I'd heard played before, but not with his style of music. I loved it.

After he finished one tune, I asked, "What's the name of the song you played, William?"

"Just an Irish ditty I made up. You like it?"

"Oh, yes. Please play another." I smiled and tapped my toes to the beat of the tune. "Lovely, thank you." I'd forgotten the pure joy music gave me. It'd been a long time, though the whir of the lathe in the wood shop had sung to me daily.

"William is quite the musician, Emeline," Sarah Cooper said. "He plays the fiddle, too. He treats us to songs after meals." She paused and turned to the young man. "You're playing your fiddle at the Spring Festival in May, right?"

He blushed and lowered his head. "Aye, along with a few other blokes. Miss O'Connor, you must be Irish, yourself? O'Connor's an Irish name, isn't it?"

My ears warmed. "Yes, William. Pa, who's now in Heaven, was Tavis O'Connor and his pa, my grandfather, is Silas O'Connor. Grandfather lives in Boston, who I met for the first time in 1890. Born in Ireland, he speaks with a similar accent." William and Jonathan were alike in build: strong and broad-shouldered, and, by his music, and his attention to me, I perceived him to be sensitive, too. But, unlike Jonathan, his manner was more casual and optimistic.

"So, then, we may have some common ancestors. I was born in Ireland, too."

The Coopers both laughed, and Sarah said, "Wouldn't that be something?"

"Sure would!" Logan said as he stood. "Break-time's over. Let's get back to work, you two. Lots to do before dinner."

I donned my white cotton apron. The strap hung around my neck, while the rest covered my front and tied in the back. "I'm ready."

We washed our hands well with soap, while William fetched the needy cow for me. On the way to the dairy barn, I surveyed the pastures, breathed in deeply, and exhaled. Without question, I preferred the wide-open spaces here to the claustrophobic streets of Boston, even though its beautiful ocean front accessed miles of fresh air. Pa's decision to leave the city for the country made perfect sense to me, but I imagined he must've enjoyed many happy memories fishing from the ocean growing up.

William guided the Jersey into the stall and stowed some fragrant alfalfa hay in the rack before her to keep her occupied. "Here you are, Miss O'Connor. This one's named Primrose — Rosie for short."

"She's beautiful. Hello, Rosie." I stroked her head and neck. "Oh, she's a beauty." She grazed contentedly on the hay.

Logan brought over a bucket of warm water from the wood-burning stove outside, two clean towels, and instructions. "Cleaning the cow's udder serves three purposes: it cleans dirt from the cow, so it doesn't contaminate the milk, it gives us an opportunity to check her for any maladies, and the warmth encourages her to let her milk down."

"It's been a few years since I've milked Nellie, and the Witherspoons don't own a cow, so I appreciate the refresher." I plunged the clean towel in warm water, washed her entire udder area, and checked her teats for any sign of disease. While I dried my hands thoroughly on another towel, I allowed her udder to air-dry. "May I have the test pail, please, William?"

"Sure, here you go." He handed me a small metal pail.

I squeezed a bit of milk from each teat and checked it for any anomalies. "It's white and creamy, as it should be." Using the larger bucket, I milked Rosie dry. Afterward, I said, "Please pass the tallow."

"Here you are," Logan said. "Sure, you're a natural, Emeline. You were born to this life."

"Thank you." Rosie's delicate skin absorbed the tallow as soon as I rubbed it over her udder. It would soften and protect her. *Born to this life.* Now *that* was a statement. Can a person be born to live a certain way? Perhaps, if it's God's design.

William said, "Bring the milk over to cool it down, now."

"This is new," I said as I carried the pail to him near a long steel table and poured the milk through a cotton flour sack filter and into a larger metal can. William set the can into a wooden box and added crushed ice around it. "What's next?"

"Give her a stir," he said, handing me a long metal spoon, which he'd first sanitized in the boiling water outside. "Keep stirrin' for about fifteen minutes; cool it as quick as you can, but not too fast. We're not makin' butter." He laughed.

Logan, hands in his overall pockets, rocked heel to toe. "Cooling it down quickly and bottling it for the icehouse keeps the bacteria from growing. Our milk stays fresh for at least six days or more when kept in a proper icebox." He pulled five gallon-sized glass bottles from the shelving on the wall and set them on the long table. Logan lifted the milk can out of the ice and they filled each bottle with care, as William moved a funnel into each bottle.

Then William capped the bottles with stiff round caps with a pull tab, which fit into a groove in their necks. "Ready for the icehouse!" He filled two wooden crates with the bottles, set them on ice, and topped them off with more crushed ice and finally, sawdust. We got the biggest smile from him when he closed the door and turned around. He clearly loved his work.

"Fascinating!" I understood Logan possessed an extensive knowledge of all things dairy. Briefly, I compared Kearney and Indianapolis. Fond of both places, it occurred to me a body could be happy most anywhere it wanted. Still, I wasn't sure about being *born to a life.*

William returned Rosie to the pasture, while Logan and I carried the pails and milk can out to the water pump to rinse them out and scrub them thoroughly with soap powder and a brush. "Make sure you brush the seams particularly well," he said.

After rinsing them with fresh water, we toted them back to the barn and set them in the icehouse with the milk. "What's next?" I asked.

"The cold and isolation in the icehouse will keep the bacteria, dirt, and bugs out. This afternoon, we'll rinse each of these with boiling water from the stove to sanitize them. Sanitation and temperature; the keys to providing healthy, nutritious milk. Before we leave, let's clean the steel table too."

Afterward, they showed me around the old barn and the chicken coop. Before they headed off to work in the fields, we ate dinner and a musical interlude followed.

I rode Dakota and observed them working with the Clydesdales, Thunder, and Titan, and then rode on to explore my acreage. Afterward, I visited with Sarah and helped her prepare food for supper. We even served two customers who turned up to buy milk and butter. Five o'clock rolled around, and it was time for the second milking of the day.

In the dairy barn, William said, "Isn't it grand?"

"It is," I said. William felt at home here, and after today, I agreed. Logan split our duties during the late afternoon session. We rotated between milking, cooling, and storing. Like a dance, we worked together and finished in about two hours' time.

William played a couple of tunes on his harmonica after supper. I beamed while I clapped my hands and fairly danced around on the porch while he played.

The routine repeated daily until Thursday, at the end of which, I said, "Thank you, William, and Mr. and Mrs. Cooper, for the lovely days and instruction. You have taught me many new things and I'll return after Mr. Pickwick's service tomorrow."

"Good night, Emeline," Sarah said with a grin. "We'll see you there, too."

Logan waved from his porch rocker and prepared his pipe for a smoke. "Enjoy your evening."

"Sure, be seein' you soon." William shook the saliva from his harmonica and set it on the porch rail to dry. Then he joined the Coopers and rocked in his chair to admire the sunset as a gentle, warm breeze blew.

Dakota and I rode back to Maude's house. What a pair of days it'd been. I shared the details with her, and she grinned. "Good night, Emeline," she said.

Exhausted, I lay my head on the pillow and slept.

Friday morning, Maude and I dressed for Mr. Pickwick's memorial service, and drove her carriage, pulled by her dapple-gray horse, Winnie, to the church. We arrived early, which was smart, as most Kearney residents turned out to pay their respects.

The weather forecast called for rain sometime today. I hoped it would hold off until after the funeral for the sake of the guests. Heavy gray clouds hung low in the sky but were not ominous. Their color matched the hewn stones of the church building. Tall, arched stained glass windows depicting various scenes from the Bible invoked reverence. I liked them better on cloudy days than on sunny ones because the colors appeared deeper, more subtle. My favorite window featured Jesus holding a lamb.

We met Audrey Pickwick inside the entrance. She extended her hand, but we each gave her a hug. "Remember, come see me anytime you'd like company," I said.

"I will. Thank you, Emeline."

"I'm so sorry, Audrey. I'll always remember Peter with fondness.
We'll all miss him dearly," Maude said.

We found our seats in the sanctuary and visited until the memorial
service began. Audrey sat in the front pew next to Andrew.

Spring flower arrangements filled the front of the room with
their beauty and scents. The pianist played 'Amazing Grace', and 'It
is Well with My Soul', as we sang along. The pastor opened with
prayer, delivered a fine eulogy, and invited folks to come forward to
offer their remembrances.

Many people did, as did I. "He was like a second father to me after I
lost my pa. When I made my trip to Boston to find Grandfather Silas,
he recommended I learn survival skills from Ole Mr. Thompson, since
I was traveling on horseback. He managed my farm for years, while I
was away in Boston and then while I lived in Indianapolis, handling
my financial interests in Kearney. I'll always remember him as my
benefactor and close friend. Rest in peace, Mr. Pickwick."

But none were as poignant as the words of Andrew, who stood
tall in front of the room. "Most of you have expressed how kind and
generous Pa was. As a child, he always cleared time for me and gave me
responsible jobs to do. As a toddler, I picked up trash and put things
away. Even then, I sensed I belonged to something important — like
I was part of a team. He made everything fun, no matter what. Oh,
yes, we fished, hiked, played catch, and more, but he even made work
enjoyable." He stopped to dab his eyes with a white handkerchief
and swallowed. "I'll never forget him — never. My goal is to become

like him: loving, protective, kind, and generous. And, God willing, I'll have a family, too. In the meantime, I'll continue the traditions he started at the Pickwick Mercantile as its new manager and co-owner with Ma."

Applause echoed in the room as emotions ran high and all but the most stoic pulled out their handkerchiefs. A beautiful ceremony, I was sure Mr. Pickwick would have been pleased.

After closing with prayer, music played as we all left for the gravesite. They finally laid him to rest. This chapter had closed, but a new one began for Audrey Pickwick, Andrew, and me.

The Decision?

"Why don't I fix a little supper while you write your letter to the Witherspoons?" Maude said.

"Alright. I may write two: one for them and one for Jonathan."

Gathering the supplies, I settled in a chair at the kitchen table. With the pen, I drew in fresh indigo ink and primed it on a fragment of newsprint. On a sheet of the thick, ivory stationery paper, I wrote.

Friday, April 14, 1893

Dear Mr. & Mrs. Witherspoon,

I hope this letter finds you well. Much has happened here.

Mr. Pickwick was laid to rest.

The Coopers are moving back to Wisconsin this year, so I need to find a new caretaker for the farm.

**Because values are down, and because of my feelings for
the farm, I've decided not to sell at this time.**

Love you,
Emeline

I neatly folded the letter and the surrounding envelope, addressed
it to the Witherspoons, and began my second letter.

Friday, April 14, 1893

Jonathan,

**I hope you're well and happy. How are things in the shop?
Please write back to keep me posted.**

**Most of the train trip went well, except for one place in
the middle of Missouri where bandits held us up. They almost
took Dakota! Fortunately for us, a gunman on board shot most
of them. One of the crew killed the last one. It was terrifying!
But I don't know if riding alone would have been less so.**

Emeline

Miss Ambrose placed a candlestick holder with a single taper on
the table and lit it for me to use for the wax seals. After addressing
the second envelope, I turned them both over and pressed down
their flaps around the letters. Now to seal them. With the candle, I

held the dark green sealing wax stick over the envelope's point and melted the end. Drip by drip, it fell until a dollop measured about a half-inch. Immediately, I stamped it, which left a lovely seal: a round design, with a raised maple leaf at its center. Finally, I licked the back of a gummed 2-cent postage stamp and pressed it on the front's top right corner. Monday, I would deliver them to Pickwick Mercantile to be collected by Carl Frick, our rural mail carrier.

Maude praised my work as she brought place settings to the table. "Nicely done." Pleased, I appreciated her compliment, and I had to agree.

"Thank you. Let me help you get supper on." I removed my letter-writing supplies from the table.

After supper, we read by lantern light. She read Louisa May Alcott's *Little Women*, while I chose to read Charles Dickens's novel, *Oliver Twist*, until our eyes grew weary, and we said goodnight.

Saturday morning after breakfast, Maude sat at her desk in the corner of the front room, with a journal. "I must prepare lessons for next week, Emeline, even though I don't expect many students this month. It may rain today, so why don't you take Winnie and the carriage this afternoon? You can raise the top and stay dry."

"Thank you, I will." I put on a belted navy-blue skirt, a long-sleeved, buttery yellow blouse, and boots. "Miss Ambrose, do you have another clean apron I might borrow? I'll wash my clothes Monday."

"Yes, of course. Take one from my bedroom dresser, second drawer."

A few times, the Witherspoons had let me drive their carriage, but this was the first time for me in Kearney. I pulled the collapsible top up, thankful for the luxury of a roof over my head. The dense clouds darkened and would soon wring rain from their soggy mass.

When I arrived, Logan waved me on to the horse barn and said, "Pull into the barn. No sense getting the rig and horse wet in the coming storm."

"Good idea. Thank you." Inside, two over-sized stalls housed their draft horses: Titan and Thunder.

"Hello." I stroked the white blaze on each of their faces and they nickered in reply. "They're gorgeous. I love their long-haired white stockings and the black manes and tails on these bays. They remind me of Penny, a Boston horse I met long ago."

"They're mighty strong helpers. We couldn't farm without them. They even pull out stubborn old stumps and boulders." He filled their racks with fresh hay and refreshed their water buckets. Pa would have appreciated a magnificent animal like this. They dwarfed my horse, Dakota.

We settled Winnie and the carriage inside the barn and then walked to the house.

Logan said, "Have a seat at the table, Emeline. We'll stay inside this afternoon, as the storm is upon us. Even so, at milking time, we'll have to brave the weather. It should quiet down by then."

William wandered into the room from what used to be my bedroom. "Afternoon, Miss O'Connor," he said.

"Hello, William. Do you live here?"

"I do. They offered to let me stay when the railroad transferred Pa to Cameron to be their Station Master. Ma went with him, of course."

"Why didn't you go with them?"

"It's not my way. I prefer to stay in one place, and I've a likin' for Kearney farm life. And I make a few bob, besides. Sometimes one day changes everythin'; sometimes years change nothin'. The day I met Mr. Cooper changed my life."

Sometimes years change nothing. I repeated this phrase and thought of Jonathan and how nothing had changed between us in years. What was it about William? Insightful? "What shall we do until milking time?" I asked.

William took a seat, Sarah poured water from a pitcher into glasses, and Logan brought a long thin box to the table.

Sarah asked, "Have you ever played Pick Up Sticks, Emeline?"

"Yes. It's great fun, and I'm pretty good at it, too. I have a steady hand."

William laughed. "We'll see now, won't we? Used to play all kinds of games of an evening with my parents."

Logan held the bunch of multi-colored sticks about two inches above the table and dropped them. Forty-one of them scattered, but most stayed in a tangled heap. "Our rule is simple: whoever ends up with the most sticks wins. We don't bother with point values for different colors. If you move any other stick but the one you're after, you must wait for your next turn. Emeline, you're our guest of honor, so you may go first."

"Alright. Tell me a little about your friends in Wisconsin, won't you?" I picked up as many easy outlying sticks as possible before I tackled the mass. "This is the advantage of being first," I said. My elbow rested on the oak table to help steady my hand as I picked two off the pile, one after the other, before I moved another stick and lost my turn. "Four, so far."

Logan said, "The Patterson and the Cooper families emigrated from Ireland and England around 1850 and have been close for decades. Both were dairy farmers in their old countries. The Pattersons have a son, Michael, 22, and a daughter, Lizzie, 25. Lizzie's married and moved away, but Michael still lives and works with them."

"Do your parents still live and work there, too?" I asked.

"Both sets of parents are still going strong on their own farms. Though dairy farmers originally, at the time they moved here, crops were more prevalent in that state, so they have adapted and grow fields of wheat, barley, oats, rye, and alfalfa, yet."

"Why did you decide to move here, then?"

"We wanted to get back to dairy farming and Missouri was the best place then. Now, dairy is coming back to Wisconsin stronger than ever."

"This is the first time I've worked on a farm, or with animals," William said. "Pa always worked with the railroads and on other equipment. I'd rather ride an actual horse than an iron one. And have roots — a place to call home."

"Sometimes one day changes everythin';
sometimes years change nothin'."

"Home. I understand, William." Looking at the Coopers, I said. "And it's *your* true place." I empathized with their desire to continue with their family and friends' traditions and clenched my teeth. They embraced their rich history.

We took turns picking up sticks for at least an hour while rain poured, thunder rumbled, and lightning flashed outside before Mrs. Cooper won the game.

We stared at the downpour from the front windows. Rivulets of water riddled the path to the barn and made a muddy mess, but fortunately, the barn sat on a slight hill, which allowed the water to run around and past it. Monday evening, I would wash my soiled clothes, but this evening, most of the mud would come off me with a sponge bath.

By milking time, the severe storm had passed, though it still rained. Mr. Cooper provided us with rain hats and coats made of oilcloth. We braved the rain and slogged through mud to milk the Jerseys. I slipped and fell flat, twisting my ankle. "Ouch!"

Logan and William both slid to my aid, helped me up, and I limped with them to a bench in the dairy barn, which was closer than the house. I rubbed the joint and moved it around, testing it.

William asked, "Are you alright? Is it broken?"

Logan provided a milking stool for me to rest my leg on and applied ice chips wrapped in a towel to my ankle. "Keep it up. Ice will help minimize any swelling."

"Thank you. Oh, my, it hurts." Grimacing, I moved the ice around when it got too cold. "I wish I could help you."

"If you must do somethin', stir the milk to cool it. I'll bring the bucket over next to you," William said.

"I can do that," I said. "Thank you."

"Aye. Anytime." He winked and went back to milking.

Would Jonathan have paid this much attention to me? Perchance. But William's attention felt different.

Muddy and soaked to the skin, we added eighteen gallons of fresh milk to the icehouse.

"That's a lot of milk." I said as I stood up and tried to walk, wincing with the shooting pain. "Agh! Oh, I'm going to need help."

"Wait here," said Logan. Soon he was back with Winnie and Maude's carriage. "William, please help her on board. You'll drive her home. I'll follow you in ours and bring you back."

"Aye, Mr. Cooper." William stood on my right side and said, "Lean on my arm, Miss O'Connor. I'll help you."

Logan continued. "And I'll not see you tomorrow, Emeline. You rest and keep your foot up until you can walk. If it isn't better in a couple of days, you might need the doctor to come out. I'm glad Miss Ambrose is with you."

At the carriage, I tried to climb up, which was painful. William ran to the opposite side, climbed in, and put his muscular arms underneath mine and pulled me up. "There you are, out of the rain now. Make yourself comfortable." He held the reins, clicked to Winnie, and we were on our way. After a few minutes, he asked, "Miss O'Connor?"

"Yes, William?"

He regarded poor Winnie in the pouring rain and then turned

toward me and asked, "This may not be the best time, but may I ask you somethin'?"

"Yes, of course," I said.

"You're the owner of the farm, and a very amiable young lady, too. With due respect, I'd like to invite you to come with me to the Spring Festival. If your ankle is better, that is. It's the evening of Saturday, May 6th, about three weeks away. I'll be playin' music part of the time, but surely would love to spend time with you when I'm free."

Though rain chilled the air, warmth rushed to my cheeks, and I smiled at him. "It would be my pleasure. Thank you, William." This was the first time a gentleman had ever invited me to an event. I smoothed my skirt over my legs and smiled.

Sunday, Maude attended church, but I rested at home. The Coopers would care for the cows today. Laid up, I'd mail my letters later. As Mr. Cooper recommended, I kept my leg raised, but each day I put a little more weight on my foot until, by the end of the week, I walked with only a limp most of the day. I drove the carriage to town and finally mailed my letters. I expected my sprained ankle would heal before the festival.

That weekend, Miss Ambrose took ill and asked me to fill in for her at school Monday morning and until she recovered. "You may sit on the stool to rest your ankle."

"Of course, I will. After all you've done for me? How could I refuse?"

She laid in bed, covered up to her neck with her feather quilt. "Thank you, Emeline. I've already prepared for the lessons. Read them over and let me know if you have questions. There won't be many children this time of year: only a handful of younger ones."

"Shall I fetch the doctor?"

"No, it's only a cold. Don't worry. I'll be well in a few days' time."

"Only a cold? Are you sure? I wouldn't want it to worsen. Remember, Mr. Pickwick."

"Give it a day or two. If it's not improving, we'll get the doctor."

"Let me take your temperature, anyway."

"I've already taken it and it's barely above normal. I'll be fine, dear." She turned away from me to face the wall.

With the pitcher in hand, I hobbled outside, pumped fresh water into it, and filled a glass for her. "Drink this down," I said. "Water helps to wash out the sickness." I prayed she would recover shortly. *No more loss, please.*

She turned over, sat up, drank, and offered a tired smile. "You remind me of my mother, child. Thank you."

I found her school journal resting on the secretary, picked it up, and began studying the lessons: arithmetic, reading, spelling, handwriting, science, and history. She had planned a full week of activities for each class. "I can handle it, Miss Ambrose." But she had fallen asleep and didn't respond. "Rest now." I laid my hand on her forehead. *Not too warm.* I let her sleep.

Monday morning, I hoped the Coopers wouldn't miss me. I dressed for school, which would begin at nine o'clock, and spent some time plaiting my hair and pinning the braids into a bun in the back, which made me appear older. Then, I fixed oatmeal for both of us. "Miss Ambrose? Are you awake?" She wasn't, but she slept peacefully, so I added more water to it and left it on a metal shelf over the stove to keep it warm.

A fluttering feeling rolled through my stomach. How would I do as a teacher? I grabbed the journal, and limped across the yard to the schoolhouse, which stood on a hill, as tall and as white as ever. Near the door, a heavy bell hung from a beam between two posts. I would ring it before school and after recess to bring children inside. An American flag fluttered in the wind at the front corner of the school.

To break the morning chill, I brought in pieces of split wood and stacked them in crisscross fashion in the wood stove's belly. Smoldering coals soon ignited the dry wood. It'd been years since I'd been inside, but it remained the same. "Sometimes years change nothin'" William had said. I chuckled.

The children would arrive any time. Outside, I lifted my eyes toward the sky. *Make me a decent teacher today.* Five minutes before nine o'clock, I rang the bell. Students lined up into two lines: only two youngsters in the boys' line, and three in the girls'. I welcomed them and asked them to enter the classroom, stow away their jackets and lunches, and take their seats.

"Welcome, class. Miss Ambrose will return when she is well. Today, I'll be your teacher. My name is Miss O'Connor. I attended this school when I was your age. First, let's get acquainted. We'll start at this end.

Will you please stand, tell me your name, how old you are, and what you like best about school?"

A few children murmured to their neighbors while others spoke. "Excuse me. No talking unless you're called on, please." Giggling, they complied, sort of.

Afterward, I had them stand, pledge allegiance to the flag in the room's corner, and recite the Lord's Prayer.

Instruction began with reading from the McGuffey readers. More excessive talking and silliness prevented genuine progress. I identified the ringleader and separated him from the group. He now sat alone near the front of the room, facing the wall. "Miss Ambrose will be unhappy with my report, if this kind of behavior continues," I said to everyone.

After that, I'd earned the respect of the children. We practiced writing, ciphered arithmetic problems on the board, and practiced spelling words. Even the privy breaks, lunch, and recess went smoothly.

At home, Maude told me she felt much better and sat at the kitchen table. I said, "The day went smoothly, after I laid down the rules and threatened them with a bad report to you. I had to move one boy to the front and have him face the wall."

I pulled over another chair, put my foot up, and joined her at the table. Miss Ambrose asked, "Who was that?"

"His name was Joe."

"The younger students mind their manners, most of the time. I'll tell them how disappointed I was to hear of their early behavior when I return, probably Wednesday. How'd you like teaching?"

"It's been but a single day, but I enjoyed it. I love helping people, probably more than anything." I smiled, adjusting my leg on the chair.

"Hmm." She paused and continued. "So, Emeline O'Connor loves to help people."

"Oh, I see. You want me to add this to my 'defining Emeline' list?" How could she read my triggers? Probably it's because she'd been my teacher for so long.

Maude smiled and continued. "*Why* do you love helping people?"

"Why?"

"Yes, why?"

I thought for a moment. "When people are sad, I want to comfort them. If they need anything, I want to help, if I can. I'd like to make a difference — to improve people or their situations."

"Write those thoughts down before you forget."

I hurried to retrieve my journal and wrote the date and the words. "Finished."

"Now, recite it for me, please."

I read her the entry which I'd memorized, by now.

"Next, list all the directions you might choose, and answer this question for each: '*how much difference will I make in people's lives?*' It'll help weight your answers and show how much impact on others you'll have. For example: not much, a little, or big."

This exercise felt like a game, but I knew it was more. Without telling me what to do, she encouraged me to analyze my answers.

I imagined various paths. "Alright, first, I'm a woodworker in Indianapolis crafting spindles and other things out of wood. I help the

Witherspoons and, ultimately, the customers, but it's a solitary type
of job. The biggest change I'm making is in the wood itself, I guess.
Pride comes from the finished work and the appreciation expressed
by them and the customers."

"Hmm. The pride comes from the finished work itself: your
workmanship. Interesting. You enjoy creating quality pieces. How
will you rate this path as it relates to other's lives?"

I paused and said, "A little. I'm helping as an employee who cares
about quality, but anyone with an eye for detail could learn to do it.
I'm not changing people — just the wood."

"What other options do you have?" She rose to pour hot water over
fresh green tea leaves with crushed mint in the teapot's strainer and
set out teacups on saucers. The steam carried the fresh scent of mint
into the air. "Hot mint tea helps clear my nose," she said.

"I love it. Thank you." Tea steeped in the teapot while I thought
of another choice. "A dairy farmer. The difference I'd make would
be two-fold." I cocked my head. "First, I adore helping the animals.
Second, families would benefit from the healthful milk I would
provide. How thrilling! Someday, I hope to have a family of my own.
I'd have to say this option would make a big difference. But it would
mean saying goodbye to the Witherspoons — and Jonathan."

"Right. You've tasted teaching, but would you consider it a
viable path? On your own, since thirteen, you've matured quickly.
At sixteen, you'd pass for at least eighteen. You've eight years of
schooling behind you, and you were an excellent student — always
an eager learner. I'd highly recommend you and offer training.

Earlier, you mentioned you missed it." She tilted her head and our eyes met.

I poured the fragrant hot tea into my cup and sat back in the wooden chair and considered this option. "As a teacher, I would improve the lives of children through education. An educated child has more opportunities afforded him as an adult. Plus, helping the children affects their families. I'd have to say this path would make a big difference, as well."

"Now, write all this reasoning in your journal before you forget."

I wrote each scenario down and glanced up at her as she sipped her tea. "Is there more?" I sat in her 'classroom', which I *had* said I'd missed. I chuckled.

"Yes, Emeline. What did you say your big dream was?"

"My ultimate goal is to marry my best friend and have a family."

"Which setting would fit this goal best?"

The choice was obvious. "The dairy because women teachers can't marry."

She sipped her tea. "True enough, though you might teach before then, if you wanted. You're young and there's no rush. I've noted the best marriages are ones where both individuals complement each other: somehow, they're better together than separately. Besides love, they need each other. By the way, have I told you I'm seeing someone on Sundays?"

"No, you haven't. Who?"

"His name is James Penn. He moved here about a year ago and opened a cordwainer shop in town. He's a talented new shoe and boot maker. Oh! I forgot to tell you this. It's incredible, Emeline. He told me about the holdup on the train recently. Remember?"

"How could I forget? But how did he hear about it?"

"*He* was the gunman you referred to in your coach! *He's* the one who gave you back your pocket watch."

"What? Honestly? I remember his face and the leather apron he wore, but I never thought I'd see him again. Extraordinary! You're fortunate to have such a gallant admirer. I'm so grateful he rode the train that day."

"He had bought some supplies for his shop in Hannibal. And you'll meet him again someday, soon."

"I can't wait. Is he courting you? And is that allowed for teachers?"

She smiled. "Not yet. We're still getting acquainted. But so far, we enjoy each other's company. In answer to your second question, no, it isn't permitted. But, fortunately, in rural towns, women teachers are given some leeway to socialize. Kansas City teachers are forbidden to socialize like this."

"Amazing. I'm glad for you. Hmm. Like me, you love helping lots of people, right?"

"Yes, Emeline, I do, more than anything — even more than having a family."

"But wouldn't it be great if the *right* someone came along, like Mr. Penn, and you could still help people?"

"Ah, it would, indeed. But as you said, women teachers must stay single. Though many rules exist for women teachers, it's still a respectable living for a woman on her own."

"Yes, but what about helping in other ways, other than teaching? I have an idea: start a small library in Kearney. Boston has a gigantic one, which assisted me in finding my grandfather."

A dimpled smile spread over her face. "An excellent suggestion. I'll tuck that idea away for later, though it would take a much larger town to support a library building, I believe."

"May we pray?" I asked.

"Of course. You begin," she said.

"Dear Heavenly Father, I pray for the clarity of my life's purpose. Thank you for the opportunities and skills you've given me. Thank you for the people you've put into my life, and for health, safety, and security. I pray for your peace about this important decision. Amen."

Maude added her prayer after mine and smiled. Her face glowed: not because of her cold, but because she loved talking about James Penn.

I returned the smile and asked, "May I ride Dakota to town before supper? I'd like to pick out some material for a new skirt."

"Yes, dear. Take your time. I'll read while you're away."

I hurried to change into my split skirt and rode Dakota for the fifteen-minute trip to the Pickwick Mercantile.

Spring Festival

At the store, I purchased yards of black and white checked cotton and some black velvet ribbon, certain Mrs. Cooper would allow me to borrow Ma's sewing machine to make a new skirt for the festival. I already owned a white blouse with flared sleeves gathered by elastic at the wrists. The ribbon would lie around the collar and tie with a Celtic knot, its tails angling downward — overall, appearing like an X. Would William recognize the Irish reference?

For the next two weeks, I continued to learn more about the business of running the dairy and farm. I still favored that foot, but my ankle had healed completely. Afternoons, Dakota and I followed along as the men plowed and sowed seeds of alfalfa, oats, and barley, with Thunder and Titan pulling the plow. Twice each day, we milked cows and collected eggs from the chickens. After suppers, we enjoyed a musical interlude provided by William, relaxed, and chatted.

"We harvest the alfalfa hay *before* the grains have formed," Mr.

Cooper explained. "But we harvest oats and barley when their seeds are ripe."

"I remember Pa did the same, but I never understood why he didn't harvest alfalfa when it seeded, too."

William said, "Before goin' to seed, the sweet hay has more nutrition for the animals, that's why." He leaned back in his rocker, raised his arms, and stretched.

From the porch swing Mrs. Cooper said, "Fresh cut hay reminds me of a warm summer day — even in winter, when I'm near the hayloft."

Mr. Cooper stood up and leaned over against the porch railing to clean out his pipe. "After we harvest the oats and barley, we harvest their short, dried, hollow grass stalks, or straw, for the icehouse, and bedding for the horses and chickens."

"Pa explained how straw was great for insulation, as it doesn't mold or attract moisture. And, like you, he rotated crops, leaving some fields unplanted. Why's that?"

Mr. Cooper answered. "A field needs to rest and recover to provide strong plants the next year."

Farming was a science, and I learned fast, although I knew *if* I was to run the farm until I found a caretaker, I would need to hire laborers for much of the field work. "May I have your new address, Mr. Cooper, in case I have questions after you've gone?"

"Of course."

As I rode home one evening, I recalled how both Clydesdales bore the weight of the plow and the farmer as they furrowed the dirt. If only Pa would have owned one of these powerful animals to help him fell that oak tree that caused his heart failure. How much different my life would be, if he were still here. Through misty eyes, I wrote in my journal.

April 28, 1893

Dear Pa,

Swirling thoughts have calmed down a little since my talk with Miss Ambrose. She's helped me discover who I am at heart: someone who wants to make a difference.

Still, managing a dairy farm scares me. Moving from Boston with Ma and settling in this place must have been difficult, but you did it and started something truly wonderful.

I won't let you down.

Love,

Em

While milking one evening, Mr. Cooper and I discussed staffing. "You'll need to hire more hands to do the work when we've gone, Emeline," he said. "There's a help-wanted board at both the bank and the mercantile."

"Yes, Mr. Kingston told me there's no shortage of people needing jobs. I have another idea about this, but nothing's decided. Don't need to worry too much about that, yet. By the way, have you fixed a moving date?"

"Yes, we've discussed it and believe it would be best to move in October after the harvest. *If* you decide to keep the dairy running, would you be willing to purchase our cows, draft horses, the thresher, and reimburse us for the material used to build the improvements? We'll make you a fair offer."

"Of course, I'm interested. At harvest time, we'll settle up."

"Perfect. Starting fresh will be easier, since we'll be sharing a house with our friends for the winter."

Through shadows of promise, my future was taking shape, though I'd made no firm decision.

Saturday afternoon of May 6th was upon us — the Spring Festival! I'd awaited this event for weeks. Sarah had allowed me to use the sewing machine two weeks ago to make my new skirt.

I swirled in the full-length black and white checked garment. Yards of fabric flowed freely at the hemline but gathered at the V-shaped yoke at the waist. Miss Ambrose helped me tie the Celtic knot in the black velvet ribbon worn over the stand-up collar of my white blouse. Though not as fine as the dresses of Boston, I considered it a success. "Won't it be fun to dance in this?" I twirled as the skirt billowed out.

"You're beautiful, Emeline," Maude said with her dimpled smile.

"Thank you." Warmth crept through my face and ears. Maude not only encouraged me, but grounded me with her mature outlook on life.

She beheld her face in a looking glass, put some beeswax on her lips, and pinched her cheeks, as was her routine. "If you're putting your hair up, you may borrow my fancy silver comb, if you like."

"We'll see." I played with my hairstyle for some time before I settled on a French plait, which gathered all my hair from each side and trailed down the back of my head. Because of the length, I looped the last of the braid into a bun at the back and pinned it. "Keeping it simple is best. Thank you, though."

"You're welcome. Mr. Penn has asked me to accompany him, so after he picks up William, they'll be by to pick us up. It should be soon, as William is part of the entertainment.

"Perfect. I can't wait to meet Mr. Penn. I haven't visited his cordwainer shop yet."

"He's eager to see you again, too. I've shared a little about you. Hope you don't mind." She blushed as she drew her hair into a beautiful loose bun and covered it with an open hairnet which matched her mauve dress.

"No, not at all." Thrilled for Maude, I imagined the changes her potential marriage would trigger. The "what-ifs" began their dance. If she married, she could no longer teach and would move to his place. Where would I live? I stopped thinking about it when the clip-clop of a horse and carriage approached.

I answered the knock on the door. "Hello, William, and you must be Mr. Penn," I said. I'd recognize you anywhere! So good to see you again.

"You must be Miss Emeline. I'm pleased to finally, and formally, meet you." He smiled, but his bushy mustache hid half of it. His eyes crinkled behind his eyeglasses. Tall and slender, he and Maude would make an attractive couple.

"How extraordinary that I would meet my savior on the train again," I said. Today he dressed well, wearing a suit, tie, and the same bowler hat. "I've often wondered if you had to defend your actions to the authorities. I should think you'd be a hero."

He answered. "I had to make a trip to Brookfield to explain things to the sheriff, but the railroad witnesses helped and they ruled my actions as self-defense, so they released me."

"Self-defense? I should think you defended everyone else on the train as well. I'll never forget you and I'm glad you weren't in any kind of trouble for it. Miss Ambrose has been my teacher and mentor for many years, Mr. Penn, and I can say without hesitation, she is a lovely woman with a heart for helping others. You'd be fortunate to win her."

Embarrassed, Maude approached and said, "My, my. Thank you for the compliment, Emeline."

"Are you ready to go, Miss O'Connor?" William asked.

Miss Ambrose answered from behind me. "We are. I see you've made introductions, except for mine and William's. Hello, William. It's wonderful to meet you."

"Yes. Forgive me," I said. "William, meet Miss Ambrose, my teacher, friend, and mentor."

William bowed. "A pleasure, ma'am."

As I climbed into the carriage's back seat, William supported my arm. "So, you'll have to fill me in on your train adventure."

After I shared that experience, he said, "Sure, that's a wild story. And to think — he's no longer a random stranger in your life." Changing the subject, he continued. "It's fine weather for the festival, don't you think?"

"Couldn't be better. I must confess something to you, William."

"Oh?"

"I've never danced with anyone before; not since I was a child with my friend Harriet. I'm a little nervous. And I don't want to push my ankle too much either."

"You've nothin' to worry about. I'm the fish out of water here. The fiddle music pleasures me and keeps me in the background, mostly."

"So, you're the shy one?"

A flush crept across his cheek. "Few know the real me. I keep most feelin's inside." He faced me and gave me a broad grin; his green eyes crinkled at the corners. "I loosen up when I'm in the pub drinkin' beer, though. Do you drink?"

"Oh, no, not alcohol. Ma and Pa frowned on it. And I've seen plenty of drunks before, none of them pleasant."

"Too bad. I wager, if tipsy, you'd be a lot of fun. I don't drink as much as I used to, though. Not since I've worked on your farm. Livin' with the Coopers puts a damper on that kind of activity."

A strange tingle ran through me. Doubts. Why did I accept his invitation while I still had feelings for Jonathan? In my heart, I knew he would never return them. Am I fickle to be attracted to a handsome young man, sweet Irish words, and music? I'd made a mistake, and I'd attempt to correct it. "Don't worry about shyness. I'm just coming with you as a friend." My hands smoothed the checkered skirt over my legs and as we lurched over a bump, I clung to the carriage's side and held on tight.

"I noticed the Celtic knot in your ribbon, Miss O'Connor. Very Irish of you."

"Thank you, Mr. Kavanaugh." I smiled as I pinched the knot in my ribbon. I was proud of my Irish heritage. He was kind enough to comment, but I maintained my distance.

"Mr. Kavanaugh? Why the sudden formality?"

"I enjoy saying it." I lied. "Kavanaugh. It's a splendid Irish name."

He let it go, and we arrived. The festival sprawled across a glade near Clear Creek. People arrived in buggies, carriages, and on horseback, migrating to the opening between stands of tall oak and maple trees. On the far end, farmers' chicks, ducklings, and goslings paraded in pens, which would sell by the end of the day. Other sale tables displayed items made by families over the winter: down pillows, brooms, embroidered tea towels, and aprons. Still others had baked goods for sale: cakes, pies, breads, and biscuits. Delightful.

"I'll tune up then. I play first." William took out his fiddle and plucked the strings, bending his ear toward them to listen for the exact notes as he turned the tuning keys. "Go on and browse around, and I'll meet up with you after the first dance." He plucked a small piece of rosin from his pocket and smoothed it over his bow.

I admired his dedication to his talent. "Alright. I'll visit the tables." James and Maude had already headed in that direction.

Audrey Pickwick lingered near the tables, and I sauntered over to greet her. "Hello. I'm glad you're here. May I join you?"

"Of course! How have you been, Emeline? Did you come with Miss Ambrose?"

"I'm fine, thank you. Yes, and with William Kavanaugh, as a friend." I turned toward him. From a distance, he saw me, held his bow up, and I waved back. Audrey grinned. Sensing her thoughts, I said, "He politely asked if I would come. I thought it would be more fun than coming alone, but I'm having second thoughts. Miss Ambrose came with her gentleman friend, too."

"James Penn? They make a lovely couple. They meet after church at the mercantile every Sunday." She chuckled, but her eyes were pensive. "Friends and family are the most precious gifts we have."

"True." We walked along, admired the wares, including Andrew's table, and chatted about my farm and their shop until the music began.

Everyone cheered and gathered in the clearing. Adults and even older children paired off and formed four separate quads for square-dancing. A man next to William clapped with the rhythm and called out moves while the pairs danced within each group. Sometimes the couples would be together, sometimes not. William played the fiddle brilliantly, while I danced in place and observed, for now. '*Oh, Susannah!* was the song he played first. It lasted for about twenty minutes, leaving most dancers breathless. Afterward, a ten-minute break gave them a rest. A new musician would play the next song.

He bowed before me. "May I have this dance, lass?"

I smiled and took his hand as we joined three other couples for a square-dance to '*Old Joe Clark*'. What fun it was! Doh-see-doh was one call, which meant we faced the same direction, but circled each other with our arms crossed. Sometimes we switched partners or held hands in a circle and danced. Afterward, we laughed and laughed. Out of breath from the exercise, we plopped down on a blanket William had brought and spread out over the grass under an oak near the clearing. A third musician would play the next song.

"'Havin' fun, Miss O'Connor?"

"I am. Thank you for inviting me, Mr. Kavanaugh. I adore music, singing, and dancing." The water in the nearby creek gurgled over rocks, making its own music. The heavy scent of lilacs filled the air.

"Singin', sure, and when you catch your breath, let's sing somethin' together."

"Do you know '*Lavender's Blue*'?" I hoped he did, as it was my favorite song.

"I do. Mother sang it to me when I was a lad."

"Good. Are you ready?" I asked.

"I am. You start and I'll join in."

I began singing.

> "*Lavender's blue, dilly, dilly,*
> *Lavender's green.*
> *When I am king, dilly, dilly,*
> *You shall be queen.*"

"Who told you so, dilly, dilly,

Who told you so?

'Twas my own heart, dilly, dilly,

That told me so."

We sang the next six verses and our voices blended well. I thought it might be a dream. I closed my eyes and marked the moment.

"Thank you, Mr. Kavanaugh. I enjoyed that."

"My pleasure, lass." He rose, rolled up the blanket, and we returned to the dance. It was his turn to play the fiddle again.

As the couples danced, I saw Maude with her partner. He bowed as she curtseyed at the beginning. Dressed up for the occasion, they were a picture. I smiled to myself.

After this dance, I approached her. "Hello, Miss Ambrose."

"Hello, Emeline. Whew! Let me catch my breath. Would you join us for some lemonade and biscuits?" she asked.

William appeared at my side before I answered. "Overheard you talkin'. Let's all go for some refreshment."

Then, I heard a familiar voice from the past. "Emeline! You're in town!"

"Harriet! Oh, goodness, what a surprise! Aren't you a sight for sore eyes?" We hugged for a long time. "How have you been?" I asked.

"I'm doin' fine, but we need to catch up. I'll be here for a few days at our old house. Come visit?"

"Of course," I said. "May I introduce you to a friend, William Kavanaugh?" Turning to William, I said, "This is Harriet Steiner, my best friend since childhood."

"Hello," William said, throwing her an engaging smile.

"Where are my manners?" Harriet turned to a tall, muscular young man. "This is my close friend, Henry Malloy — Huck for short."

Huck bowed to me and said, "Hello, m'lady."

I laughed, "No need to stand on ceremony. Hello, Huck. We're going for lemonade. Will you join us?"

We all chatted about the festival, what we've been up to, and more. For a moment, my mind skipped ahead to the long visit with Harriet tomorrow. It'd been years since we've talked, except through occasional letters. *Oh, how I've missed her!*

Soon, the dancing changed from square-dancing to the waltz and the two-step. The finale was a round of Virginia Reel. After the food disappeared, the festival ended. Customers purchased what they would at the tables and pens. Andrew packed up the few things left on his table. Our eyes met for a moment, so I waved, and he returned it. William bought two cherry pies: one for Maude and me, and one for himself and the Coopers.

On our way home, instead of talking, we hummed a few of the tunes from the afternoon together, and I was glad to keep personal conversation to a minimum. "Mr. Kavanaugh, would you do me a favor?" I asked.

"I'll. What is it?"

"Please tell Mr. Cooper I won't be in tomorrow because I'll be visiting Harriet while she's in town."

"Consider it done." He pulled the cart up to the house and helped me out. At the door, he said, "Thank you, Miss O'Connor. I enjoyed your company very much."

"I'm glad. I enjoyed yours, too. See you later, Mr. Kavanaugh."

I smiled as he bowed and hopped into the carriage seat, as if gravity had no effect on him. James delivered Miss Ambrose to the porch. Then the men left.

I would not make this mistake again, though my intention to stay just friends might prove difficult with his Irish charm. I couldn't abide growing close to someone who drank alcohol, especially to excess. And, technically, he was the Cooper's hired hand, and I was his boss. How would it look? Had I already burned that bridge by attending the festival with him today? I sighed.

Harriet & Huck

A gentle rain fell through the night, which brought the temperatures down into the fifties by morning. The floor chilled my feet as I stepped across the wood floor to the washstand to cleanse. Finding the pitcher empty, I threw on my khaki riding skirt, a blue blouse, and boots to go outside and draw water from the pump. I cleaned up and brushed my hair. Where was Miss Ambrose? Hungry, I went to the kitchen to fix something for breakfast: a slice of wheat bread, some white cheese, and a glass of water.

The door opened, and the teacher entered. "Morning, Emeline," she said.

"Good morning. Have you already eaten breakfast?" I asked.

"Yes. I rose early — couldn't sleep. I've tended to the horses."

"You couldn't sleep? Were you thinking of Mr. Penn?" I smiled.

Maude chuckled. "I suppose. We had such a great time at the festival." Her face shone whenever she spoke of him. She washed her hands in the washstand's basin, where the chamomile soap released its sweet apple scent.

"I did, too, though I must admit, on the way, I entertained second thoughts about the outing. Though William acted quite the gentleman and we both love music, I kept our footing on friendship ground."

While styling her hair, Miss Ambrose asked, "Oh?"

"Yes. Physically, I'm attracted to him, but our values differ somewhat. He drinks, although he tells me he doesn't drink as much as he used to. And I kept thinking I'd made a mistake. Jonathan popped into my thoughts, and I wasn't as comfortable as I might have been with William. Plus, I'm his boss. How does socializing with an employee look?"

"I see. My. Sounds like you've whipped yourself into a frenzy over these two men. If I were you, I'd stop dwelling on it and do something completely different. What plans do you have today?"

"I'm visiting Harriet at her house, and I can't wait. It's been such a long time since we've visited alone, face-to-face. Do you have plans?"

"After I've cleaned up the schoolhouse a little, Mr. Penn has asked me to go out for a carriage ride and picnic lunch. I'm thankful I teach in the country, where socializing with a man is permitted without judgement."

"Do you think it's getting serious?"

Her smile spread across her face, and a blush colored her cheeks. "Yes, possibly. He's easy to talk to, and we find plenty of topics to discuss: our likes, dislikes, interests, favorite things, dreams, you know…"

After breakfast, I cleaned up, and stopped by the door. "I'll be back for supper. Have fun, Miss Ambrose."

"You, too, dear."

Dakota and I cantered to Harriet's house, about a ten-minute ride from Miss Ambrose's. The weather was balmy, and the birds entertained me with their lively chorus. My favorite was the mockingbird, with its varied vocals. I could have walked, taking time to enjoy the flora and fauna along the way, but I wanted as much time as possible with my friend. She was waiting for me on the wraparound front porch of her family's white, two-story farmhouse. "Harriet!"

"Emeline!"

I dismounted and ran into her open arms. We hugged for a long time. "Oh, how I've missed you," I said, my heart beating wildly. We had been inseparable as best friends during our childhood, but had been separated for too long, and I yearned to refresh the bond we used to have. Exchanging letters a few times over the years wasn't enough. I tied Dakota's reins to a rail.

"You're the one who left first, ya' know. I've missed ya', too," Harriet pointed out. "Let's share some tea inside and visit for a spell. Afterward, we can go for a walk or somethin'."

The inside was about the same as I remembered it. Although some of the furniture had changed, it was cozy. We sat across from each other in two hickory chairs with cushions stuffed with feathers tied to the seats and backs. Covered in dark blue heavy cotton, the cushions provided comfort and appeal. "How does your pa like working construction in Westport?"

"He loves it. They've kept their home in Kearney and hired men to plant and harvest crops. Pa says it's paid for and there's no sense to be sellin' it yet. I think he worries about not havin' a place to live, in the unlikely event he loses his job."

"Your pa is wise. He probably makes a profit from the harvests after expenses, too. But what about you? What have *you* been doing all this time?"

"I still live with them in Westport. Ma and I clean the houses of some of the wealthier folks. It isn't difficult or glamorous; not like I've learned a trade like you've done with woodworkin', but it helps pay our bills and keeps us occupied."

"I see. And are your parents doing well physically?"

"Fine, just fine. They'll be glad you've come back. Ya *have* come back to stay this time, right? Don't tell me no!" Her eyes pierced mine, insistent.

I chuckled. "For now. I didn't expect I would, but with the way things are, it's the best solution. I'll live with Maude until the Coopers leave — or until she gets married. Not that she is, yet, but she and Mr. Penn spend a lot of time together. If they marry, I'll live in my farmhouse, I guess, which means William Kavanaugh will have to move elsewhere. But I'm getting ahead of myself."

We moved our chairs closer to face each other. "Sounds like a game of dominoes," she said.

"I love that game. Yes, it's similar. Good analogy, Harriet." I sipped some tea. "Mm. This is delicious."

"Thank you. What about the fella you raved about in Indianapolis? What's his name — Jonathan? Is that over? I thought it might be, since you went with William to the festival."

Jonathan. Had he read my letter, yet, I wondered? Then I answered her. "Although smitten with Jonathan for years, I was naught but a friend to him. When I left, he'd set a date with Ruth, the new teacher in town. But I adored the Witherspoons too, as they took care of me like parents. I'd planned to go back to them after settling business here, but complications have arisen."

She sipped her tea and said, "From the looks of things at the festival, ya' might have found a diversion in William, no?"

My face wilted. "That's what people think? No, no, Harriet, we're just friends and I'm his employer. I shouldn't have gone with him, but I enjoyed the music and dancing." I drank deeply from my glass and turned the conversation toward her. "What about you? What's the story between you and this Huck fellow?"

She set her glass down on a thin wooden coaster on the hickory end table and stood up. Harriet gestured whenever she talked about something exciting. "We met in Westport. About a year ago, he was deliverin' food to a house Ma and I were cleanin'. I helped put away the food he brought in the kitchen for the Mrs., and we got to talkin'. This happened several times before he *finally* asked permission to spend time with me after work. Ma asked for Pa's approval, and he gave it. They adore Huck, and he's a perfect fit for me. We've talked about gettin' married someday, but it's not official, so keep it *quiet*. Shhh!"

I jumped out of my chair. "Oh! I will." I crossed my heart, but inside, it fluttered. First Maude, and now Harriet, were in a significant relationship.

Then, an idea occurred to me. "Let's go for a ride, shall we?" I asked. "I want to show you something new."

"Sure, it's a gorgeous day. Since Huck has the horse and carriage, may I ride with ya' on Dakota?"

"Of course. This is perfect. I'll introduce you to the Coopers, if they're available, and you've already met William. Prepare to be amazed, Harriet."

She sat behind Dakota's saddle and held onto my hips, while her legs hung loosely down his sides. I held my Morgan to a walk, and we noted familiar landmarks and commented on the colorful May flowers and ideal weather. Upon our arrival, I tapped on the screen door.

Sarah came to the door and opened it, wiping her hands on her apron. "Come in, come in! I'm cleaning, but I can stop anytime. Housework never ends, does it?" Her round face with ruddy cheeks gave a genuine smile, which crinkled the corners of her eyes.

We remained outside. "No, thank you, Mrs. Cooper. Not to interrupt your day too much. I'd like you to meet my best friend in the world, Harriet Steiner."

"Nice to meet you, Harriet."

Harriet smiled and nodded.

I continued. "We grew up together. Her family's farm is just north of us, but they've moved to Westport for a while, and she came up for the festival and a visit. Do you mind if I show her around?"

"Not at all. Please do. As the men are working the fields today, you probably won't see them or the draft horses."

"Thank you, Mrs. Cooper. We won't be long," I said.

"A pleasure to meet ya', ma'am," Harriet said with a smile. Sarah returned it, nodded, and closed the door.

Beaming with pride for the Cooper's enterprise, I gave her a brief tour, which included the pasture, the old horse and cattle barn, the new milking parlor and creamery, and the icehouse. "Isn't it fantastic? They've built a thriving dairy business, which should continue, as many Kearney families depend on them for their healthful milk, eggs, and butter."

"Impressive," she said.

We stood in the creamery while my mind developed a new scenario. "Harriet, do you enjoy living in the city and cleaning houses, or do you miss living here and farm life?"

"To be honest, I never wanted to leave the farm. Westport was Pa's idea. He wanted more for us. You were gone and nothin' tied me to Kearney, so I went with them. And then, I met Huck." She smiled and clasped her hands over her chest. "He's the thing I love most about Westport…not the city itself. Workin' with Ma is fine, but cleanin' houses is a means of makin' money, not my dream." She glanced toward the pasture where the Jerseys grazed. "Besides the farm, I miss bein' with ya', my friend."

"I miss you too, Harriet, terribly." I sighed and asked her the burning question. "The Coopers are leaving after the harvest this fall — moving back to Wisconsin and their family and friends. So, I have a proposition for you. Tell me, truthfully, whether you're interested."

She turned toward me; her soft amber eyes fixed on my hazel ones. "Sounds like an important question. What is it?"

"Alright. Here goes," I said. "What if…" I hesitated. "What if you moved back to Kearney, learned the dairy business, and become my caretaker for this farm?" I laced my fingers behind my back, grinned, and raised my eyebrows. Silently, I awaited her response.

Her jaw dropped, and her mouth gaped. "That *is* a big idea, Emeline. But I wouldn't leave my Huck."

Undeterred, I continued. "You know him well, right? Might he be interested, too? There's plenty of work and money to be made for all of us. The three of us can discuss it if you like."

"Wow! Maybe. Let's talk about it. Huck's dream is to be a business owner someday. This is a business, right?"

"It is, but at first, we'd all be working together with me as the property owner."

"He might not be interested then, but I'll ask him, just the same. But where would he live?"

"He would live with the Coopers and William in the beginning. After the harvest and the Coopers move, you and I would move in, and the men would live at your house. Your pa might enjoy having Huck and William monitor the hired help, too. We can hire extra help in the spring and fall seasons, if we need it."

"It's sure somethin' to ponder…and a tremendous opportunity, Emeline."

"I want you to be certain this is the life you'd choose. Dairy farming is a full-time commitment. Dairy cows don't take time off from milking. Every day, twice a day. And there's planning for calving, and lots more." I held my breath and clenched my hands together, hoping she would agree.

"Let me talk it over with Huck. He's stayin' with a friend of his near town, but we'll be together for supper."

"That's fine. If you need me, I'll be at Miss Ambrose's house evenings, or here with the Coopers most days. When are you two returning to Westport?"

"Day after tomorrow. I'll discuss it with Huck this evenin'. Will ya ride over to my place again tomorrow mornin' about ten o'clock? If he's interested, I'll ask him to meet us then."

Trembling with excitement, I said, "Absolutely." I couldn't wait to tell Maude about it. I prayed a silent prayer as we rode back to her farm. My fears diminished as I recalled the verse promising God doesn't give you anything you can't handle, without a way to escape. Would this be the answer? *Dear Lord, You must have planted this idea in my mind. You work all things together for good. Thank you for planting this seed. Water it and nurture it, that it may grow into a sturdy tree for your glory. Amen.*

Wide-eyed, I talked this idea over with Maude during and after supper. Scarcely eating, I saved most of my food for later. Lacy tendrils of the sprouting seed crept through my mind as I imagined my future with it. The more I thought about it, the more I wanted it. "It's a fine idea, isn't it?" I asked.

"It is, if it suits them, Emeline. It's their decision, not yours. You asked, but it's too soon to say if they will be your caretakers or someone else, perhaps."

"True."

"This brings some verses to mind. Let me read them to you." Maude rose from the table to retrieve her Bible. She sat back down, turned up the lantern, and read Matthew 7, verses 24–27, aloud. In them, Jesus compared the wise man who built his house upon a rock with the foolish man who built his house upon the sand. When a flood came, the house on the rock stood, while the other fell.

"I understand, Miss Ambrose, and thank you for the reminder. I'll pray, rest, and trust in Him alone, my rock." *But, somehow, a caretaker must surface.*

The next morning, I helped with the seven o'clock milking and shared my idea with the Coopers and William at breakfast. They were supportive, as I'd expected.

Between bites, Logan said, "Anything we can do to help before we leave, we'll do with pleasure. Keep us informed."

Easygoing, William said, "The more, the merrier!" He shoveled sausage and biscuits into his mouth and drank down a glass of fresh milk.

"Of course, I will. Enjoying the food, Mr. Kavanaugh?" I stared at William with his voracious appetite as I answered Logan. "Thank you for your help, Mr. Cooper, and for the delicious breakfast, Mrs. Cooper. I'll be back tomorrow morning."

William smiled, unable to speak with his mouth full, but he waved goodbye, fork in hand.

The next morning, I rode to Harriet's and knocked on her door. I trembled inside.

"Come on in, Emeline," said Huck with a grin. He was much taller than she, and his shoulders and arms were herculean, no doubt bolstered by lifting in his delivery job. "Have a seat."

He motioned for me to sit in a cushioned chair next to where Harriet would sit. She stood in the kitchen. "Hi, Harriet. How are you this morning?" I asked.

"Doin' fine, thanks. I made some tea for us. Would you like some?"

"Yes, please."

She poured tea into cups and brought them into the front room. Huck pulled over a wooden chair, turned it around, and sat spread-eagle over the seat in the backwards chair. "None for me yet, Harriet." He rested his chin on his arms, which were crossed over the top rail of its back.

"I'll set yours aside for now," she said.

Huck began. "Emeline, Harriet's told me about your big idea of involvin' us in your dairy farm business. Is it because you're losin' your caretakers and can't sell it outright?"

"In a nutshell, yes, Huck. But also because Harriet's my best friend and I believe she'd prefer the farm life. In fact, I've decided not to sell right now. I'm definitely not returning to Indianapolis until I manage things here."

"Really?" She fairly burst into tears as we both rose to hug, with smiles and laughter. "Oh, Emeline, I'm thrilled!" She pushed me away and stood with her hands on her hips. "But I want you to stay *forever*. If we become your caretakers, does that mean you'll leave?"

"We'll see." We swiped the tears from our faces and sat down again. "Back to business, now." After a deep breath, I continued. "I want you both to contemplate seriously the time commitment you'd be making and spend some time there before you make a final decision. You must enjoy the lifestyle." I paused for a moment, then continued. "Huck, what about you? Are you fond of city life? Have you ever lived on a farm? Are you happy working as a deliveryman? What's your dream?" I set my tea down, leaned forward, and gave him my full attention.

"Such a lot of questions! Shucks, bein' a deliveryman's fine, but my dream is to own a business. I want to be in control, not just an employee. How much control would I have at this dairy farm?"

"An excellent question, Huck," said Harriet.

I was ready with an answer. "As caretakers, the Coopers have always overseen their business. We would be partners for a while. I would actually own the property and dairy, for now, but would work and share profits with you and Harriet. I've lost Mr. Pickwick, who was my manager, but Andrew Pickwick says he'll manage as long as I need him. By the way, the Coopers say they'd be happy to teach all of us the ropes."

I hoped my offer struck a chord with them. If they agreed, the dairy would continue. They would free me to live with the Witherspoons, *if* I decided to, and Harriet and I would be close — even if only by mail. If not, I'd remain in my Kearney home, managing it with William and unknown hired hands. I prayed silently. *Please, oh Lord, please.*

"How much control would I have at the dairy farm?"

I continued. "We would divide the farm's proceeds equally between us. Regarding living places, Huck, you would live in the farmhouse until the Coopers leave. Then, you and William could live in Harriet's house, with Mr. Steiner's permission. Harriet and I would live at the farmhouse until we settle things." I smiled at them, though my hands wrung together in my lap conspicuously. The teacup shook slightly as I brought it to my lips. I knew they would marry, eventually, but I kept that to myself. "Of course, Andrew would insist on a legal contract for everyone's protection." I sipped.

"What do ya think, Huck?" Harriet asked after she swallowed some tea.

"Aw, I tell ya. I'm sorely tempted, I really am. I grew up on a farm and believe I *do* prefer it over city life. Quieter, cleaner, more space to breathe. And I have an idea burnin' in the back of my mind, which I won't share yet. I'm for tryin' it — a trial, so to speak. What about it, Harriet?"

"I think we should take the next steps and see how we like it."

"It's settled then," Huck said. "Tomorrow we'll talk to the folks in Westport and get their permission. We're practically grown and on our own — eighteen, both of us. Let's go for a two-week trial. If we decide against it, no hard feelin's, right, Emeline?"

"Never! Like I said before, the decision must be the right one for you. Pray about it, too."

"We will," Harriet said. "Thank you, Emeline."

Huck shifted in his seat, then stood and stretched. "Excellent! We'll come back in two weeks. That'll give us time to get ready. Will you make the arrangements with the Coopers?" he asked.

"It will be my pleasure, Huck." I squelched a squeal of excitement and prayed silently. *Thank you, Lord.*

June

June's morning sun warmed me as I traveled up the road to downtown Kearney. Herds of Black Angus and Hereford beef cattle dappled the fields of grass on the hills. Occasionally, I caught a whiff of the colorful, fragrant wildflowers growing alongside the road: blue chicory, purple thistle, and small yellow buttercups. Other times, if the cattle grazed close to the road, the less-pleasant whiffs of manure permeated the air. But it all made me happy. *Maybe I am meant for farm life.*

Harriet and Huck would return soon, so I had to discuss the business with Andrew today. Arriving at the Pickwick Mercantile, I tied up my horse and entered the store. "Hello, Mrs. Pickwick… Andrew," I said. Audrey waved from the back as she swept the wood plank floor.

From the counter, Andrew said, "Good morning, Emeline. What brings you in today?"

"I'd like to meet with you, if possible, to discuss a contract for two potential business partners: Harriet Steiner & Huck Malloy. Do you have time?"

Andrew walked toward me but checked with his mother. "Do you mind watching the store for about an hour, Ma?"

"No problem. Take all the time you need." Audrey smiled, swept up the small pile of dust, and put her broom away. She started toward the counter but stopped and turned to me. "Oh, Emeline. You received a letter." From the post office, she pulled a letter from the back and handed it to me. "That'll be two cents, please."

I always carried some change in my pocket, so I paid her for the postage. She said, "Thank you. It's difficult sometimes to get people to pick up their mail and pay for postage due. It would be helpful if senders always paid the postage."

I smoothed my hair and said, "I imagine it might take days or weeks to collect the money." I peered down at my letter. It was from Indianapolis — written in Jonathan's hand. It would have to wait. I shoved it into the pocket of my dress, sat at a table with Andrew, and tried to forget about it.

"How can I help?" he asked.

"I've spoken with my best friend, Harriet Steiner, and her friend Huck Malloy about working with me as caretakers and, potentially, owners. If they decide to do it, we'll need some kind of contract outlining expectations for us. Is that something you can write, or would I need to hire a lawyer?"

"Hmm. I can draft a first document for a lawyer's approval. Will you get us some glasses of water while I grab my notepaper and pen?"

"Of course, Andrew." I didn't know him well, but I felt confident he would do a decent job of it, since his pa must have taught him a lot about business. Plus, he had graduated last year with a business degree from the Kirksville Mercantile College.

Although lanky, Andrew's shoulders were broad and capable. Unsure of his age, I thought he might be around twenty — about the same age as Jonathan. An indoor pump provided cool water for our glasses, which I filled and set on the table. "I'll be right back, Andrew." Opening the door, I hurried to the privy to read Jonathan's letter. I couldn't think straight without reading it first. I tore through the seal and opened it.

May 10, 1893

Dear Emeline,

Things have taken a turn in the trim shop, and I'm not referring to the spindles. Few people are requesting railings and moulding because of the decrease in new construction in Indianapolis.

Perhaps your call to Kearney came at a good time. The Witherspoons don't share details of their business, but I've noticed a decrease in their trips to town. I never thought I'd have to worry about job security, but from reading the papers, it's something to consider. It's far worse, farther east, at least for wage-earners like me.

Sometimes the new teacher, Ruth Dugan, comes by after school. You met her once, remember? She's helping with a few chores in the shop since you're away. She sweeps, sharpens chisels, and helps Mrs. Witherspoon with gardening, and such.

I hope you're well and finding the answers you need for your farm. We all miss your smile and encouragement. See you soon?

Your friend,
Jonathan

"Your friend, Jonathan," I said to myself. Ruth. The shop. The economy. If only I still worked in the trim shop, I might grow closer to Jonathan: closer than a friend or a sister. But fiddlesticks! *I'm here. And Ruth's there.* Exasperating, that's what it was. I stuffed the letter back in my pocket and slammed the privy door behind me.

Upon my return, Andrew sat at the table, pushing a shock of dark, wavy brown hair through his fingers and out of his face. "Let's see now, Emeline. Tell me their names again."

I sat and regarded his mustached face and, for the first time, realized how intense his dark brown eyes were, like the black-brown stain of walnuts. "Yes, Andrew." I repeated their names, spelling each one. "Tentatively date it July 1, 1893."

He wrote these details down and said, "What kind of arrangement did you have in mind?"

He and I had come to happy terms:
we were like brother and sister.

I sat up straight in the chair and leaned toward him. "A partnership. I would be the actual owner, for now, and initially, we would share the work and the profits from the enterprise. Eventually, they could run it without me."

"You? Run a business? How old are you, Emeline?"

"Sixteen, but I'll be seventeen next month. I can manage details and I'm very organized. The Coopers have already taught me so much."

"Not that you couldn't do it, but you don't have the experience to manage all the finances by yourself yet. Would you mind if I helped you out? I'd only ask ten percent. That would leave thirty percent for each of you." He paused. "One moment. I need to grab a textbook."

He returned with a thick book about types of business organizations. "Let me skim the partnership section for a moment."

While he was reading, Mrs. Pickwick filled the coffee grinder with whole coffee beans and the candy jars with sweets: black licorice whips (my favorite), peppermints, and Tootsie Rolls.

Andrew leaned toward me and continued. "We'll need to identify who has control over what. I'll need time to study and draw up a draft, so can you give me about a week's time?"

"I will, thank you. I knew I could count on you."

"Emeline, you can *always* count on me." He smiled, his teeth straight and white, his dark eyes creased at their corners. "I'll see you soon." He stood up, tucking the notes inside his book.

"Thank you, Andrew."

He walked me to the door and opened it for me. I turned, smiled at him, and left for Maude's house.

Maude would be home this afternoon after running errands. I fueled the wood stove in the kitchen for later. With trembling hands, I made myself some coffee, washed my hands and face, and sat in a rocker in the front room. Finally, I drew the letter from my pocket and re-read its contents.

Why did my hopeless attraction to Jonathan persist? Was it merely because of the challenge, like forbidden fruit? It was pure silliness to keep pretending. Jonathan simply thought of me as a friend, a co-worker, nothing more. *Get over it, Emeline. Accept it! Stop wasting time mooning over someone with whom you have no future. Someone who wants no future with you, other than friendship.* I swallowed the truth like a bitter pill.

Weary of the struggle, I resigned myself from my one-sided infatuation at last. Oh, I was still happy for him, as a friend. He'd found what he wanted in Ruth, and I wished him well. All things worked together for good, right?

Horse hooves clip-clopped in front of the house, signaling Maude's return. I tucked the papers and the letter into my rucksack and strode toward the kitchen to make us some dinner before I left for the farm again.

Miss Ambrose entered the front room. "Hello, Emeline. Making dinner? Nothing for me, please. I enjoyed a meal at the Kearney Café with Jim."

She called him Jim now, rather than Mr. Penn. "Alright." I beat two eggs with a fork in a bowl, coated a slice of bread with the eggs, and browned one side in melted butter in the pan. "What are you learning about him?"

"One thing I love about him is how he listens and asks deep questions. And he's not afraid to open up emotionally to me, either. He's polite and shows respect for me. How was your morning?" Maude asked.

After a minute, I turned the bread over to brown the other side. "Andrew's working on a partnership agreement for us, and I received a letter from Jonathan in Indianapolis." After removing the toast, I added a bit more butter to the pan and scrambled the rest of the eggs. A glass of milk completed the meal.

"Oh, what did Jonathan say?"

"I'll sum it up by saying we're friends. That's it. He won't be the reason to return to Indiana unless I want to be a woodworker or an unofficial adopted daughter." Carelessly, I brought my dinner to the table and ate.

"You're not disappointed?" she asked. "You're giving up?"

"Oddly, not as disappointed as I thought I'd be, no. Giving up? I'm tired of fighting it. Maybe it's because I've moved on emotionally, or perhaps it's because of time and distance." I couldn't help thinking of William, my ambitious, tempting farmhand. "It wasn't to be, I guess." I sighed.

"Be patient, Emeline. You know in your heart what you really want — what will bring you peace. True joy doesn't come from people or circumstances. Those are fluid and ever-changing. Always remember, God is your rock."

"Yes, and for that, I'm thankful." Isn't it strange — the difference between joy and happiness? Happiness came from earthly things, but joy... to have joy in good times and bad — *that* was a treasure. I cleaned up my dishes and put them away. "Miss Ambrose, I'll be at the Coopers' all afternoon and early evening, but I'll be home before dark. Okay?"

"Right. See you then, Emeline. Be careful."

I left the house, excited to work after weeks of recovery from turning my ankle.

I took time to brush Dakota all over first, including his mane and tail. He sighed and leaned into me as I brushed, extending his lips forward — thoroughly enjoying the attention. Then I tacked him up. "You'd like to run today, wouldn't you, boy?" He snorted as I climbed into the saddle.

As soon as I arrived at the Cooper's horse barn, I took everything off him but his halter, and released him in the south pasture. He ran, kicked, whinnied, and then ran some more. How he loved his freedom and exercise! Where were the cows? Had they moved them to a different pasture? "Have fun, Dakota." I shouted. I didn't see anyone anywhere, so I went to the house and rapped on the door.

Sarah opened it, her round face smiled and her eyes brightened, though red and puffy. "Emeline! I'm so happy to see you again. Come in quick, once. How's your ankle?"

"Good as new, thank you. How's everyone here?"

She hesitated, but said, "There's been a calamity, Emeline. Have a seat at the table and I'll get us some biscuits, honey, and hot tea."

"Oh, no!" Eager to hear about it, I offered to help. "I'll make the tea." Usually, a discussion with food and beverage was weighty.

With the table ready, we settled in the wooden chairs. "Our cows are gone." Her chin quivered. "It's likely they've been stolen. We don't have any idea who did it, but we're not the only farm missing animals lately. We fear some of the unemployed are turning to thievery out of desperation."

"Even my old cow, Nellie?"

"Yes. I'm sorry. It must have happened while we were sound asleep last night. Mr. Cooper and William blame themselves, but it isn't their fault."

"Did you report it to the sheriff?" I lifted the teacup with a shaky hand and sipped the hot tea, as my mouth had gone bone dry.

"That's the first thing Mr. Cooper did. And he's reported it to the marshal. They've contacted both the railroad and the stockyards in Kansas City in case the thieves try to sell them, but, so far, they've found no clues. The Clay County Sheriff says stealing Jerseys is unusual." She sniffed. "They're smaller than Hereford or Black Angus, and they need to be milked. We're… devastated! They were our… our livelihood." Her voice broke as tears trailed down her cheeks. "I'm so worried about our poor cows."

I held her hand and let her cry. Shocked, I said, "I'm speechless." I took a biscuit and drizzled honey over it. The food distracted me while I processed this dizzying news. "How does *anyone* keep their cattle safe from thieves?" Saddened for the animals, I wondered if these horrible people would milk them or let them suffer and sell them to the highest bidder. If we didn't find them, our dairy enterprise together would end. I bowed my head and shed tears along with Mrs. Cooper. Somewhere, deep inside, anger welled up. This lawlessness must stop. First, the train hold-up and now this. Frantically, I searched for ideas.

Sarah wiped her eyes with a kitchen towel. "Maybe we should've had a watchdog or something."

I said, "Or perhaps barbwire on our fence — and a gate at the entrance to lock at night." Crying, I wiped my eyes with another towel Mrs. Cooper handed me. She sipped some tea and continued. "The men feel lost. They're working the fields now, but they'll be back for supper soon." She sighed. "What will we do with no dairy cows? Where will our money come from until harvest time?"

The Coopers had moved the stove outside to the summer kitchen, where a pot of ham and potato soup simmered. Its flavorful scent filled the air and wafted through the open windows of the house. "We should pray."

"Of course," she said. We bowed our heads, and I prayed: "Dear Lord, we are grieving the loss of our beloved cows and the source of our livelihood. Please help the authorities find them or show us a way to recover from this terrible event. We love you and thank you for all you've done, do, and will do for us. Amen."

"Perfect, Emeline." Then she added her heartfelt prayer, which included care for Logan and William. She stood up and said, "So, let's get the table ready for supper, then."

We stacked chunks of cornbread on a plate in the center of the table, and set out four bowls, spoons, and knives for the butter. The wooden honey dipper stuck out from the jar of golden sweetness. Its grooves reminded me of the spindles I used to love to make at the Witherspoons. After we'd filled four glasses with fresh spring water, the men arrived.

First to enter the room, Logan said, "Oh, hello, Emeline." He poured water from the pitcher into the basin to wash his hands and face. Sarah handed him a towel. "Did Mrs. Cooper give you the bad news, er no?"

William came in and said, "Miss O'Connor, it's good to see you again. How's your ankle? Healed up?" He washed up, too.

"Yes, I've heard the news, and my ankle is right as rain. Thank you."

All four of us went outside, filled our bowls with soup, and brought them back to the table to sup.

Logan gave thanks and started the conversation. "So, what shall we do about our problem, eh?"

I wanted an immediate solution to return our lives to normalcy, but unfortunately, conflict resolution was not my strength. Why couldn't things go smoothly? "Unsure. How can I help?" I asked.

William devoured his soup and cornbread in silence. As a farmhand who lived here, he understood it wasn't his place to make these kinds of decisions. But between mouthfuls, he checked my face to estimate my mood. He was an intuitive person, I'd discovered as time marched on.

Logan continued. "Well, I'll tell ya, if they don't find the cows within a week, we might have to move sooner than expected. We can't stay here without income for long."

Sarah sighed and grinned. "Really, dear?" Her facial expression grew sunny.

She's eager to move home. This was an unexpected reaction. Besides the loss of the cows, I'd be losing the Coopers sooner. How can I keep them here? The answer hid itself from me. In a frenzy, I asked, "Would you mind if I discuss this with Andrew, my manager, before you decide? There may be something we can do."

Logan wiped his mouth with a cloth napkin. "You may. But we'll need to decide in about a week. Obviously, this will affect your friends coming to learn about dairy farming, too. You'll have to tell them quick, once, hey."

"In the morning, I'll speak with Andrew and return for dinner, if that's alright."

"That'll do, Emeline," Sarah said.

"Depending on what we know, I'll speak with Harriet and Huck."

A New Plan

Dakota had covered himself in grass from rolling on his back. I quickly brushed him off, tacked him up, and rode home. Downhearted from the loss, I tended to Dakota, then opened the squeaky screen door of Maude's house. "Hello?"

She was nowhere in the house. I walked through the back door to the summer kitchen. "Oh, there you are," I said.

"Hello, Emeline." She stood by the stove, now covered by a tan canvas awning, but the hot flue pipe didn't touch it, nor the roof of the house. "Jim and his friends moved the stove outside to the summer kitchen today and put this cover over it."

"Oh, now you can cook even while it's raining. That was good of him." Looking for the men, I surveyed the land behind the house and towards the schoolhouse.

"They've left," she said. "It's about time we did this. The weather's too warm to cook indoors now."

"You're right. Um, Miss Ambrose?" I blurted out my question. "May I talk to you inside about something pressing?" I reminded myself that God was on my side, so I gathered my strength and courage.

"Of course." We made ourselves comfortable in the front room's rocking chairs and she asked, "What is it, dear?"

I delivered the bad news and asked, "What should we do?" I'd come to rely on her sound advice, as she'd mentored me for much of my life, especially now.

She leaned forward and said, "Emeline, you're already familiar with the process."

"I am?" She wouldn't give me a direct answer this time, forcing me to think for myself, causing me to admire her even more for pushing me, but I lacked patience.

"Yes. List your possibilities, like you've done before, then write them down and prioritize them the way they would best fit into your life's goal."

"Alright. Surely, I can do that." Inside, I felt my confidence growing, little by little. All I must do is slow the swirling thoughts and stifle the panic.

"Yes, of course you can. I can't decide for you, as you're a responsible young woman now with a sound mind and a promising future. Only you and the Lord understand the best way for yourself, and no one else. Don't forget to pray." She winked at me, stood, and faced me. "Will you excuse me, please? I need to write some lesson plans, so I'll leave you to it."

"Of course. Thank you," I said. It was her way of giving me time to think. She moved to her desk chair in the room's corner and began writing in her school journal.

I fetched my journal and pen from my rucksack and began listing options. I enjoyed this exercise. It allowed my mind to play with scenarios, as anything was possible.

1. Provide financial support to the Coopers until after harvest. They would still train Huck and Harriet before they left. Buy new dairy cows, a guard dog, and barbwire for the fence and gates.
2. Partner with Huck and Harriet regardless of the type of farm.
3. Allow the Coopers to leave early. Move back to the farmhouse and decide then what to do with it. As a single man, William would need to find a new place to live, and I would have to hire extra help at harvest time.
4. Not have a dairy farm, at all, but raise beef cattle instead: Hereford or Black Angus. Still use the icehouse for chilling beef.
5. Eventually, when the market improves, sell the undeveloped land, keeping only 95 acres of the 160 acres Pa settled. The woodland would provide much needed income and developing it for my use was unlikely.
6. Or live at the farmhouse, sell the entire place when the market improves, and find some other way to make a living — even move back to Indianapolis... potentially.

I reflected on these and added new ideas as they came to mind. For now, I wanted to brush Dakota, my old friend. Being around him relaxed me. With the currycomb and brush, I walked to his stall. He snorted his pleasure at seeing me. "Dakota, here we are again, boy." I hummed, brushing him all over from head to tail. He leaned against me till I nearly fell over. "Hey! Stand up, boy." Silently, I prayed for direction.

The next morning was cool and rainy, so Maude allowed me to borrow her horse, Winnie, her covered carriage, and some of her clothes for my business meeting with Andrew Pickwick. I stared at my reflection in Maude's looking glass. With puffed sleeves, her loden green jacket made me look older than my years and attractive, I thought. I wore my hair in a low, loose bun in the back, and the fancy straw hat of Miss Ambrose's sported a contrasting soft pink ribbon tied in the back with a bow.

When I arrived at the mercantile, I found him busy filling the coffee grinder with fresh roasted beans. "Those beans smell heavenly, Andrew," I said as I walked toward him.

"Emeline, welcome. Would you like a fresh cup of coffee?"

"Yes, please, with a smidgen of milk." I set my payment on the counter while he poured it.

"It's on the house," he smiled and said, "You sure look lovely today."

Picking up the pennies, I said, "Thank you, Andrew. Will you join me? I've something to discuss."

He looked at the clock and around the store. No one else had arrived yet. "Yes, but if someone comes in, I'll need to excuse myself. Ma's over at the church for a bit. It's morning, so we'll likely have some time. I haven't finished your partnership agreement yet. You're early."

After we took our seats, I set my journal on the table, opened it, and turned it towards him. "You can wait on that, probably," I said. His eyes seemed kinder today, softer, though still deep brown. I updated him with our news. I removed my hat and hung it on the top corner of another chair. "How would you like to be a sounding board for me? Talking over things helps me process." That was the truth. Writing thoughts on paper helped, too.

He read over the list. "Alright. Let's see. How do you feel about buying new livestock and paying the Coopers out of your savings until they move?"

"It would cost a lot for me to pay them, buy cows, a guard dog, and barbwire. I would have to be positive about continuing the dairy. You sell milk here and must buy from other dairies in town. Where do you purchase your supply?"

"Two other dairies in town sell to us, but I'd have to admit the Coopers' products have been our best sellers. No one's ever reported any sickness from drinking their milk."

"Hmm. That encourages me to continue it somehow, not just for myself, but for the people of Kearney."

He continued. "What about the second choice? Partner with Huck and Harriet, regardless of the type of farm."

"Yes, I wish to partner with them if they do. As I don't have control over that option, I shouldn't commit to it."

"Fine. Next, how do you feel about the Coopers leaving early and just hiring workers at harvest time? I see no livestock investment in this choice."

"Andrew, I really don't mind this option. I've worked with them long enough that I believe we'd do well, even if I decide to continue the dairy later. You should have seen Mrs. Cooper's face when Mr. Cooper suggested they might leave early. She lit up like a four-wick candle."

"Alright. Now, what about this idea of raising beef cattle instead? How do you feel about that?"

"You tell me. Which kind is in more demand in Kearney? Plus, I know nothing about raising those, and I'm not sure how I'd handle killing and butchering." A sour expression crossed over my face.

"Most farmers in Kearney raise beef cattle." Andrew said. A little bell over the door announced a customer. "Excuse me, I'll be right back. Give me a few minutes."

From the counter, he filled the customer's order of sundries. "Thank you, Mrs. Martin," he said. The little bell rang again as she left. I loved how he addressed everyone by name. Such a friendly and intelligent man, Andrew Pickwick.

He returned to his seat across from me. "Beef or dairy?"

Smiling, I said, "Dairy cows. At least I'm familiar with them. But down the road, I could add a few head of Black Angus, Hereford — or even sheep."

"Don't mix sheep and cattle, whatever you do. You'll have a dickens of a time keeping your pastures green. Besides, Mr. McGregor has that market sewn up in this area."

I threw my head back and chuckled. "Ha-ha! Fine. No sheep. If I get a hankering to knit something, I'll visit the McGregors."

"Now the last option you've written is about selling part or all the property whenever the market improves. Is that something you *really* want to do?"

"No, not really. The farm is part of who I am, my heritage, my legacy. Pa and Ma would cringe if I sold it off. But if it comes down to it… I might have to."

"Alright then. And I'm thrilled to see that Indianapolis is almost out of the picture entirely. I, for one, love having you here, Emeline." His smile beamed, but he broke eye contact as he brushed his black wavy hair back from his forehead again.

"I appreciate your listening to me. This helps. I think I've decided, but I'll pray about it before I see the Coopers tomorrow morning. May I tell you tomorrow afternoon?" I positioned my hat back on my head and stood up from the table.

"Yes, you may. I'll look forward to seeing you then."

"Thanks, again. See you tomorrow."

Rain slowed to a sprinkle as Winnie and I drove to the Coopers. It was dinnertime, about one o'clock, and everyone was in the house. I took my journal inside and removed my hat. "Good afternoon," I said.

William jumped out of his chair and pulled out the fourth chair for me. "You look lovely today, Miss O'Connor." He grinned.

"Thank you, Mr. Kavanaugh." My wardrobe must need updating, as two compliments on the same outfit meant something.

Logan asked, "Would you like something to eat or drink, er no?"

"Thank you, no. But I'd like to go over some ideas with you."

In a low voice, Logan said, "We've been on pins and needles since you left yesterday. What are your thoughts?"

"I've decided if we don't find our cows, I'll buy more Jerseys. I'll check with the two other dairy farms in town first. If they don't have any to sell, we'll travel to the Kansas City stockyards to see if they have some. Also, I'll buy a guard dog and barbwire for fencing above the perimeter fences and gates. We'll build a new gate to close and lock over the entrance at night."

"I see," Logan said. "But what will we do for income before the cows can produce? It may be some time, especially if you start with young ones."

I leaned on the table with my forearms crossed and locked eyes with him. "If you'll stay until after harvest, I'm willing to support you with necessities like food and you won't need to pay rent. But if you'd rather go north to Wisconsin early, I'll understand. With the training you've already provided, I feel confident that, with help, I'll manage." I stared at William for a moment and then back at Logan. "It's your decision."

"Oh, Logan!" Mrs. Cooper cried into her napkin. "Excuse me." She left the table and returned momentarily.

Logan held my gaze and replied. "That's a mighty generous offer, Emeline. We hoped you might come to such a conclusion, but I have a counteroffer." He paused. "We'll stay for two weeks to train your new helpers, even without a cow. Afterward, we'll accept your offer of allowing us to head home to Wisconsin early. I'll share with you the names of some reliable men and boys I've used in the past who can help bring in the harvest."

"Wonderful. Then we have a plan." Leaning against the back of my chair, I let out a heavy sigh of relief. Everyone around the table smiled and chattered happily, and I was glad for them. And I was pleased to *have* a plan — even if it changed down the road. *If nothing else, I've learned flexibility.*

"When they come for their two-week trial and make their decision, which I hope is to stay, we'll need new housing arrangements. But we can work that out when the time comes, Mr. Kavanaugh." Our eyes met. Certain he could find a living arrangement elsewhere; he must realize he couldn't live here with me.

"Not a problem," he said. "Sure, one thing I'll need is a horse to ride back and forth to work. You and I could shop for one in town, aye? I've some bob saved up. No doubt the farrier will know of some available animals."

Logan wagged a finger at him. "No need, William. Our neighbors to the south, the Johnsons, have extra horses, I believe. You and

I'll visit next week and you can take your pick. Emeline can come along, too, if she likes."

William smiled, but averted his gaze. "That'll be grand, Mr. Cooper." But his voice revealed his disappointment.

"Perfect. I'll be off to update our manager, Andrew. And, as I'm traveling to Westport to advise my friends, I won't be back for a couple of days. I'm much obliged." I rose to leave.

Outside, Logan asked, "To Kansas City by yourself? You should see about someone going along, Emeline. Perhaps we should accompany you, to be safe."

"Yes, Miss O'Connor. Let's all go together," William said, his eyes brightening.

I smiled, donned my hat, and climbed into the carriage. What could happen on a four-hour ride on a well-traveled road?

Downtown, I surprised Andrew by coming back on the same day. Both he and Audrey were busy attending customers, so I took a seat and waited. She came by first.

"Why, hello, Emeline. I'm sorry I missed you this morning. How are you?"

"Fine, thank you, and you?"

"Doing well. I'm filling my days between the store and activities at church." She smiled. "I love working with others to decorate for events like holidays, memorial services, and weddings. Someday you may have a wedding in your future." She raised her eyebrows.

I laughed out loud. "Ha-ha! That would be something, wouldn't it? No time soon, I imagine, but who knows?" She gave me an odd look, which I dismissed as whimsy.

"Would you like some fresh coffee on us? With milk, right?"

"That would be lovely," I said. She returned shortly with the cup. "When Andrew gets time, may I speak with him for a few minutes?"

"Yes, in fact, he's finishing with Mr. Orrick now. I'll take his place and send him over afterward."

"Thank you, kindly."

Soon, Andrew sat across from me. "I thought you were coming back tomorrow," he said, sliding his chair toward the table.

"I was, but our meeting necessitated I come today. Tomorrow morning, I'm riding to Westport to speak with Huck and Harriet about their trial and the Coopers' decision."

He leaned forward. "How'd the meeting go?"

"They're thrilled about moving back to Wisconsin early. I'd be surprised if Mrs. Cooper isn't already packing. But they offered to stay long enough to train my friends for two weeks. I'm staying with the dairy for now." I threw my hands up in the air, my mouth gaping open as I smiled. "Can you believe it? I can't."

"That's fine, Emeline. I'll be here for you whenever you need anything. In fact, I'll accompany you to Westport, if you don't mind. That's a long trip for a young woman to make alone. Kansas

City and Westport have some mighty seedy areas. The stockyard is one of them."

I chuckled. "You understand I traveled across the country alone when I was thirteen, right?"

"And you nearly died, Pa told me. If I hadn't been away at college, I would have gladly made safer arrangements for you. And what about that train hold-up incident?"

"Hmm. Yes, well, you're right, but won't the two of us traveling together as far as Westport give people ideas?"

"I'm simply your manager," he said.

"If you can spare two days for travel to and from Westport, you may escort me *as my manager*, Andrew. Strictly business." I grinned and gave him a side-long glance as I stood to leave.

"Fine. I'll arrange for someone to help Ma with the store and pick you up at eight o'clock in the morning." He beamed, stood, and walked toward the door to hold it open for me.

Such a thoughtful gentleman.

For the trip, I wore my black and white pinstripe dress, added Ma's cameo brooch to a black velvet ribbon at the collar, and a matching belt around my waist. Today, I plaited my hair, rolled the ends, and tucked them under a contrasting white net in the back. Then I pinned the netting to hold it. My figure had grown quite

womanly this past year. It curved in all the proper places, just like Ma's. I smiled.

Outwardly, I'd always displayed courage, but I'd often feigned confidence, although, through faith, it had grown stronger. As a child, I surrendered happily to the authority of my parents and my teacher, Maude Ambrose. On my journey to Boston to meet Grandfather Silas, had it been courage, or stubborn determination to keep my promise to Pa? Dependent upon others, I'd lived with benefactors: the McCarthys in Boston, the Witherspoons in Indianapolis, and now Maude.

I sighed. Someday I'd grow to be a confident woman, regardless of circumstances, wouldn't I? Time stood still, it seemed. What was it William had said? Sometimes one day changes everythin'; sometimes years change nothin'. An intriguing viewpoint, but what if we remained the same on the inside despite external changes? Jonathan had said something, too. What was it? Change is healthy. Jonathan and William might've made good friends.

I packed my rucksack with extra clothes and toiletries. Horse hooves sounded outside — Andrew Pickwick's carriage. After stuffing my coin purse with a little money and Harriet's address, I snapped its strap around my belt, grabbed my rucksack and canteen, and met him at the door. "Good morning, Andrew."

"Good morning, Emeline. Are you ready?"

"I am." I stepped onto the porch, locked the front door, and slipped the key into my purse.

"It's much warmer today than yesterday. No need for a jacket," he said.

"It's perfect weather: not too hot, not too cold."

"That's a lovely dress and I like the brooch you're wearing. Was it your ma's?"

"How'd you know?" I hadn't worn it in years because it brought back painful memories. Now, I welcomed them, though I would always miss her.

"Just a lucky guess." He grinned as he held his arm out for me to balance as I climbed into his carriage.

"You look rather dapper yourself, Andrew, without your customary apron." He wore tan pants and an olive-green tweed vest with a bright white shirt. A gold pocket watch chain gleamed and attached to a button on his vest.

Making the trip to Harriet's to discuss the dairy business, currently without cows, was one thing: important and timely. But to make it with the companionship of Andrew Pickwick was another. I regarded his tanned face with its dark mustache, newly waxed, and turned up slightly at the ends. He was a handsome man, mature, like Jonathan, but a business owner rather than an artisan. I held the side of the carriage as we jostled over bumps and ruts in the dirt road. This would be a memorable trip.

Westport

On the way to Westport, Andrew asked, "So, Emeline, why do you want to be a dairy farmer?"

It would be several hours before we reached Westport. "Excellent question, Andrew, and if you'd asked me when I first returned from Indianapolis, my answer would have been, I don't. Turning spindles day after day fulfilled me. I'd become close with the Witherspoons, and with their apprentice, Jonathan. At least, I thought so." I rubbed my hands over my arms.

"What's changed your mind, then?"

"First, your pa passed away." I regarded his face. He stared straight ahead. "I'm so sorry, Andrew." I paused. "Besides that, the economy has prevented the outright sale of the farm, which was my initial plan." I paused again as we jostled through deep wheel ruts in the road.

"Sorry. I'll pull to the side more to get out of the ruts," he said.

"That's alright," I said, holding tight to the carriage's edge, as I continued. "I guess because I'd been away for so long, it became an obstacle to overcome. A thing without life. But since I've been back, my emotions for Pa and Ma's farm have been rekindled. Now, I'm even questioning my place and purpose in life." I sighed.

"Hmm. Go on."

"The Coopers have impressed me with their dairy mastery. And you've testified that no one's ever complained about their products."

He glanced my direction and asked, "Why not live at your farmhouse, as you did as a child? You've seen the notices people post on the board in the mercantile: jobs wanted, things to sell, and so on. I'm sure plenty of hired hands are available to work for you. And you've already got William. It would surprise me if Mr. Cooper hasn't listed names of those he's called on for help in the past. You're aware milk is but part of his income from the farm."

"Yes, I am, and he's already given me his list of people to help with the harvest. I'd also forgotten how much I adore caring for animals and helping people. A dairy meets both these desires nicely."

He asked, "What about your love for woodworking? Are you ready to give it up entirely and not move back to Indianapolis, for certain?"

I peered at him from the corner of my eye and said, "I suppose, if I wanted to, I might work for someone who does woodworking here, but, no, my interest in returning to Indianapolis has diminished." I didn't mention Jonathan. "Personally, I believe working with animals and people is more fulfilling than working with pieces of wood, even if appreciated."

"So, Emeline, why do you want to be a dairy farmer?"

"You're a well-educated young woman. Why not teach someday?" he asked.

"Miss Ambrose suggested that too. It's not that I wouldn't enjoy teaching. I love children. But, if I taught, I couldn't marry. Someday, I hope to find and marry my best friend and settle down. In the end, that's all I really want. That, and to have confidence in myself."

His eyes were on the road, but he smiled. "I see."

Silent for a few minutes, he continued. "You don't believe you're confident? That surprises me, after all your travels."

"What did I have when I traversed the country to find grandfather at the tender age of thirteen? Courage? No, I was afraid. Confidence? No, I wasn't sure I had what it took to succeed. What I had was the stubbornness to honor Pa's last wish, because I always honor a promise. That's conviction, but not confidence. Looking back, if I'd known of all the trials I'd encounter, I'd never have left alone like I did."

"Then you've matured because what I see in you is a bright young woman, ripened beyond her years, who knows how to problem-solve, and manage details. A confident young woman, strong and determined. You've plenty of admirable qualities."

I smiled, and my cheeks warmed at the compliment. "Either I'm believing in a lie I'm telling myself, or you're looking at me through rose-colored glasses. I'm still uncertain of my place and purpose right now. But enough about me. How about you? From what you said at your pa's service, you enjoy working at the mercantile. What else do you like? Do you have other dreams?"

He smiled. "I like change. I get bored otherwise. On the surface, the mercantile work appears routine, but in fact, I love moving things around, bringing new displays, products, and services into the mix. I appreciate most people and learn a lot of what's needed by talking with them both inside and outside the store."

I faced him and said, "Change equals uncertainty and I'm not fond of it, as I'm more the steady, predictable type. Comfortable with routine, I'm rarely bored with repetitive or prosaic tasks. I find joy in the simplest things, even a bird twittering in a tree."

"You're like Ma, that way. I'm good at big-picture possibilities and analysis. And I can read people, too. During the Spring Festival, I couldn't help but notice William's fascination with you, while you seemed unsure. Oh, you danced, had fun, and were friendly, but not in the same way. I saw it in his face and in the way he moved around you."

"I only went with him as a friend. That's all."

He lifted his eyebrows. "Then clarify that with the young man, unless you're open to learning more about him. He's mad about you."

"I told him I came only as a friend, *and* I started calling him Mr. Kavanaugh at the fair for emphasis."

"I believe he's the idealistic, hopeful type of fellow and won't give up so easily. Mark my words."

"You think so?"

"Yep."

"Oh my. I've been interested in someone else for some time: Jonathan McFarland in Indianapolis. He's the reason I moved back to their home after Boston. I regret accepting that invitation at all, considering I still am fond of someone else."

"Tell me more about this McFarland fellow. What's he like?"

Why would my manager need to know about Jonathan? "Oh, just a man about your age whom I've had a crush on since I was thirteen. Let's leave it at that, for now."

With a knowing look and a smirk on his face, he said, "Fine."

For the rest of this leg of the trip, we shared less personal information. My favorite seasons were spring and fall, as were his. He enjoyed playing baseball and wanted to buy and learn to ride a bicycle soon. I shared my enthusiasm for animals: riding Dakota for pleasure, watching wildlife, singing, and taking care of the cows and chickens. I guessed it was beneficial for a manager to understand his client well.

Farms and homes appeared, a few at first, then more densely. In Westport, tall brick homes stood separated by slender grassy areas, differing visually solely by diverse front doors. Andrew brought a map, so we found Harriet's address with no trouble, but no one was home. "They're probably working," I said.

"This trip is a treat for me, anyway," Andrew said. "Houses are quite different here, aren't they? Mostly stone and brick, tall, and awfully close together."

"Yes. They remind me a little of the houses in Boston. The stench of manure on the roads is familiar, too. There's a beauty about the buildings, but I prefer the openness of the simple sprawling farmhouses and outbuildings of Kearney. The air is clearer and fresher in the country, too — and there's more sky." I covered my mouth and nose briefly with my hand.

Andrew pulled over and stopped in front of a café, which provided Stormy with much needed water and complimentary hay. "We might as well stop for dinner and a walk to stretch our legs. Stormy needs a break, too." He stepped out, stretched, tied off his horse, and then came around and offered his hand for balance as I climbed down to the ground.

"Thank you." Stretching felt marvelous, but I teetered a little on my legs. "Where's my balance?" I asked.

"It'll come back soon enough." Thirsty, the gelding guzzled water from the trough. Andrew chuckled and opened the door to the café, and we took seats on opposite sides of a table. "I'm hungry, aren't you?"

"I am."

A short older woman in a calico pinafore said, "Hi. Welcome to Boone Café." She handed each of us a menu and a glass of water. "The dinner special today is the meatloaf meal, which includes mashed potatoes, peas, and a fresh-baked roll. I'll return in a few minutes for your order."

"What a treat, Andrew." We studied our menus. Choices included fried chicken and catfish. Desserts included various pies and cakes. My stomach growled. "Now I'm famished."

"Is the meatloaf alright for you?"

"I've never had catfish, but I love meatloaf."

When the waitress returned, she brought white cloth napkins, silverware, and two tall glasses of water. "Have you decided?"

"Yes. Two specials please," Andrew said.

"Very good."

She left, and we waited. Andrew opened the map and studied it for a minute or two. "Hmm. We're close to the stockyards. Shall we pay it a visit while we're here?"

"We have time, so why not?"

We devoured the delicious meal, Andrew paid the bill, and we headed toward the Kansas City Stockyards. He smiled and peeked at me from the corner of his eye, as our carriage rambled through the city streets.

"Many thanks, Andrew." I smiled.

Horses, carts, and people filled the earthen roads. Drivers, riders, and pedestrians navigated the crowded streets with caution at intersections. One riotous block differed: most establishments on it were bars or saloons. William called them pubs. Drunken patrons sat idly on the wooden sidewalks, others shouted colorful words, some fought. Some ladies, dressed in revealing clothing, enticed men. Instinctively, I drew closer to Andrew.

Before long, the stockyards loomed ahead. "Look: a bridge crossing the river," I said.

"That's the Hannibal Bridge. The train you took from Cameron to Kearney comes here." Thousands of animals stood in pens: cattle, hogs, and sheep. I cupped my hands around my nose and mouth.

"Whew! The stench is vile, but I guess that is to be expected."

"The Kansas and Missouri Rivers join here. They built the yards at this junction so they could conveniently dump animal waste into the river."

"Oh! Remind me not to fish downstream." Several railroad tracks ran right alongside the building leading to the train depot, which stood directly to the east. We reached the three-story red brick building, tied up Stormy, and opened the heavy front door. Inside, the ceilings were at least twelve feet from the floor, I estimated, while a long hallway housed offices on either side; each door identified its purpose with lettering on its window. We opened a door to one of them — *Kansas City Cattle Company*.

"May I help you?" A heavyset man in a suit and tie sat behind a wooden desk with a leather top — just like our banker's. "Take a seat, won't you?"

After we sat in chairs in front of the desk, Andrew inquired about our Jerseys. "We're curious whether you've purchased any Jersey cows recently. Ours are missing and haven't been located yet."

"No, sir, we haven't. We don't deal in dairy cows, just beef cattle: Black Angus and Herefords — and a few Texas Longhorns, too. We sell to local ranchers who raise them for beef, and we're a stop for beef cattle headed elsewhere. But you might check with the local dairy farmers in town. Sorry I can't help."

"Thank you, sir," I said. "Do you have addresses for these farmers?"

"No, sorry. You might check the library at 9th Street and Oak."

"We appreciate your time," Andrew said.

"Wish I could've helped. I hope you find your cows, or some replacements."

We left his office and climbed into our carriage again. "So, more research," I said as we climbed back into his carriage.

"I'll venture Huck will know the whereabouts of dairy farmers. We'll find some Jerseys, yet."

I giggled. "I hope so. Shall we check to see if Harriet's home?" *I couldn't have imagined a better manager or friend.*

"We shall." He clicked his tongue for Stormy to step lively, and soon we were back in front of the Steiner's house.

This time, when I knocked, the door opened. "Emeline, what a surprise! When did ya arrive? Why are ya here? How long will ya stay?" Harriet twisted her body and shouted down the hallway. "Ma, Emeline's here. Isn't that grand?" She turned toward Andrew. "You're Andrew Pickwick, right? I haven't seen ya in *years*. Sorry, I'm babbling."

I let out a hearty laugh as we hugged. "You're hilarious, Harriet."

"Nice to meet you again." Andrew smiled and leaned against the doorway.

"Where are my manners? Come in, come in. Let's all sit in the parlor. Huck and Pa are tendin' to the horses and will be in soon. Huck's joinin' us for supper."

Harriet and I snuggled into a long, overstuffed sofa while Andrew sat in a wooden rocker. Mrs. Etta Steiner joined us with a tray of beverages. "I figured you'd be thirsty." She placed the tray on a side table and sat on the other side of Harriet. Presently, Mr. Conrad Steiner and Huck joined us.

Conrad said, "What a pleasant surprise! What brings you folks to Westport?"

I wasn't sure if Harriet had discussed the dairy trial idea with her parents, but she sensed my concern and spoke first. "They probably want to talk to us about the business trial I spoke with ya about. Right, Emeline?"

"Yes," I said.

Huck stood in front of Andrew and said, "Hello, name's Huck Malloy, and you are?"

Andrew stood and shook his hand. "Andrew Pickwick, Emeline's manager. It's a pleasure to meet you."

Huck sat in a wooden chair, with his long legs sprawled apart, as if they couldn't find their place.

"Yes, we want to discuss the dairy, but before we go into it, how have you all been? Do you enjoy living here more than Kearney?"

Conrad Steiner expressed his views first. "I tell ya, this town is boomin'. There's more buildin' of homes, businesses, and roads than I've ever seen in my life. A bricklayer's work is hard and repetitious, but it pays well. There's enough money to rent this beautiful home, plus pay others for the plantin' and harvestin' of crops on our farm in Kearney. I figure I'll do this for a few more years, then we may move back to Kearney. I miss the quiet and slower lifestyle."

Etta said, "Me too. Not that I don't appreciate this gracious home and all." She smiled demurely at her husband.

Harriet voiced her opinion. "I agree. I don't mind workin' to clean this and other people's houses, but I've found all I want in Westport."

"You mean Huck," I said with a grin.

"Exactly." Harriet sat on her hands and bowed her head, but a shy smile stretched across her face. She couldn't hide her feelings from me, nor from anyone else.

Andrew nodded for me to continue. "Remember the idea of you and Harriet becoming my partners and new caretakers?"

"Yes," they said together.

"We must tell you of an unfortunate incident, but it doesn't need to stop our plans, at least for now."

"Oh, Emeline, *please,* just tell us!" Harriet said with round eyes, which made Andrew chuckle.

"We're missing all the cows and a bull. As of today, there's been no trace of them: not in Kearney, at the train depot, the stockyards, or anywhere, according to the sheriff. Even poor old Nellie's gone." With a corner of my sleeve, I soaked up tears that rimmed my eyes. Andrew passed me a handkerchief from his pants pocket, which I accepted.

"How terrible!" Conrad said. Everyone murmured their displeasure.

"That's awful," Harriet said.

"It is. But Mr. Cooper has agreed to train you, yet, for two weeks — even without the animals." After a pause, I continued. "Have you already decided, or do you have questions?" I eyed Andrew. "Andrew has been working on a partnership contract and will help manage the finances for a while."

Huck leaned forward in the chair, crossed his arms, and rested them on his knees. His eyes were on Harriet. "We've consulted our folks, and talked with each other, and have been leanin' toward acceptin' this opportunity." He turned toward Andrew and me. "But I'm afraid I'm the one holdin' us back; income is the uncertainty. Kansas City is growin', even durin' this difficult time."

Andrew leaned toward Huck and said, "Each year, farmers take risks. Weather or disaster may spoil their profits one year but soar in others. The difference is, it's their business. Alone. They don't work for anyone else and earn pennies per hour or split profits with an owner." Andrew faced me. "Correct me if I'm wrong, Emeline, but this partnership is but a starting point for the four of us. As soon as you are willing and able, she would like to sell you her farm, and you and Harriet would own the whole ball of wax. I'm merely included as the manager at ten percent until then, while each of you would split the other ninety percent equally."

"Understood," Huck said. He gazed at Andrew, his interest piqued.

Andrew continued. "Moreover, Kearney is also growing. The railroad runs from Kansas City to Chicago and stops at Kearney and/or Cameron several times a day. Railroads bring in businesses, more residents, churches, and schools."

I smiled, watching each of them.

Andrew offered more encouragement. "It's a comfortable life in the open spaces of Kearney. One that will support you as you grow with the town. I speak from experience, as part-owner of the Pickwick Mercantile."

"But with no cows to milk, how long will it take to get back to makin' money, Emeline?" Harriet asked.

"That is uncertain," I said. "First, we must purchase more, some hopefully pregnant. I have the funds for this, plus cash will come in from the crops this fall. If we buy animals that are already giving milk, that would be perfect."

Andrew spoke again. "I understand you deliver dairy products and cold food to people every morning. You must know the dairy farmers, right Huck? Would you check with them for any available Jerseys, specifically gravid ones? Emeline's determined to have Jerseys because of their milk's high cream content." He bent toward me. "How many do you think to start, Emeline?"

I shifted in my seat to face him. "We owned a herd of seven cows and one bull. A full-grown bull isn't necessary, but I'm not opposed to buying a weaned bull calf, or a couple of yearling heifers. Three cows in milk are probably plenty to start with." We turned to look at Huck.

The idea of negotiating for bovines that could one day be under his ownership and care brought a smile to Huck's face as he said, "It would be my honor. I can spot a good milker."

"I trust you can pick them, Huck, but make sure they're healthy. Mr. Cooper taught me they should be of a generous weight, not too lean or heavy; have clean udders with no sign of mastitis, and the teats should not be extended; have trim feet and strong teeth; but most of all, they should have a gentle temperament; calm and easily led."

"Give me some credit, Emeline! I can pick 'em. Consider it done," he said as he stood in front of Harriet. "Shall we proceed with the trainin' trial before the Coopers move, Harriet?"

Harriet checked my expression. Surprised by Huck's stern comment to me, she said, "Oh, yes. Definitely. I've always been for it." She put her arm around me and tugged my shoulder.

"Alrighty then," he said. "We'll come up in two weeks; perhaps with a cow, if you'll give us the money to pick one up."

"I'll wait to purchase," I said. "Just shop the dairy farms, please, and if you find one you like, ask if they'll hold it for a week or two." I stood and grabbed Harriet's hands and smiled. "Thank you both for testing the waters." Working with close friends appealed to me immensely, as I missed her desperately, more than *anyone* in Indianapolis, in fact. And she and Huck were perfect together, like eggs and bacon. Though he was controlling, I understood why she loved him, as she'd always been insecure — the same reason she and I had become close friends. *I hoped he and I wouldn't clash over control of the business or cause a rift between us.*

After Andrew moved the carriage and tended to Stormy, we shared mealtime together. Later, I fell asleep in Harriet's room upstairs, while Andrew slept on the sofa downstairs.

Tomorrow morning we'd travel again, and I, for one, anticipated conversing more with my manager. A gentle rain fell on the roof and lulled me to sleep.

Control

On our return trip, we conversed about the progress made. Grateful for my hat and long sleeves, the cloudless sky allowed the sun to shine brightly this June day.

"I have a question for you, Andrew. You've been in the mercantile all your life, you're smart, and full of ideas. Have you ever considered doing anything else? I would think, with your education, you'd succeed in any business you'd like."

"Growing up in the general store, as I have, I know the business inside and out. I've always felt it's a vital part of the town. Residents of Kearney depend on us for so many things: fabric for sewing clothes; staples like flour, sugar, salt, potatoes, dairy products, meat; the receipt of mail — we even boast of a small café. It's essential."

"True, but you wouldn't have to own it if you didn't love it, absolutely. Down the road, you could sell it, if you wanted, as I could sell my farm, eventually."

"Touché, Emeline. If I wanted to. Right now, I'm devoted to it, and successful. Above all, I want Ma to be comfortable, provided for, and proud, since she's the most important person in my life, at present. I'd never sell the mercantile Pa worked so hard to build from under her nose."

His words pierced my soul. Why didn't I have a similar devotion to Pa and Ma's farm and cherish it as they did? Why did I think of it as an inconvenience in my life? Growing up, I had loved the farm: Pa, Ma, its land, the house, the animals, the seasons, and its very air. How could I have forgotten? *Did forgetting make losing them easier?* No, it didn't.

"I understand." Nearing home, we rode along in silence, each deep in thought. Andrew pulled Stormy up to the front of the house, climbed out, and supported me as I stepped down. "Thank you, again, for allocating two days for me. I'm blessed to have you as a manager — and as a friend."

"Glad to assist. Just ask when you need to make another trip."

I smiled and waved as he turned toward town and then walked inside. Maude napped in her rocker, her head snuggled against an ecru crocheted blanket, with a herringbone pattern, draped over the chair's back. An open book lay face-down on her side table. It was Saturday at two o'clock, a perfect time for an afternoon's rest.

What a great idea! I joined her after I read a little from my Bible, centered on the side table next to the room's other rocker. I read all of Philippians 4, but this verse resonated with me today.

"I can do all things through Christ which strengtheneth me."
(Philippians 4:13)

I reminisced about my childhood: family fun and work on our farm, school days, and my friend Harriet. I thought of the other places I'd lived and loved and concluded that every choice always resulted in an outcome, just as each path or river always led somewhere.

It was time for quiet reflection: to hush all the voices in my head and listen to the Lord's leading. I prayed again. *Dear Lord, words aren't enough to thank you for all you've done for me. You know my heart and have drawn me here for a purpose. I don't need to know exactly where you're leading. I'll continue taking small steps as I listen — to You. Amen.*

With a peaceful smile on my face, I closed my eyes and rested. My thoughts wandered through the past, the present, and the unpredictable future.

After a little while, Maude jostled my shoulder, waking me from slumber. "Emeline, time to wake up."

"Umm. Oh, hello." I scooted to the edge of the rocker, arched my back, yawned, and stretched my arms wide.

She asked, "Are you hungry? I've set a place for you at the supper table."

Am I? "Yes, I am, because we didn't have a noon meal. I'll be right back." After visiting the privy, I washed my hands and came to the table. "How was your day, Miss Ambrose?"

"Relaxing. After I finished my lesson plans and swept and dusted the house, I spent the rest of the day reading."

"That's good, and so is this cornbread. Mm. It's sweet enough on its own, without honey or jam." I washed the crumbly bread down with water and cut into a slice of smoked ham with the side of my fork.

"Tell me about your trip, which I'm sure was more interesting." Maude smiled before she took a bite of the savory ham.

I summarized the trip and then asked, "Remember when I reported the missing cows to you? How you told me *I knew* what to do next? Then, I listed scenarios?"

"Yes, I do."

"I guess God works through *you,* Miss Ambrose, because now I know what I must do."

"Oh, my! What's that?"

"I will take one step at a time, listen for His leading, and move toward whatever brings me joy. I finally understand how to iron out difficulties and cope with conflicts."

"That's profound — and vague, Emeline. I'm glad I could help, but what's your plan now?"

"One step at a time: that's the plan. The first move is to complete Huck and Harriet's dairy training before the Coopers leave. That's it. They'll be here in two weeks, and I'll figure out the next step later."

"I see. So, you're not considering any consequences, planning, or anything?" She said, alarmed by my new attitude. "No thinking ahead?"

I didn't blame her. As a teacher, she was used to scheduling everything. "I've lots of ideas rattling around in my mind, and I'll play those out, of course. But I'll wait until their training is complete and they've resolved to do the work first. I hope to have one gravid Jersey cow to milk, though."

"You're continuing the dairy, then?"

"Having one cow, one who's expecting a calf, would thrill me, but I'm not one hundred percent committed to a large dairy, yet. We'll see what develops."

"Anytime you need to bounce ideas off of someone, remember, I'm here for you."

"Thank you, Miss Ambrose. Sincerely, thank you."

The next week, I learned about the business side. We were cleaning the tables, containers, and shelving in the creamery when Logan said, "Not only do you need to milk the cows and process their milk correctly, but you must also learn how to keep the cow's milk flowing."

"Oh, you mean getting the cows pregnant," I said.

William swept the floor close by. "Aye. Joel Cunningham has some fine Jersey bulls. When you think it's close to her time, just take her over for a visit."

"Exactly." Logan said. "Come over here quick, once, hey." He pulled out a notebook filled with details about each of the stolen cows. "You'll have to record information on every animal you own. Track their names, dates, amounts of milk given, illnesses and treatments, fertility cycle, birth records and notes, and everything else. Do the same thing with the chickens and any other animals."

I examined his meticulous journal entries. "This is an impressive account, Mr. Cooper. We will."

Inside the farmhouse, Sarah introduced me to a stack of hardcover journals. "This green one's for customers, the yellow is for crop records, the blue for business and house expenses, and the black is the bank book, which summarizes totals from all the others." She opened each to show its contents.

"Thanks for sharing these important steps with me. Will you help me set up my own books?"

"Sure, I will, with every detail." Sarah smiled and set all the journals back on their shelf.

The next day, I rode to the Pickwick Mercantile. The familiar little bell tinkled as I opened the door. Audrey was placing fresh banana bread slices under the glass domed plate, which sat on the countertop. But something was amiss. Bare floor appeared where barrels and bags used to sit, and the food shelves were empty. "Hello, Mrs. Pickwick. How are you today?"

With tired eyes and a feeble grin, she said, "I've been better, Emeline. What can I do for you?"

"I need to buy some journals." After a pause, I asked, "What's wrong? Something's happened."

She smiled, but her heart wasn't in it. "Let's take care of business first, please, then I'll tell you all about it. Do you like any of these?" She pointed to a shelf with colorful books: some with lined, and others with grid-lined paper.

What on earth was wrong? "Yes, please. I'll take five of the grid-lined books in different colors — you pick."

She assembled my purchases. "Okay, that will be $3.50."

I paid her. "Now, can you tell me what's wrong?" I followed her to a table, and we each took a seat.

"It's Andrew. Last night, some people broke in and stole everything out of the icebox — all the meat and dairy products — and all the tins of food from our shelves, even the barrels and bags on the floor. No other damage, thank goodness. I guess they just needed food. As they were leaving, they made enough noise to wake Andrew. He ran downstairs with his gun just in time to see the door close and a cart drive off."

"Oh, my! Where's he now?"

"He's devastated and at the insurance office."

"I'd like to speak with him. May I wait?"

"Of course."

I prayed for words. "At least they didn't hurt anyone. I'll buy a slice of your banana bread and some coffee." I handed her the coins, which she accepted this time, and she prepared my food and brought it to a table for me.

Then she resumed her post behind the counter.

After about an hour, Andrew arrived and saw me. "Hello, I wasn't expecting to see you today," he said, downcast, as he pulled out a chair to join me.

"I needed a few things. Your ma told me what happened. I'm so, so sorry. Thankfully, no damage or injury occurred. Will your insurance cover your losses?"

"We lost food, which wasn't enough to meet the deductible, so no. I declined to file a claim. But I found out from the insurance man that your pa had coverage on the buildings of your farm. My pa added the new dairy barn and creamery buildings to it, but I'm afraid your policy doesn't cover any loss of animals or crops."

"I hadn't thought about insurance. Obviously, I still have things to learn about running a business, don't I? What would I do without you?" Even now, though depressed, a smile grew and spread across his face at my words. I loved his smile.

"It pleasures me to help you, Emeline. I've been thinking about security for both of us. Dogs. Shall we shop for two: a shop dog and a farm dog? I'll do anything to keep those *dastardly* vandals out." Anger temporarily replaced his pleasant smile. "I'm even getting bars on the windows and doors. The blacksmith is making them for me and will install them. He's making me a strong metal door latch with a lock, too." His face grew stern. "I love the mercantile and will do all I can to protect it." He pounded his fist on the table.

"May I share a verse Miss Ambrose brought to mind recently?" I recited from memory.

I continued. "Realizing we're not in *complete* control lifts a tremendous burden. Think of the pressure you put on yourself, otherwise!"

"Easy for you to say, Emeline. As a man, and a business owner at that, I'm in command. What would happen if I lost control?"

"For myself, I believe I should control all I possibly can... I just acknowledge that, sometimes, situations fall beyond it; things that aren't my fault. For example, you couldn't help what happened to your pa, could you? Curing his illness was beyond the doctor's power, too. And the weather can't be controlled. I believe God works everything together for good, don't you?"

"Yes, I do. Thanks for reminding me." His smile faded briefly, his eyes closed for a moment, and I knew I'd struck a chord. When he checked my face again, he said, "We should learn from our recent losses. The first thing we should do is get those dogs!"

I asked, "You have a recent copy of the *Kansas City Times*, right? Let's check the ads." Controllable safeguards would be the subject of our conversation today — something we both needed.

He smiled. "Does Carter have little liver pills? Of course! We have today's issue. I'll get it." He retrieved the newspaper, a sheet of writing paper, and a pen.

We pored over the advertisements in search of the perfect dogs for us. "I'd like a massive dog, like a St. Bernard," I said. "Here's one!" I jotted down the name and address. "I understand they're wonderful family dogs and excellent at guarding livestock. He or she would intimidate intruders, and the cows couldn't accidentally step on them."

"For the store, I need a smaller dog, like this one." He pointed to an ad for a wire-haired fox terrier. "I've heard they're friendly to trusted people, but excellent watchdogs." He noted the contact information on our paper. "Looks like we'll be traveling back to Kansas City. This time, we'll drive a cart, and bring money."

I continued. "While we're in town, we might find a Jersey cow, too! Let's see." I peered through the livestock advertisements. "Here are a couple of ads for Jerseys." I copied their information on the sheet of paper. "Isn't this fun, Andrew?"

"It is." His engaging smile returned.

I asked, "Where should I buy barbwire for my fencing? You don't carry it here, do you?"

"Where else? You don't see it on the shelf, but we have it. And I can order more if needed. Next time you're there, take a measurement of the length of fence you need to cover, and I'll deliver it."

I noted his pride and grinned. "When can you get away for another two days?" I asked, delighted at the opportunity for another trip. "I'm sure we can stay with Harriet's family again for the night."

"Let me check." He stepped to the counter to consult with his ma.

She checked her calendar and said, "Other than this Wednesday, I'm available, and if I need to, I can get our church friends, Mary Dawson or Jacob Jennings, to help me."

Walking toward me, he said, "Let's go this Friday and Saturday, June 16th and 17th, Emeline."

"Perfect! I'll notify everyone. This gives me a few days to measure the fence, set up my record books, do my laundry, and pack. Shall I take the money from the safe now, or will you bring it?"

"I'll bring some money."

"Oh, Andrew, you're the best manager."

While I was getting up to leave, he winked, smirked, and pulled my chair out. So polite.

Sarah stopped me. "Oh, Emeline, I almost forgot. You received another letter." She tripped over a loose board on the floor on her way to the post office. "Oops!" She caught herself on the back of a chair.

Andrew rushed over. "Are you alright, Ma? Sorry. I've been meaning to fix that. I'll nail it down today."

"A letter? How much do I owe you?"

"Just two cents," she said.

I recognized the handwriting as Clara's and traded the fee for the letter. "Thank you," I said as I departed, stuffed the letter into my skirt pocket nonchalantly, and mounted Dakota for the return trip home. I knew what the contents of the letter would be — I thought.

Home Again

While Maude taught, I sat in her rocker and tore open the letter from Clara.

June 7, 1893

Dear Emeline

 I regret to inform you that Mr. Witherspoon fell from a cart and has broken his leg in two places. With his crutches, he can only work briefly.

 Jonathan is managing as work has slowed down, but we miss you. Would you be able to come back and help, even if only for a couple of months?

 Please let us know.

Love,

Clara Witherspoon

I felt awful for them. *Two months of help is the least I could offer after all they've done for me.* But what about the timing? I leaned back, folded the letter in my lap, and sighed. I knew making a list would be next, but I remembered my new mantra: one thing at a time.

The side table held my Bible, journal, and a pen — everything I needed. First, I opened the Bible to Proverbs.

"Withhold not good from them to whom it is due, when it is in the power of thine hand to do it." (Proverbs 3:27)

First, I prayed for wisdom, then opened my journal to a fresh page and started writing a list to process.

1. Record books with Mrs. Cooper tomorrow.
2. Friday, Andrew and I would visit Kansas City.
3. The following week, install barbwire on the pasture fence, and make and install a locked gate at the entrance.
4. Huck & Harriet would train with the Coopers for two weeks and make their decision.
5. The Coopers move, leaving William alone in the house, with a cow and a dog in the pasture, possibly.
6. Miss Ambrose would be busy teaching all summer.
7. Andrew could check in at the farm, occasionally.
8. It would cost money to travel by train: money that I'd planned to use for support and the farm.

With no dairy duties at present, and the crops busy growing, we had time to put up the barbed wire and gate. Depending on Huck and

Harriet's decision, I might move into the house and find normalcy. But without knowing, it was impossible to determine exactly what I'd be doing for the rest of the summer. But who would oversee the farm during my absence if Huck and Harriet declined? *William?* Maybe.

I cut some potatoes into chunks and boiled them until they were almost done. After pouring off the water, I added some fresh milk, butter, chopped onion, shredded cheese, seasoning, and a little chopped bacon. I stirred the potatoes frequently and cooked them until they were done, then moved the pot off the heat. Maude will be pleased that supper's ready, won't she?

"Potato soup!" Maude said, as she entered and settled her things on the desk. "I'm famished. It's been a long day. Thank you so much, Emeline."

After supper I bounced ideas off her.

She smiled and said, "I'm proud of you. You're becoming quite a mature young lady. You've made a well-reasoned decision, all by yourself."

"Thank you." I blushed and lowered my eyes. It wasn't essential to have her approval, but it bolstered my confidence. I smiled.

"But you must have everyone else's approval first, of course. And enough money to handle both efforts during these trying times."

I arrived at the Coopers' the next morning after breakfast with my grid-lined record books in my rucksack. Sarah and I spent the morning copying the headings, or categories, into my new books. It was fun using my new fountain pen to print names neatly over the columns. I used a wooden ruler to separate the columns along the pre-printed grid lines.

While I wrote, Sarah ground beef and pork to make a meat loaf. She mixed cornmeal, cubes of bread, onions, and seasonings with the ground meat and made a loaf in a pan. She also kneaded dough for a fresh loaf of bread. Then she baked both in the oven in the summer kitchen outside. Potatoes boiled in a pot on the stove, too. Meanwhile, I prepared all five books.

"What are the men doing today?" I asked.

"This morning, they drove Titan and Thunder to the farrier to tend to their feet. I expect they'll be back shortly and starved. Will you be a dear and set the table for us, please, while I mash the potatoes?"

I arranged the place settings for four and filled the water glasses. "The bread smells heavenly, Mrs. Cooper. So does the meatloaf."

"It's about finished baking. Just a few more minutes." She smiled as she mashed the potatoes with some milk and butter and then spooned them into a serving bowl. She pulled the crusty wheat bread out of the oven, placed it on a breadboard on the table, along with fresh butter and a knife. Outside, I cut a few stems of black-eyed Susans and put them in a vase of water at the center of the dinner table. Their bright yellow petals added a colorful cheer to the room. At last, the meatloaf was ready and set on a plate on the table.

"It's taking longer than usual. I hope he didn't run into problems with the horses." Hungry, I was eager to eat, but even more so to share my new idea with the group. We didn't have to wait long. They drove in, loosed Titan and Thunder for a pasture romp in their new shoes, and joined us inside.

"Mm. Dinner! Thank you, my love," Logan said as he kissed her cheek.

William said, "Ah, look, we have a visitor as well. Good day, Miss O'Connor. How've you been, lass?"

"Very well, thank you. And you, Mr. Kavanaugh?"

"Grand, just grand."

With everyone seated, Logan gave thanks, and we passed the plates and bowls around. Afterward, our stomachs filled with the savory food, the men meandered to the porch, while Sarah and I cleaned up. William played his harmonica, which made it a quick and pleasant task.

Once we were all outside and relaxed in the porch chairs and swing, I began. "I received a letter from Mrs. Witherspoon of Indianapolis yesterday. Poor Mr. Witherspoon has fallen and broken his leg in two places. I'm afraid he's unable to work much at all. They've asked if I can return to help for a couple of months until he recovers."

"Oh, no," Sarah said.

I saw questions written all over their faces. "I've thought about it, and prayed, and I think I might accommodate them, with your help. Could you still train Huck and Harriet for two weeks without the cows — or me before you move? And, William, are you available to oversee the farm after the Coopers leave and until I return, with or without Huck and Harriet? I would still pay you, of course."

"I'll surely do what I can. Not to worry." William leaned back and put his feet on a porch rail.

Logan leaned forward in his chair and then stood to pace the porch floor. "Let me think, now. As we don't have many animals to care for, we only need to harvest the barley and alfalfa, but I can arrange for help to bring it in, *provided* you leave me some money to pay the wages. I think the best two months to be absent are July and the first part of August. You'll need to be here to arrange for more harvesting help then, as we'll be gone."

"I appreciate your flexibility. I must discuss it with Andrew Pickwick, too. I'll keep you informed. Speaking of him, he wants us to measure how much barbwire we need so he can deliver it. I'll celebrate my seventeenth birthday while I'm away: July 15th." My rucksack sat inside the house, so I excused myself for a moment to retrieve the calendar I'd made. "Look. This Friday, June 15th, Andrew Pickwick and I will visit Kansas City to buy a couple of dogs and, hopefully, a gravid cow who's still giving milk. I want a St. Bernard pup to protect the farm, while Andrew wants a fox terrier to live at Pickwick Mercantile. Someone robbed them of food recently, so they need a dog, too."

"I hadn't heard that," Sarah said. "What's wrong with people today?"

"That's terrible," William said.

Sarah stared at her husband, who nodded. "This should work out if we can settle up before we part ways."

"We can. My manager will need figures from you in the morning. Unfortunately, I can't reimburse you for the cost of the missing cows, as the insurance did not cover them. I'm sorry. Don't forget to add more for the harvest labor you need."

"We understand," Sarah said. "You're a fine person, Emeline. It's been a blessing to oversee your farm and we appreciate your giving us this opportunity when we first moved here."

"You can count on us," Logan added.

"Aye," William said. "Don't give it a worry."

"Thank you, all," I said. "You've blessed me as well."

"May I have a word over by the pasture, Miss O'Connor?" William stood and proceeded across the yard to the fence around the pasture.

I followed. "Yes?"

"Just a quick question for you." He shuffled his feet and stared off into the distance, then at me. "We're only friends, aye?"

"And you're my employee, as well. But, yes, we're friends."

"Right. I noticed you call your manager Andrew, yet you call me Mr. Kavanaugh. In fact, you didn't start calling me that until the Spring Festival. We enjoyed ourselves then, didn't we? Can you explain?"

"I'm glad you brought this up. Remember when I injured my ankle, and you drove me home and invited me to the festival?"

"I do, of course."

"I shouldn't have accepted — not because of you, but because of me. At the time, my feelings for someone else made being with you awkward. I'm sorry. Calling you Mr. Kavanaugh created distance between us. Distance I needed."

"We may never have a close relationship, but I'd like to be friends, at least. And friends call each other by their first names. Please, call me William."

"I will. Thank you, William." I gave him a smile. "Now, I need to see my manager to get his approval. Will you excuse me?"

"Aye. Have a good afternoon, Emeline."

He'd never called me by my first name before. I liked it, but I shook it off and reminded myself that *he's just a friend.*

That afternoon, I visited Andrew again. Steel bar panels leaned against the inside walls of the store.

"Hello, Andrew. Mrs. Pickwick. How are things today? It looks like your bars are ready to install."

"Yes. The blacksmith is coming over later this afternoon," she said.

Andrew came over to a table. "Won't you have a seat? May I treat you to coffee this morning?"

"Thank you. I'd love some." He came back with two cups and sat across from me. I told him about the letter, Mrs. Witherspoon's request, and my list. "The Coopers and William are on board. Logan is gathering the figures for you so we can settle up before they leave. He'll have them ready in the morning."

He stared at my list with a solemn expression. "You can make this happen alright, but I highly question the last item — money. While everyone in the country is scrimping and saving, is it wise to spend money without monetary return? While I admire your devotion to your friends, you shouldn't spend money on travel. And, with all that's at stake at your farm, I'd highly recommend you stay put. Surely, the Witherspoons have local friends who could help."

Aghast, my mouth dropped, and I stared at him, motionless. "Andrew, I didn't expect this from you."

"I'm sorry to disappoint, but I'd be a poor manager if I advised otherwise — in this day and time. Isn't it enough that you must pay wages to bring in your harvest, pay for new animals, and who knows what else? Oh, I imagine you'll defend your position by saying you'll eventually sell your farm and regain the money spent."

"No, no, no. Oh, Andrew, I haven't told you. I've reconsidered selling all of it. I've realized that I've been pushing down my feelings for it in trying to get over the loss of my parents. I do care, from the bottom of my heart, for the farm and all the land it sits upon. While I'm happy to sell part of it to Huck and Harriet eventually, I now want to keep the forested acreage for myself, and for Pa and Ma." My mouth quivered as I smiled at him. "I know. It's a revelation to me, too."

"My, my." Andrew sipped his coffee and leaned back with a sigh. "What of your original plans for Indianapolis, then? Returning to the Witherspoons — and your friend Jonathan?"

"So much has happened in a few short months, hasn't it? As far as the Witherspoons go, I'll always treasure their friendship, but I don't need to live there to show it. We can communicate by letter.

And Jonathan has clarified, he'll be nothing more than a friend. He even has a girlfriend, Ruth."

Folding his arms on the table, he leaned forward and with a slight smirk, he said, "Welcome home, Emeline O'Connor."

That evening, I wrote another letter. It was difficult to write, and I hoped they would understand.

June 21, 1893

Dear Mr. & Mrs. Witherspoon,

I regret that I'm unable to help at this time due to pressing developments at the farm that require my attention, and also due to money commitments.

I love you both and wish you the best, but recommend you hire someone new to train, or get help from a carpenter friend.

I'll keep in touch, but my return is doubtful.

Love,

Emeline

After an emotionally draining day, I tossed and turned on my pallet, but eventually, sleep prevailed.

Shopping

I packed the usual clothes and things, plus some food and two canteens of water. Andrew drove a larger wagon this time. "Will Stormy be able to handle pulling this by himself?" I asked. Andrew stepped out and gave me a boost up to the seat, which was much higher than the carriage. Then he lifted my rucksack into the wagon.

"Yes, he'll do fine. He's bigger than your horse. If we were hauling something heavier than dogs and straw, I might need two horses. If we find a cow, she can walk behind." He had piled bales of straw in the middle of the wagon.

"Why the straw?"

"I thought the pups might like a soft place to lie on the trip home. They'll be able to see, but not jump out, hopefully." His dark eyes sparkled as he smiled. Casually dressed this time, he looked the part of a farmer in his overalls, western hat, and boots.

I wore a comfortable, forest green dress with long, slightly puffed sleeves. The color of the simple frock highlighted the green in my eyes. I'd pulled my hair back into a loose bun and secured it with hairpins. A riding hat sporting a dark purple ribbon complemented the outfit and would protect my face from the sun.

We were on our way, and the morning sun warmed the air quickly. Soon it would be hot. "I'm glad for the few streams close to the road for Stormy's breaks," I said.

"Me too. I've a barrel of water in the back — always carry it on long trips, just in case. Are you as excited as I am about this trip?" Andrew asked.

"I'm quite excited about the animals, but a little nervous about the upcoming dairy trial. Do you think they'll like it enough to leave the job security in Westport?"

"I think they will, but time will tell. Jobs aren't as secure as they once were, right now."

Breathing deeply, I sighed. My eyes found his. "You're a godsend, Andrew."

"I don't know about that." Changing the subject, he said, "Mind if I ask you a personal question?"

"It depends. What is it?"

"Is there anything you're afraid of?"

Quiet, I thought about it. I'm sure he didn't mean things like spiders or snakes. I held up one finger to ask for time to answer. What was I afraid of? In good times and bad, I'd leaned on my faith for strength.

*I don't think there's anything you couldn't do
if you put your mind to it.*

I thought back to my childhood. Back before Pa had died. Before Ma had died along with the baby. I still missed them and wished they were here — but that was impossible. "I'm afraid of being alone, Andrew," I said. "More than anything, I miss Pa and Ma — our family. I hope someday to have that again with someone — someone who's my best friend."

"I understand and feel the same way about family, but I don't fear being alone. Someday I won't be. And I still have Ma."

I continued. "Despite my efforts to do what's right, I still believe I'm not good enough, smart enough, or talented enough. I believe I need other's help to accomplish my goals." Andrew had touched the deepest part of my psyche. My moist eyes searched his face.

"Time to rest and water the horse and grab a bite to eat." Andrew pulled Stormy and the wagon off the road to a grassy area, climbed down, drew water from the barrel into a bucket, and gave it to Stormy. Then he scrambled back up and helped me to the back of the wagon. We sat on the straw bales and enjoyed the bread and cheese I'd packed and drank water from our canteens.

"Thanks for sharing with me, Emeline. Isn't it peculiar that others see us differently than we see ourselves? In my book, you're one of the bravest, most confident, and *competent* young ladies I've ever met. I don't think there's anything you couldn't do if you put your mind to it. And it isn't a weakness to enlist the help of others, by the way. Managers do it all the time. It's called delegation." He smiled, lifted his canteen to his mouth, and guzzled water down, some escaping to run down his chest.

"What about you, Andrew? Do you have dreams or fears? You seem like the solid one to me: logical, honest, hardworking, trustworthy."

He laughed. "That was Pa."

"Does the apple fall far from the tree?"

"Not too far, I guess. I don't think Pa worried as much about control as I do. I mean, he started the business, after all. He always had control, as much as anyone could. Sometimes I wonder if I have what it takes to keep the mercantile up to his standards and protected." He shooed a fly from his face.

"I don't think anyone could do better." I moved back on the bale of straw to face him. "Have you ever written in a journal — to write down your thoughts?"

"No, can't say that I have. Mainly, I look at the facts and use logic to solve problems, although being robbed angered me considerably. I rarely share my deepest feelings with anyone, even Ma."

"You should try it sometime. Everyone has emotions."

"True, but some lose themselves in them and I find that foolish."

"Maybe find a balance? I mean, you're human, after all. Even a dog has feelings."

We both laughed at that, and he said, "Let's get back on the road. We should arrive in about two hours." Andrew jumped down and hung up the water bucket while I returned to my seat.

Before we arrived in the city, we watered Stormy again and let him graze. We used this time to study the map and locate the addresses published in the newspaper. "We should see about the St. Bernard pup first," Andrew said.

As we traveled, I asked, "Are you hungry, Andrew?" We shared deep drinks of water from his canteen.

"I am. After we look at this pup, we'll stop in town for a bite. Here we are." The two-story farmhouse with its wood shingled roof was unusual in that they built it primarily of stones of various shapes and colors. Muntins divided the open windows' multiple panes. Behind the building stood a carriage house. Andrew pulled up to the entrance, tied off Stormy, and knocked on their front door.

This time, a heavy-set man answered. "May I help you?"

"Yes. Do you have St. Bernard pups for sale?" Andrew asked.

"We do. Go on around to the back and I'll meet you."

Andrew helped me down from the wagon seat, held my hand, and led me around the house. *He held my hand!* Unfamiliar stirrings warmed my insides. What did this mean? In the back, a fenced area housed the dogs: mama and four pups. My heart melted at the sight of them. "Oh, they're precious. How old are they?"

"Nine weeks, Miss. Let me introduce myself. My name is Geoffrey Wilson. And you are?"

Andrew spoke for me. "I'm Andrew Pickwick and this is Emeline." We've come from Kearney in search of a dog to guard dairy cows at our farm, and we've learned that the St. Bernard is perfect for this work."

"They are, indeed. We raise sheep and these dogs protect them from predators and would-be thieves with their intimidating size and warning barks. But they will warm to people you accept and are most affectionate with family members. They need basic care, including a thorough brushing now and then. They drool, but if they're outside, it's not an issue."

"I realize they're massive dogs. How much do they weigh as adults?" I asked.

"Females run about 130 pounds, while the males are about 150 pounds or more."

I looked at Andrew, agog.

He nodded and raised his eyebrows. "That's why I can't have one of these in the mercantile!" he said. "But aren't they beautiful and perfect farm dogs?"

"They are. May we go inside the pen?" I asked.

"Sure. I'll come in with you." He opened a small gate, and we all entered the area.

"Hello, mama. You're a good girl." I said to the mother, who panted heavily as the pups played with each other.

Mr. Wilson patted the mother dog and picked up each puppy for me to hold. "Two females and two males." One puppy showed me special attention. Whenever I walked away, it followed and tried to lick my legs. The other three were busy playing and tugging on a stick.

"Andrew... Andrew." I paused. "Is this a sign?"

He shoved his hands in his pockets again, with that sidelong smirk on his face. "You know it is."

I checked underneath. It was a girl. "How much is this one?"

"She's $10.00. A bargain for a farm guard dog, if you ask me."

"We'll take her," I said. "I've named her already." Winking at Andrew, I held the pup, extended her paw toward him, and said, "Hello, my name is Mabel."

Andrew grinned, paid the man, and the three of us were off to downtown Westport. We found a small restaurant, which served fried chicken, mashed potatoes, and green beans. We tethered Mabel to the cart's wheel and gave her a bowl of water. Then we ate our fill of the delicious food inside, even though Mabel yelped the whole time. She didn't fancy being alone, either.

"Andrew, I have a question for you," I said.

"What is it?"

"Why didn't you let me introduce myself when that man asked who I was? And why'd you use your last name, but not mine?"

"Ah, good question. You're very perceptive. You and I are a man and a woman traveling together. Some might think it unseemly. So, I thought it best to let people think we're a married couple. People in Kearney know us and that our relationship is one of business, but not so here."

"Oh, I see." I adjusted my hat and held out my left hand. "Should I hide my hand then? I have no ring."

He laughed. "Sometimes people take off valuable jewelry. Don't worry."

The sky clouded over, which made the day cooler, but would it rain? The wagon gave no shelter.

Our stomachs full, we studied the map to locate our next stop and resumed our travel. Mabel surveyed the world from her place in the back of the wagon, happy to be with us. Upon our arrival, Andrew knocked on the front door and an older woman answered.

"Yes?"

"Hello, ma'am. My name is Andrew Pickwick, and this is Emeline. We've come about the wire-haired fox terrier pups you advertised."

"Fine, come on in. My name is Mrs. Ingersoll."

Andrew helped me down and held my hand again as we walked into the house. Was he just being protective or was this part of the appearance of marriage?

She led us to the mudroom in the back of the house where the pups rested in a crate with their mama. "We have two boys left, and one girl. May I ask why you're considering this breed?"

"Our business, the Pickwick Mercantile in Kearney, was recently robbed. We need a dog that will alert us to intruders, and possibly catch mice if they should take up residence. But we need one that's also friendly to our customers and stays relatively small."

"You've done your homework. This is the perfect breed for your purposes, then. Well done, young man. Which pup do you fancy?"

Smiling, Andrew picked up each pup and studied them.

"Go ahead, take them out of the crate and see which one takes a shine to you," Mrs. Ingersoll said. "They're ten weeks old and weaned."

He sat on the floor with the three dogs, which crawled all over his lap and tried to lick his face. "Can you tell, Emeline? They all seem friendly to me."

"Stand up and walk away and see which one follows," I said.

That didn't work. They all followed him. "I guess I'm the Pied Piper, or something." He appeared helpless.

"Ha-ha!" I laughed. "Which one, which one? Only you can pick," I said.

"This one." He chose a saucy boy: mostly white, with color blocks of tan and black on his head and back. "I'm calling him Gus."

"Gus?" I wrinkled my nose. "Gus?"

"Yes. It suits him. How much do I owe you?" He put his hand in the top pocket of his overalls, where he kept his money clip.

"He's $6.00 and a fine choice." She smiled.

He handed her the money, thanked her, and we left the house. We introduced the pups in the wagon, and because they were so young, of course, they got along. Andrew helped me up to the wagon seat, and we headed to our next-to-last stop: Hampton's Dairy.

I held the newspaper and map while he drove to the address. It was a sprawling acreage on the southeast side of town, far from the stockyards, thank goodness. Dozens of cattle wandered over their hills. A sprawling two-story farmhouse stood on one end, while an extensive red barn, and a creamery, larger, but not unlike the one the Coopers built, stood downhill from the house. Barbwire fence surrounded the perimeter of their property, while other farm fences divided fields. We pulled up to the house and tied Stormy to the hitching post. Andrew hopped down and came around to help me off the wagon.

"Thank you," I said.

"My pleasure."

A woman emerged from the house, wiping her hands on her apron. "May I help you?"

"Mrs. Hampton?" Andrew asked.

"Yes."

"Hello. My name is Andrew Pickwick, and this is Emeline. We're responding to your listing in the paper and would like to see your available Jersey cows."

"Oh, yes. Let me walk you down to the creamery. My husband can help you."

We followed her to a massive white building with red doors; three times the size of our creamery. On the far west side, a tall lanky man in overalls stood with his hands on his hips, as deliverymen unloaded bags of ice into his icehouse. "Hello!" she shouted.

"Hello." He walked toward us, his hand outstretched. He shook Andrew's hand firmly. "Name's Joel Hampton. Yours?"

"I'm Andrew Pickwick and this is Emeline."

"These folks have come for a Jersey," Mrs. Hampton said. Turning to us she added, "People say we've the best milk in the city. I'll leave you to it." Her chocolate-brown dress, covered in part by a crisp white apron, swished as she whirled on her heel and marched back toward the house.

"We shared your reputation in Kearney until our cows went missing. Could you show us the Jerseys you've advertised, please?"

"Certainly. Follow me." With long strides, he led us to their pasture where at least fifteen Jerseys contentedly grazed on grass. Farmhands worked in the field pumping well water into a trough and shoveling manure into a wagon, no doubt headed for the compost heap. "All our Jerseys are healthy, excellent milkers, and provide lots of cream. Are you after just one cow, then?"

"For today, but we may return later for more." Andrew shifted his feet and leaned with his arms on the fence rail.

"Might you have any that are gravid?" I asked. "We need to rebuild our herd."

"All our cows are currently giving milk, and most are gravid and due to calve next February through May. We've raised some bulls, which spend most of their time in another field."

"Why are they wearing bells around their necks?" I asked.

"The primary reason is for their security, so we can locate them if they stray. But also, I engraved each bell with the cow's name for easy identification and for recording." He turned to us and smiled. "Plus, I love naming them."

Andrew stood up and pointed to the bell on the nearest Jersey. "Why are the bells made of wood rather than metal?"

"The noise from metal bells disturbs the cows, so we use wood for a softer sound and, also, it's easier to engrave wood with their names." Mr. Hampton said.

I turned to Andrew. "Interesting. We should do that too."

Mr. Hampton opened the gate and let us inside the field. "I have some extra bells to sell. Let's pick out a cow first. Do you see one you like?"

I roamed cautiously among them, checking their udders, their feet, their weight, and their eyes. I chose one and stroked her neck. She lifted her head as if to say, "whoo are yoo?" She had a beautiful shape and butterscotch coloring with huge, dark brown eyes and long lashes. Her bag and teats were clean and healthy — no sign of mastitis. I peeked at her bell, which was engraved with the name 'Maggie-Moo'. "May I halter this one and walk her about, please?"

Still by the fence, Andrew, hands in his pockets, smiled at me, then shuffled his feet in the soft dirt.

Mr. Hampton said, "Sure. Have one right here for you." He pulled it from a fence post, brought it to me, and I strapped it on Maggie-Moo to walk her around.

I loved her instantly and brought her close to the fence. "Is she calm when you milk her?" I lifted my eyebrows and held my breath.

"She's an easy one. You'll see, she's a calm girl," Mr. Hampton said. "I'll fetch her records to give you all the information."

My eyes locked with Andrew's. "What do you think? Isn't she a beauty?" I hoped her records wouldn't reveal anything negative.

He returned with a book opened to her page. "She was born three years ago on April 24th, 1890, and gave birth to a heifer on April 3rd, 1893. Clover is now weaned and doing fine. And on June 15th this year, we bred Maggie-Moo to one of our bulls, Noah. Her calf will be due March 23rd next spring."

With a wry grin, Andrew nudged me with his elbow. My mouth gaped open, and I sputtered, "We'll take her." I smiled at Andrew, then Mr. Hampton, and finally, Maggie-Moo. "We have a rope in our wagon for her, and I'd like to buy three wooden bells as well."

"Fine. Walk her up to the house and we'll make a handwritten copy of her records and complete the sale."

With Maggie-Moo tied behind, two pups and a bag of bells in the wagon, we were soon on our way to our last stop: the Steiners' house.

A Surprise

The air, heavy with humidity, felt like it would rain sooner than later. Our entourage arrived in front of Harriet's house at last. Andrew checked his watch. "Four o'clock. They'll be home soon."

"Won't they be surprised to see — all of us?" I asked.

"I'm sure they will. But they're farmers at heart, so they'll love our new companions."

Within the hour, they arrived home. "Emeline!" Harriet shouted from their wagon.

Conrad Steiner waved, but drove his horse to the livery stable at the end of the block. While he tended to him, Etta Steiner, Harriet, and Huck ran back to welcome us.

"I see you've been buyin' some animals. Ya came all the way to Westport for them? Goodness, they're gorgeous." Harriet blubbered over them, one by one.

"Nice job picking this one," Huck said. "Now we'll have a cow to milk durin' our trainin'." He smiled.

"Yes, and thank you," I said.

Etta addressed Andrew in the wagon seat. "You'd best get your horse and cow put away in the livery stable. You'll find plenty of empty stalls. Emeline, bring the pups into the house and we'll bed them down in the mudroom." She climbed the steps, pushed open the front door, and disappeared.

"Andrew, hold on and I'll give ya a hand with the animals. Emeline, allow me to help ya down." Huck, always helpful and in charge, assisted me and then led Stormy and Andrew down the street to the stable. I overheard Huck say, "Looks like rain. At least you'll have shelter tonight."

"Thank you, Huck," Andrew said.

Once everyone was inside, we enjoyed a simple supper and conversation. Harriet even played a song on the piano.

We still needed to milk Maggie-Moo. Etta, Harriet, and I cleared the table and cleaned up the kitchen. Afterward, Etta gave me the supplies. I washed two buckets and gallon jars thoroughly. Then, Harriet and I left for the livery stable with one bucket of water, an empty one, and two towels. Maggie-Moo munched on the hay, pleased to be still. "Sorry this isn't as warm as usual, girl, but we have to clean you off." I washed her udder all over and expressed some milk into the pail to check it. Perfect. Soon her milk nearly filled the pail. I covered it with the clean, dry cloth and we carried it back, taking turns every couple of minutes. The pail was heavy, and the walk seemed long. In the kitchen, we poured the fresh creamy milk through the dry cloth into the gallon jars and capped them. "Do you have an icebox, Mrs. Steiner?"

"Of course we do."

"You'll enjoy this fresh milk. We'll have more in the morning, too."

We washed the towels and bucket and set them out to dry overnight. She smiled and took the jars away to cool.

That night, before I fell asleep in Harriet's room once more, I prayed in silence, giving thanks for safety and provision. Lightning flashed, followed by deep, rolling thunder in the distance. Finally, rain poured, and wind blasted it against the windowpanes. I loved sleeping through a storm.

First thing in the morning, Andrew and I walked the pups, gave them a little food provided by the Steiners, some water, and then milked Maggie-Moo. She wouldn't need to be milked again until this evening. She'd give less milk too, with less grazing, water, and more exercise. We cleaned up in the kitchen, which was a breeze with a pump right inside. What a wonderful convenience. "I'd like to put a pump in our kitchen at home someday," I said.

"No reason not to." Andrew dried the pail and hung the clean towels outside on the line, even though a light rain persisted. Then he left to ready our wagon for the return trip. I hoped the rain would let up soon.

Etta was making bacon and eggs for all of us. "Thank ya for the milk, Emeline." From the icebox, she brought a cooled jar from last night. "We'll have some with breakfast."

"You're welcome. We must milk her, after all. It's I that's thanking *you* for your hospitality. Let me set the table."

"I appreciate ya. We'll eat in a few minutes."

After breakfast, we said our goodbyes, walked the pups once more, and double-checked the knot in the rope tethering Maggie-Moo. The rain diminished to a mist, and the sky showed streaks of blue between the light gray clouds. Rain had washed away dust and grit to reveal deep, vibrant colors in everything from bricks to plants. Andrew and I finally started back to Kearney with our pups and a cow in tow.

Maggie-Moo's bell added a mellow sound to Stormy's clip-clopping. The trip home would be a long one, as the animals would require more frequent breaks. Andrew let me hold the reins while he studied the map.

"Looks like a shortcut, see?" He showed me a trail that avoided part of the city to connect with the main road again outside of town. "It might be narrower, but we'll avoid the crowds. What do you say?"

"Fine with me." The trail meandered through open meadows. Less traveled, we were grateful for a grassier path, and fresher air.

Before we joined the main road again, we stopped to rest and water the animals. We let the pups have some free time to play and do their business. Being young, they didn't have the desire to roam far. I followed Mabel to the other side of the wagon, while Andrew and Gus stayed on theirs.

A horseback rider galloped up from behind us, stopped abruptly, dismounted, and grabbed me without a word.

I shouted. "Andrew!"

The wretched man pulled me tightly in front of himself, my back against his front, his beefy arms crossed, pinning my shoulders to his chest. He bellowed at Andrew, who ran toward me. "Give me your money, *now*, or I'll hurt this one." He clenched my shoulders tighter, and I groaned, arched my back, and tried to bite his arms. All my squirming and wriggling just made him laugh; his foul breath made me gag. Startled, Stormy reared up, neighed, and pulled the wagon down the path, with the bellowing Maggie-Moo in tow.

Andrew pulled his money clip from the top pocket of his overalls and threw it towards him — but only about halfway across the road into a little patch of blue wildflowers. "It's not much, but take it."

The slovenly beast of a man was unshaven, dirty, and reeked of body odor, smoke, and alcohol. He released me and I ran to Andrew, who pushed me behind himself. The thief staggered as he grabbed the cash and headed for his horse. But quicker than you can say Rumpelstiltskin, Andrew wrestled him to the ground and punched him repeatedly until he gave up, dropped the clip, and stumbled over to his horse like the drunken man he was. With difficulty, he mounted it, turned, and rode back the way he came, blood oozing from his mouth and nose.

Andrew and I stared at each other, panting through open mouths. Out of breath, he asked, "Are you… alright?" He regarded his bloody hands, used to bludgeon that vile man.

"Yes," I said. "Are you?"

"Yes, I'm fine." His face grew angrier than I'd ever seen it. "I'm done with lawless people. No more. **NO MORE!**" he shouted. We gathered the pups and caught up with the wagon. Pups in the back, I comforted Stormy for a moment while Andrew washed his hands under the water barrel's spigot. He helped me up, clambered to his side, then took the reins and said, "Giddup."

We rode in silence for at least an hour. Back on the main road, at last, I took off my hat. "I wish that hadn't happened, Andrew. Thank you for what you did. I must say, you surprised me." I tried to read his face, arranged my mussed hair, and re-positioned my hat.

"Why?" He turned toward me.

"I've never seen you fight anyone." In truth, I hadn't witnessed many fights in my lifetime, unless the train hold-up counted. I recalled I'd been driven to fight for myself three times on my journey to Boston. In one instance, I'd used a knife, and in another, a cast iron pan. When I'd almost died, I'd no weapons at all.

"As your manager, I'm here to protect you, Emeline. What would have happened if you'd made this trip alone? I shudder to think!" He stared at me; his face earnest. "Which leads me to the next thing I'm compelled to say."

My eyes hadn't left his. He stopped Stormy, and the wagon came to a halt. Then he turned toward me and grabbed my arms. "Tell me you'll never travel unaccompanied again. Never. Promise me. I need to hear these words from you."

My heartbeat raced and my eyes closed for a moment, then I gazed up at him. "I don't know how to thank you properly for all you've done for me, Andrew. You're much more than a manager. Alright, if you insist on it, absolutely. I'll never travel alone again. I promise." He valued me, which pleased me greatly. Something stirred inside, and it wasn't hunger or sickness.

His focus shifted forward into the middle-distance, as he fumbled with the reins. "There's something else, Emeline." He paused. "I'd love to become *more* than your manager." He shuffled his feet and his eyes found mine again. "May I court you? I'd ask permission from your parents if they were alive to ask."

"Andrew Pickwick!" We eyed each other steadily as I hesitated. He understood me well and possessed many admirable qualities. We might complement one another, but was I ready for this? I'd never be with Jonathan, but would William and I stay just friends? Quickly, I sent a silent prayer to the Lord.

Sensing my apprehension, he said, "We'll take plenty of time to become acquainted." He raised his eyebrows and grinned. "You can call it off any time, if you want to."

Blushing, I returned his smile and said gently, "May I give you my decision in a day or two?" Though he'd said he wasn't the emotional type, he'd certainly expressed emotions today.

"Of course." He smiled, focused ahead, and released a held deep breath.

Complex and wonderful, Andrew might be for me, but this would be a gigantic step — one of which I had to be certain. But wouldn't it be fun...learning about him?

Business & Pleasure

On Monday, I worked at the farm. This week, we needed to calculate how much barbwire we needed, make a gate, and get William's horse. After the morning milking, I asked William to help me measure. "Will you fetch the measuring tape while I get a paper and a pen?"

"I'll." He smiled and ran to the barn for the tool.

I met him at the farm's front entrance, ready to make notes. "Fine. Let's measure the distance across the entrance. How should we make the gate, William?"

"Mr. Cooper and I have discussed that. The blacksmith could make a wrought iron one, but that would be heavy and too expensive. Since money's tight, we're plannin' to weave wire between boards. We'll secure it with a latch and a keyed padlock. Sound good?"

"Sounds perfect." I held the fifty-foot tape. "I'll hold it here while you take the tape to the other side of the path."

"Right." The smooth tape slid out from its round case. "What does it measure?"

"Looks like twenty-five feet." I set a rock where I stood. "Use a rock to mark the spot for the post."

He selected a nearby stone and placed it where he'd been. "Look what I've found. Here, take it."

"What is it?" He placed a copper penny in my hand.

"A penny, of course. 'Find a penny, pick it up. Pass it on and have good luck.' I'm in for some luck now." His smile flashed.

I laughed and slid the coin into my pocket. "Maybe you'll get a fine horse. We're riding to the Johnson's this afternoon."

He inched toward me. "You'll help me pick one, won't you, Emeline?"

I stepped back. "Oh no, William. Picking a horse is a personal thing, and it's not about luck. Only you, and the horse, will know which one suits you. And, mind your distance, please." His advances made me uneasy. Though charming, could we ever be more than friends if we talked and shared our thoughts on a deeper level, like Andrew and I had?

"Aww. No harm done, lass. Say, the Fourth of July picnic is comin' up. Would you like to come with me, or are you still thinkin' of someone else?"

"Thanks for asking, William, but I must decline. I'm sorry. You're a fine, sensitive young man and I'm sure you'll find the right young lady."

"Had to ask. Thanks for your encouragement, but I'd still like to know you better. I'm patient."

"I care for you, as a friend, and hope we can work together as such," I said. *This wouldn't be easy.* Andrew was right when he said William wouldn't simply give up.

We continued measuring until we completed the total for Andrew. After dinner, Logan, William, and I headed to the Johnsons to see about a horse.

We followed Mr. Johnson to the fence where several horses grazed and swished flies from each other's backs. "Not all are for sale, but we have two to choose from. They're powerful animals: they'll do any kind of work you need, and they're both broken to ride." He pointed to a bay with black legs, tail, and mane. "The reddish one is Cimarron, a two-year-old gelding with a spunky personality." He pointed in another direction toward a pale buckskin, also with black legs, tail, and mane. "That's Driftwood, a two-year-old mare who's as gentle as a kitten. Is this your first horse, son?"

"Aye."

"Do you have a preference, William?" I asked.

"May I see them up close — even ride them? Are they the same price?"

"Yep. $200.00."

William's eyebrows rose.

Logan said, "That's a fair price for an animal that's trained and ready to ride and work, son. A quality horse is an investment. Besides the initial cost, you'll also have upkeep, feed, vet care, farrier expenses, and such. Are you prepared for this commitment, er, no?"

"Aye. Been savin' up money for a couple of years now. I'm ready."
William bent over the fence, pulled out his harmonica, and played
a happy little tune.

Wouldn't you know? All the horses gathered toward William
to see what made that sound. Amazing.

"May I go inside and check their hooves, legs, and teeth?"
William asked.

Mr. Johnson said, "Go ahead. You'll find them all strong
and healthy."

William climbed between the rails and stood next to Cimarron
first, then Driftwood. Both passed his test, but Cimarron's eyes
showed some nervousness, while Driftwood's revealed a calm
demeanor. "I'd love to ride Driftwood. Shall I ride her bareback
here, or should we saddle her up?"

Mr. Johnson threw a halter toward William. "Halter her and
bring her over to the gate. We'll take her to the stables and get her
ready. Will you need a saddle? I'll sell you hers, a blanket, and the
rest of her tack for an extra $50.00."

William said to Logan and me, "I see what you mean about an
investment. This oughta keep me out of the pub, eh, Emeline?"

The pub? Since I've known him, he hasn't imbibed once, to
my knowledge. But he had said he enjoyed beer. Now I worried
owning a horse would give him the freedom to ride to the pub in
the evenings, and who knows what else. Ah well, as long as it didn't
affect his work, why should I care? *One more reason we'd remain
only friends.*

"Aye, I'll need them, Mr. Johnson." He brought Driftwood through the gate and to the stables. She followed faithfully. Gorgeous horse. Intelligent, well-set eyes.

Patiently, she stood as Mr. Johnson changed the halter for the bit, demonstrating techniques to William as he continued to saddle her.

He mounted her and rode around the yard and toward the road. "Be right back," he said. About ten minutes later, he returned. "She's a dream. I'll take her and her equipment."

Now William Kavanaugh had a way to and from work and independence. It would be interesting to watch how he handled his newfound freedom.

Tuesday, I rode to Kearney to meet with Andrew after morning milking to order the barbwire and speak to him about the partnership contract. And I was ready to give him my answer if he asked. *Oh, I hoped he would.*

"Hello, Mrs. Pickwick, Andrew." I stepped to the counter to buy some coffee and a piece of banana bread.

"It's on the house," Audrey said. She smiled as she wiped down the countertop.

"You're spoiling me. I'm happy to pay."

"She loves spoiling you. Take a seat. I'll be there in a moment." Andrew stepped into the back room and returned with some papers, his coffee, and a slice of bread. "I've started drafting the partnership agreement but still need to go over it with the lawyer. When your friends arrive next week, it will be ready for all of you to review. I've addressed several important considerations."

1. Contributions: time, effort, and equipment.
2. Distributing profits: who gets paid first? Salary? How much?
3. Ownership: handling changes if sold, in the event of death, bankruptcy, buy–outs, non–compete clause.
4. Decision–making: voting? Who has final say?
5. Disputes: mediation
6. Developments: how might partnership be modified? Process for changes.
7. Dissolution: legal steps to dissolve partnership.

"Andrew, you've thought of everything, as usual. Thank you."

"Do you have any other items of business to discuss?" he asked.

"One more thing to get out of the way." I handed him the layout and measurements for the barbwire. "Here's our order for barbwire. We'll need some smooth wire, too, to make the gate." I pointed to the farm's entrance on the drawing.

He took the drawing, folded it, and stuffed it in his pocket. "No problem. I'll write up the bill and deliver it tomorrow. Now then, is our business concluded, Miss O'Connor?" He swallowed a mouthful of the moist bread and sipped his coffee. "Emeline, can't you tell my stomach is in knots? Do you have an answer for me?"

We laughed, which helped release our tension. "My answer is, yes, Andrew. Yes, a thousand times, yes. I would love to be courted by you." *Oh, my.*

He looked around to see if anyone was in the room and, finding no one, he reached across the table and held my hands. "You've made me the happiest man in Kearney today, Emeline." He released my hands, beamed, and with a twinkle in his eyes, sat back and pulled a small black velvet-covered box from his apron pocket and set it in front of me. "Open it."

"What's this?" I opened the box, which housed a beautiful necklace: a gleaming golden chain with a solid gold heart pendant. "Oh, my… Andrew. Is this just for courtship?"

"Do you like it?" he asked, unable to stop smiling.

"It's beautiful. But what does it mean? I'm not sure how courting works."

He pulled the necklace out, walked behind me, and fastened it around my neck while I lifted my hair. "There's not much to it, really." He returned to his seat. "To stay respectable, we'll meet in public places like here, or before or after church, or at public gatherings to become acquainted." His smile dazzled me. "But if we go somewhere where we'd be alone, such as trips out of town, Mrs. Dawson, Mr. Jennings, Ma, or someone else must chaperone us."

I rubbed the little heart between my fingers and observed him. "And how long does courting last?"

"It depends. Unless one of us calls it off, it could be just a few months, or as long as years. Whenever both of us are comfortable moving to the next step, we'd take it."

"Which is?"

"At some point, I would ask for your hand in marriage. That would begin our engagement, which again could take as much time as we like. Then, the last step, of course, is our marriage."

"I see. Well then, let's get started!" I wanted to learn everything about him, so I asked about his childhood. "Why don't I remember you from school as a child?"

"Excellent question, Emeline. Incidentally, may I call you Em?"

Ma and Pa always called me Em. No one else ever had. Not even Harriet. "Yes, you may." I grinned.

"Em, when I was in school, I sat in the back with the older children while you were in the front. You probably don't remember me because I never caused much trouble, and you were more interested in children your age, like Harriet. I saw you, but of course, I hung around with the older ones. We would have been four years apart, which is a lot when you're only ten."

"And by the time I was ten, you had finished there?"

"Yes. By that time, Pa took over my education here and when I was sixteen, he sent me to college to earn a degree in business. 'Education is important, son. I want you to have every advantage in the coming world,' he'd said."

His eyes returned to mine when I said, "My parents said that, too, and I believe it's true. Look at you. You're running your own successful business now, besides managing mine, and you can do anything you like with the mercantile. I admire your entrepreneurial spirit."

"Isn't that curious? I could say the same about you, Em. You're different from other young women. You've a fire inside, courage, and you're smart. Your spirit captivates me the most, despite your attractiveness and freckles. That's a bottom fact."

Unused to receiving such high praise, I raised my shoulders up and covered my chest with my hands clenched together around the heart pendant. "Thank you." Then I relaxed and grinned.

Sunday, Maude and I attended church, as usual. This time, Huck and Harriet attended. Men sat on one side and the women on the other to maintain modesty and attention to the service. "Harriet." I said. "I'm glad to see you." We sat together in the wooden pew, Bibles on our laps. She looked pretty, with her hair pulled back into a neat bun covered by a thin hairnet. Her cheeks glowed. Was it because an engagement ring now glimmered on her left hand?

She asked, "Come for a visit after church, won't ya? Hey, new necklace, Emeline?"

"It's a courtship necklace," I said. "Andrew Pickwick." I blushed and couldn't hide my smile.

"Go on… you and Andrew? I had a feelin' about you two. Congratulations!"

I smiled. "It's a courtship, not an engagement. We're taking time to learn about each other."

"Aww, it will be, I'll wager."

"Anyway, yes, I'll visit you afterward. And if Huck is here, ask him to come too." I smiled and turned my attention to the front, as the service began and we sang 'When the Roll Is Called Up Yonder', a brand-new hymn this year. Lovely!

After the service, Maude and I fixed a quick dinner, and then I rode to Harriet's house. Naturally, I loosened Dakota in the pasture and watched as he shook his mane, ran a bit, and then settled to graze on the long grass. "Too hot to run much, eh, Dakota?" Then I turned toward the house and knocked.

Harriet hurried to let me in. "Come in, friend, come in. You've probably eaten dinner, but I made some tea for us, anyway." She handed me a cup. "I wish it was lemonade, but I haven't bought food yet."

"Thanks. I love fresh lemon in the summer. It's so refreshing. They may have some at the mercantile, but it's hit or miss with some produce, like citrus fruits. Trains coming from California and Florida this year are undependable." *How long would this economy be down?* "I notice you're wearing an important piece of jewelry on your left hand, Harriet. Congratulations! When did that happen?"

We set our cups on the side tables and settled into her cushioned chairs. "I tell you; Huck is no mystery to me. I knew something was on his mind because he was quiet and a little distant all day until after supper one evenin' last week. We sat with Ma and Pa, who were suspiciously quiet as well. Of course they were. They already knew, because he'd asked them first. I guess he wanted to ask before the trial."

"And then?" I smiled and leaned forward, gripping the sides of my seat cushion.

"He got down on one knee, said he loved me, and asked if I'd spend the rest of my life with him as Mrs. Malloy. Needless to say, I jumped up from the chair. He stood up, too, and I said yes. Absolutely. I love him so much, Emeline! Then, he reached into his vest pocket, pulled out this ring, and slid it on my finger." She held it out for me to admire — a plain gold band with a single diamond recessed in the center.

"That sounds like him, and your ring is stunning." I smiled and clapped my hands. "You two were made for each other. Have you set a wedding date yet?"

"Yes. We're plannin' to be married after the harvest: Friday, December 1st at noon."

We hugged for at least a minute before a knock on the door announced Huck's arrival.

Smiling, she rushed to the door to let him in. "Hi, Huck." They continued to hold hands even after they took their seats near me.

"Hello, Emeline. Good to see ya. We're thrilled you're home," he said.

"As am I. Congratulations on your engagement, Huck. You're a blessed man to have won Harriet."

"I am. Thank ya," he said with a smile.

"Huck, look at Emeline's necklace. Just look. Andrew's courting her," she said.

"Fancy. Well, well… love must be in the air this summer," he said.

"It must be," I said, and then changed the subject. "I'm excited to train tomorrow, aren't you?"

"Naturally. We'll fly in with the birds in the mornin'. I'll pick you up at six o'clock, Harriet, and we'll head over."

Monday, June 26th, marked the beginning of the trial. By July 10th, we'd have their answer, just before my birthday.

Cooper Dairy

After the first week, Huck and Harriet had already proven they could handle the dairy end of the farm. The Coopers taught them about farming the crops, too: when to plant, what to plant, when to harvest, and the rotation of crops. And they covered bookkeeping. Fortunately, both had previous experience with both crops and animals, so the training was more or less a refresher course with a few new techniques explained.

One day in front of the farmhouse, my necklace drew William's attention. "New necklace? Haven't seen it before," he said.

"Yes, it is. Andrew Pickwick gave it to me."

"As an early birthday present, I assume?" His soft brown eyes checked mine, and he grinned.

"No, William. It's not a birthday gift. Andrew is courting me now." I couldn't help smiling back, but his countenance fell.

"I see." He picked a black-eyed Susan from the flowerbed

near the pump and handed it to me. "Congratulations, then. Still friends, are we?"

"Of course," I said. "Still friends, William. I'll always enjoy your musical talents and rely on your hard work here. It's not as if I can't speak to you anymore."

"True." He bucked up and said, "Remember, I'm a patient man, Emeline. We'll see how it goes." With a wink, he walked toward the creamery.

Oh my.

By the end of the first week, Andrew had completed the contract with the lawyer. Near the end of the second week, on July 7th, I popped the question after supper at the Coopers. "Have you two decided? Shall we meet with Andrew to review the partnership contract?"

Huck took Harriet's hand and turned toward the Coopers. "We've loved every minute here. I'm most impressed with the successful business you've built. It would be our honor to continue your work, make it our own, and grow it in the future — with home delivery."

"Splendid! Welcome to your new home." I stood, along with everyone else, and shook everyone's hand, except Harriet and Sarah, whom I hugged. "Thank you, thank you all." Turning to William, I asked, "Would you mind playing a little something by way of celebration?"

"Aye. Right away." Excited, he flew into his room and brought out his fiddle. With gusto, he played and sang 'Whiskey in the Jar', a rousing Irish song which made us all dance around by the end.

Breathless, I said, "William, you're an amazing musician." His talent couldn't be denied. I wondered if Andrew played an instrument or sang. No matter. We would make music together somehow.

Monday morning, July 10th, we met at Pickwick Mercantile to review the contract with Andrew. We pushed two tables together and Audrey Pickwick treated us all to coffee. Huck and Harriet sat on one side, while Andrew and I sat on the other. Andrew brought a pen for signing and the contract, of course. Then he explained all the concerns, which were addressed with his lawyer's help.

Huck read each line carefully and asked questions. "Mostly, I understand everythin' and am agreeable, but I'm confused about when and how much we're paid."

Andrew clarified. "You'll keep records of your income through dairy products and crops, and that money must be deposited into a business account at the bank. Also, you'll record all expenses incurred. Each month, we'll meet over those records and split the profits: 30 percent for each of you, and 10 percent for me."

"A month seems like a mighty long time to wait. Can't we make it weekly?" Huck asked.

"Let's take a vote. How many would rather meet weekly on Saturdays?" Andrew counted three hands. "Weekly it is, then." He amended that part of the contract. "Anything else?"

Harriet asked, "What are we calling our business?"

"Good question, Harriet," I said. "Since the Coopers made it the success it is, and it's known by that name, I suggest we call it Cooper Dairy, until — and if — you both decide to buy the farm."

Andrew asked for another show of hands and we voted the name in and Andrew scribed it in the document. "Questions?"

Huck said, "One more question for Emeline. How soon would ya be willin' to sell?"

His question caught me short. I blushed and stammered something of an answer. "You know, I've been giving that some thought. I'm not backing out but must disclose my feelings. In the past few months, I've discovered I've distanced myself from Pa and Ma's farm because it reminded me of their passing — which is painful. Actually, I've flipped sides. Now, I embrace it as my heritage and my parents' legacy. I don't mind selling the eighty acres of existing farm, pasture, and cropland to you and Harriet, plus fifteen acres of woodland. But I'm thinking of keeping the other undeveloped sixty-five acres of woodland for myself, and for their legacy. Will that satisfy you?"

"Aw, sure. It's plenty. I'm glad ya explained this. We must be open with each other — above board — so to speak." Huck said. "What about William? Do you think we need him? Money's tight these days."

I said, "Harriet and I can handle the garden, milking, and housework, but what about the heavier field work?"

With forearms folded on the table, he leaned forward. "We can hire people temporarily to help with plantin' and harvestin'. We don't need William full-time."

After a round-table discussion on the matter, we had differing opinions. How could I back the decision to sack William? It was too soon — and too harsh. I asked, "How much difference could it make between hiring extra hands at harvest and keeping William on? He's become like family, or at least close friends. No, I couldn't support this decision. Not yet."

Andrew observed them during my discourse. I sensed the wheels of his mind turning and I'd hear his analysis later. He said, "Since all decisions must be unanimous, William Kavanaugh will stay employed full time, for the present. We can re-visit the matter again later if you wish. If there are no other questions and you're ready to sign, here's the pen."

Huck asked, "Harriet, Emeline, Andrew… are there any more questions?"

We all murmured we didn't and passed the document around for all our signatures. And the Cooper Dairy business was born, at last. Happy birthday to me!

Huck and Harriet left, but I stayed to talk to Andrew. "What do you think?"

"I think Huck is the take-charge type of commander and will do well. I only hope we can trust him to deposit all the money into the bank account I'll open today."

"What?" His comment shocked me.

"No reason to believe we can't. But today I sensed something suspicious about him. He must prove he's trustworthy. I'd like you to inventory your products. You'll be aware of how many gallons of milk are produced and sold, and after sales, how many should remain. But be discreet. After a few months, if he's proved himself trustworthy, we'll stop this cautionary action and it'll be full speed ahead."

"Andrew, why? He's been honest and upfront about everything. Harriet and I trust him completely. Are you frustrated because you don't have, but want, complete control over Cooper Dairy?"

He clasped his hands in front of him on the table and asked, "Don't you get the idea he's bossy and domineering?"

"Well, yes, I do. That's why he and Harriet are perfect together. He's a leader, and she's a follower. But he's not dishonest."

"Alright, you win this one. It's not my business, is it? I'm merely the manager. But, if you don't see enough money being deposited, and you're suspicious, don't say I didn't warn you. And, also, why did you champion young William's employment? What did you mean when you referred to him as family or a close friend?"

"Oh, Andrew, really."

"No, no, I'm serious, now."

"I meant what I said. There's a lot of work on the dairy farm. Too much for two women and one man, I imagine. William has worked there for years and knows more than any of us how things should go. He's valuable. Yes, he's a friend, but that's all. I promise." Reaching for his hands, I held them. "*I promise.* And I always keep my word."

We smiled at each other, and he said, "We've survived our first quarrel."

"I hope there aren't too many of them. That was tough."

"Another reason I adore you, Em: you stand up for yourself. For the record, Mark, the blacksmith, is looking for an apprentice. If things don't work out for William, you might suggest he apply. He might make more money, too."

The Coopers had moved, and the contract was signed. It was time for the next steps. William enjoyed a break, with Mabel curled up at his feet. She stood quietly when I arrived. "Hello, Mabel." I gave her ears a rub. "Good afternoon, William. Are you ready for milking?"

"Sure." I followed as he went to fetch Maggie-Moo. After tethering her, he brought her to her stall. William had cleaned it, spread fresh straw on the floor, and stocked some alfalfa hay in the rack for her pleasure. "Would you like to do this today?" he asked me.

The hoofbeats of approaching horses drew our attention, and Harriet yelled, "Wait up! I want to show ya what I've learned." They tied up their horses by the house and hurried to the porch. Today, she covered her hair with a net. "I'll be there as soon as I wash up." She and Huck ducked into the house and were back out in a few minutes.

She grabbed two buckets. Using a small pail, she pulled simmering water from a pot on the stove outside the barn and poured some into each bucket to sanitize it. Then, she pulled two clean towels from a shelf: one to wash the buckets, and then Maggie's udder and a second to dry her hands. "Logan taught us to clean everythin' first: our hands, the buckets, and the whole udder — even the back part — so we don't get germs, hair, or dirt in the milk. He also said to let her udder air dry before milkin'." When her teats had dried, Harriet expressed some milk in a test pail. Perfectly creamy. Gentle Maggie-Moo was a dream.

"You've learned well," I said. I sent silent thanks to the Lord.

Mabel panted in the barn's doorway, while William leaned against it, chewed on a piece of straw, and waved off occasional flies. "They know what they're doin', Emeline. Just watch."

While Harriet milked, Huck got the milk can ready by sanitizing it again with hot water. He placed it inside a barrel and surrounded it with crushed ice he'd scooped from the icehouse. Finally, he covered the top of it with a thin cheese cloth as a filter. Then he sanitized several gallon jars and set them on the steel table.

After they poured the milk into the can, I asked, "May I help you cool it down?"

"Sure, ya may," Huck said, as he handed me the long stirring paddle.

"What's your favorite part of Cooper Dairy, Huck?" I stirred slowly.

"I think part of it is pride. Pride in ownership and pride in havin' the best quality dairy products around. But aside from that, I love workin' with the animals and the farm's peace."

"I know what you mean," I said. "How about you, Harriet? What do you enjoy the most?"

"The same things, but also, I like that it's ours and we're not working for anyone else, except with you, Emeline."

"Someday, this farm will be all yours," I said and then thought. *And I'll settle the woodland acreage next to it.*

After milking, we collected eggs from the chickens and tossed them some grain. Then we enjoyed supper: French toast, scrambled eggs, and fresh milk. "Did you make this bread, William?" I asked.

"No. I'm not a cook or baker, no. I bought it from the mercantile."

"It's delicious. Thank you. Oh, I meant to ask, how do you like riding Driftwood?"

"Wish I'd bought a horse a long time ago. She's wonderful — gentle, smart, and doesn't spook easily. And I can come and go as I please. Bought that bread at the mercantile, didn't I? Now, I can run errands for you." His smile lit up his face.

"Will you favor us with a song this evening?"

"I'll. Any requests?"

"Whatever ya like, William," Harriet said.

The next morning on the farmhouse porch, I approached our employee. "William, since I'm moving my things into the farmhouse this afternoon, and Harriet is doing the same, will you please move your things to Harriet's family farmhouse today to live with Huck?"

"Not a problem. Been expectin' this. Not much to move. I'll be out this afternoon." He threw me a sidelong glance and grinned.

"And something else, between you and me. Huck felt we could handle all the work here without you, but I said we couldn't." He froze and waited for my next words. "He thought we could hire part-time help during planting and harvest seasons, money being tight and all. But I said we need you full-time instead. I wanted to tell you, in case Huck says something to you."

He patted Mabel, who sat next to him. The silence was palpable.

I continued. "Just in case you're interested, though, Andrew says the blacksmith is looking for an apprentice. He's always busy making things with metal and shoeing horses. You might make more money, too. It's a valuable trade skill to have."

"Andrew," he said. "He's a good man. Like him better than that Huck fella."

"What don't you like about Huck?"

"Bossy fella, he is. Watch your back, Emeline."

"Oh, he's a leader, but also a nice person."

"That blacksmith job sounds promisin'." He stood up and faced me. "Mind if I leave with my things now? I can pack everything in a bundle and tie it behind Driftwood's saddle."

"No, that's fine, William. You can stay with Huck at the Steiner's house for as long as you like."

He smiled at me and said, "No, that won't be necessary. I'll find my own digs, thanks all the same. It's been a pleasure workin' here and knowin' you, Emeline. Thank you for sharin' with me. Shows you do care after all. I believe I'll go speak with the blacksmith directly, if you don't mind."

"Not a problem, I understand. Please tell me, or even Andrew, what happens. I wish you all the luck an Irishman can get." Remembering the lucky penny I still had in my pocket, I pulled it out and handed it to him. "God be with you."

"Keep that penny. Takin' it back would be bad luck, it would. I'll tell one of you where I wind up. Hope to see you soon. May the saddest day of your future be no worse than the happiest day of your past."

"Thank you, William."

Then, he saddled his new horse, packed up, and rode away.

After that difficult conversation, I gathered my clothes and things to move back to the farmhouse. Like William, my belongings fit behind my horse's saddle. "We're moving back to your old barn, Dakota." I left a note thanking Maude Ambrose for her generosity over the past months, as she was busy teaching. I would see her again, even if only at church on Sundays.

Back at the farmhouse, I first made Dakota at home in a stall, hung up his tack, and groomed him. Then I moved back to my old room. So familiar. I loved the bed with its soft green, blue, and yellow patchwork quilt Ma had made, the nightstand with a kerosene lamp, the curtained window to the back garden, and the four-foot-tall Shaker dresser with deep drawers for my clothes and personal items. Hooks on the back of the bedroom door would hold dresses and my wool winter coat. A shelf on the wall offered a place to display flowers or books. Harriet would have the larger bedroom, as she and Huck would eventually marry and need the space.

Soon, I learned William had become the blacksmith's apprentice and loved it, and this outcome pleased Huck. July and August flew by, and we kept busy.

One week in August, the four of us, Andrew, myself, Harriet, and Huck, traveled to Kansas City with two wagons and bought four more cows from Mr. Hampton. William generously offered to milk Maggie-Moo while we were away, besides working his new job, and I compensated him for it. Our new cows were as wonderful as Maggie-Moo. Their names were Annabelle, Buttercup, Penny, and Millie. Penny and Millie were yearling heifers, not yet bred or able to provide milk. My savings dwindled, but we'd covered our biggest expenses. With our herd restored and our harvest coming in soon, what could go wrong? Plenty, it turned out.

Money Troubles

On Friday afternoon, September 15th, Harriet and I rode to Pickwick Mercantile to shop for material for her wedding dress. It surprised us to see people congregated in small groups along the street. A sign in the window of Kearney Bank & Trust said: "CLOSED — Come Back in October".

"Oh, no!" I said. "The bank's closed." I held my breath. What would this mean to our business and to the community? I tried not to panic.

Animated groups of men discussed the dilemma. Anger subsided, diffused by rational people who encouraged working together rather than fighting a useless battle. In Kearney, there were few strangers in town, and fewer secrets. Camaraderie, neighborliness, and fellowship usually prevailed.

"No, this can't happen. I won't have money for the fabric." Harriet said. "And what about food? Is it foolishness to spend money on a weddin' dress?"

"I'll cover it until you can repay me, Harriet. Please don't let the bank's closing spoil our fun." Mr. Kingston, the banker, impressed me as an optimist, which is why he wrote 'October,' on the sign. I hoped so. "At least the Pickwick Mercantile is still open. Harvest time should help us, anyway. We'll have to save our earnings at the house until the bank reopens, too."

"Thank ya, Emeline. I'll never forget this kindness." She squeezed my hand. "Ya know how I hate spendin' money, especially now."

The door and windows wore bars on them now, like the bank. When we entered, Gus yapped excitedly and ran to greet us. Like a metronome, his short tail stood straight up and wagged rapidly. Ah, the simple life of a dog. What did a dog understand about money? Or a horse, or a cow, for that matter.

"Hello, Gus," I said, as I stooped to pet him.

"He's adorable. What kind of dog is he?" Harriet asked.

"He's a wire-haired fox terrier: a perfect watchdog for the mercantile."

My eyes searched the store in vain for Andrew. Audrey Pickwick greeted us from the counter. "Hello ladies. May I help you today?"

Harriet smiled and stepped up to the counter, and I followed. "Yes, please. I'm lookin' for fabric for my weddin' dress. Do you have any?"

"Yes, I believe I do, but I keep the finer materials in the back. I'll get them for you. While I'm gone, if you're looking for a pattern, please browse through these Butterick selections to see if you like one." She gave us a crate of enveloped patterns and stepped away, with Gus at her heels.

"Oh, Emeline, look," she said, thumbing through the envelopes.

"Have you ever worked with a store-bought pattern before?" I pulled one out and read the information on the back: notions needed, amounts of fabric for each part sorted by size, and more. "My!" Later, I would have to try one of these myself.

"Oh! Look at this one, Emeline." Harriet selected a beautiful pattern. The satin A-line skirt of the dress hugged the waist and then fell gracefully under the ornate, fitted bodice with its unique, detailed sleeves. They featured three narrow, folded bands on the top of the arm and then puffed out at the shoulder. A cap of material, with the same appliqué detail, sat atop each puff. The neck was high with the same lace appliqué around it and a soft lace edge on top. "This is it! Isn't it gorgeous?"

I held the pattern and stared at its pictured views. "It's the most beautiful dress I've ever seen. Sewing it will be a challenge, but I'll help. Won't Huck be speechless when he sees you in this? He'll melt into an absolute puddle." I smiled broadly, excited for her. Secretly, I wanted to see Huck toppled, for once.

"I hope so. Well, not too speechless. He needs to say his vows, after all. We can't let him see any of this before the weddin'. Promise?"

"I promise. We'll work on it by night with all the lanterns lit. Or for shorter times while he's away harvesting."

Gus ran ahead of Audrey, who returned. "Here we are." She carried four bolts of fabric and set them in front of us. "Did you find a pattern you liked?"

"Yes, ma'am. I love this one." Harriet handed her the envelope.

Audrey moved the crate. "Oh, it's lovely. Let's see." She pulled out an ivory brocade, a white linen fabric, and a snowy satin for our consideration. "The brocade is too heavy for the design of this dress and would compete with the cutout lace overlay. You need a softer, more flowing fabric. The satin would be my choice, but it's your decision." She unrolled part of the bolt of netting. "This will be perfect for your veil, after you edge it with a lovely lace, which we can order by catalog."

"I love the satin fabric. Look at its sheen, and it's so soft and flowin'. Can you manage the cost, Emeline?"

"How much is it, Mrs. Pickwick?" I asked.

"Forty cents per yard." She checked the back of the pattern. "I estimate you'll need about seven yards of it. The lace will cost more, but the netting is the least costly. I estimate it will cost roughly $10.00 to make, counting thread and the buttons you'll cover."

"That's only half the cost of a cow, Harriet."

She laughed.

"It's your wedding dress. Of course, it must be the nicest one you'll ever have. Let's do it."

"You're precious, Emeline!" Harriet's eyes teared up as she embraced me.

We spent another hour figuring how much fabric we'd need and cut it, ignoring the grumbling outside. Then we chose the lace and appliqué from her catalog and placed the order. Harriet folded the fabric neatly and packed it with the pattern into a canvas bag she'd brought along, while I paid for it.

Audrey took this opportunity to speak privately with me. She held my hand and said, "I just knew you and Andrew would hit it off. I'm so glad." She pressed my hand between hers and smiled. Her eyes glistened.

I returned her smile. "Me too, Mrs. Pickwick. Incidentally, where is he?"

"I'm not sure. He said he had something to do, but he'd be back soon. Didn't say where he was going. But I don't believe he's involved with the bank ruckus. I'll tell him you were here."

"Thank you. Say hello to him for me." Harriet and I left and returned to the farm, where we discussed the events of the week, but we avoided the subject of money for now.

After supper at the farmhouse, the three of us chatted together outside. Huck started a conversation about money. "I worry about the bank closin'. How will people be able to buy and sell things? We can have the healthiest milk products and crops, but who'll be able to pay?"

"It depends on how long it stays closed, I guess," Harriet said.

We all remained quiet and solemn for a few minutes. "Let's pray," I said. We prayed aloud, one after the other. Our spirits lifted, and I continued. "My cash reserve is dwindling, but I can pay for the harvest help and for our food and supplies for a while longer. Surely the bank will be open before I'm out of money completely!"

Huck spoke for them both. "That's fine, but we'll keep track of all the expenses so we can reimburse you. We can close our Westport bank accounts and use that money, too, provided those banks are still open. But if we run out of money, then what?"

I said, "People need to eat. Even if we must lower our prices temporarily, we'll still make some money from the sale of milk products, eggs, and the harvest. As a last resort, I could try to sell the wooded acreage I own, even if I don't get full value. But only if I'm absolutely forced to." Pa and Ma would cringe at that thought, and so did I.

Harriet eyed me and said, "I hope it doesn't come to that. I know how much that property means to ya."

Huck said, "I wonder how Kansas City and Westport are doin'. I should ride in and close that account and check on our parents. Just for a couple of days. Can you girls manage?"

We smiled, "Of course, Huck," Harriet said.

I said, "Don't come back and tell me you want out of the partnership to move back there." I covered my mouth with both hands in a prayer pose.

"Don't worry, Emeline. I need to see what's happenin', that's all."

"Alright. When will you leave?" I asked.

"Tomorrow mornin' after the milkin's done."

The next Monday morning was rainy, and we delayed milking until late morning when Huck returned with his update. He hung up his raincoat and hat on a peg in the creamery's wall and sat on an upturned barrel. "I won't lie. Business there is declinin'. Some banks have closed, but fortunately, I withdrew the money out of ours." He showed her a bag from under his coat. "We'll put it in a safe place in the house. You think it's bad in Kearney with a few hundred people? Imagine thousands of people."

Looking at Harriet, he continued. "Your ma and pa are even thinkin' of returnin' to their farm. Your pa says construction has slowed between owners not bein' able to pay, and sellers not bein' able to get materials here due to railroad bankruptcies. They're barely meetin' their rent and food expenses. At least in Kearney, they won't have rent to pay." He prepared the milk can, while I sanitized the jars and lids on the steel table.

Harriet kept milking Maggie-Moo, though her hands shook. Even the cow showed concern, as she mooed and turned her head to look at her. "At least you got our money. And it will be wonderful to have Ma and Pa back home again, even if it's sooner than expected. They'll be there to better manage the crops ready for harvest."

"It's fortunate you made that trip, Huck," I said. "Harriet, will you still live with me if they come back, or will you go home?"

Turning toward Huck, she asked, "Would it be alright if you live with Ma and Pa while I live with Emeline until the weddin'?"

He smiled. "Of course. I'll see you here every day, anyway. And your folks will chaperone us when you visit."

That night, as I lay in bed awaiting sleep, I wondered if animals ever worried about tomorrow. Wasn't there a verse about this? I reached for my Bible and read from Luke.

"...Therefore I say unto you, Take no thought for your life, what ye shall eat, neither for the body, what ye shall put on. The life is more than meat and the body is more than raiment. Consider the ravens: for they neither sow nor reap; which neither have storehouse nor barn; and God feeds them: how much more are ye better than the fowls?" (Luke 12:22-24)

The rest of the chapter held even more solid promises. Closing my eyes, I prayed for strength, wisdom, and patience. I clung to hope. There was much to be thankful for, even in desperate times. *Regardless of people or circumstances, I can find joy and strength within myself.*

Harvest Time

Late September and October always brought cooler weather for the
autumn harvest season. Logan Cooper had kindly given me the names
and addresses of workers he'd hired in the past, so Harriet, Huck, and
I rode to their various homes and offered them work. Fortunately,
most were available and willing, and each received a schedule and
weekly rate of pay. We relied on my savings and their Westport bank
money for this, but we recorded the expenses in our bookkeeping
journal for future settlement.

From a bird's-eye view, my farm appeared much like Ma's patchwork
quilt… with varied shapes and colors, depending on the season. Dark
brown, lifeless, fallow fields laid next to green or golden ones. We
rotated crops of alfalfa, oats, and barley. Composted manure from our
cows and horses, fertilized the fallow fields for the next year's planting.

While cooling Maggie-Moo's milk, I said, "I'm so glad the harvest
is in. Harriet and I enjoyed making food for everyone. I love harvest

time when everyone comes together. It makes the work fun." When at our house, people filed in and out during dinner and other break times. We reciprocated, helping others at their farms. Women and girls fixed all kinds of delicious foods and enjoyed watching the smaller children and visiting, while the men and boys worked, ate, and worked some more. The men's laughter and song made for a quick day's work.

In the creamery two weeks later, Huck said, "Harvestin' is fun when working shoulder to shoulder with our neighbors. The barley's harvested, thanks to the McCormick reaper, and Mr. Spencer, who came around with his steam-powered thresher. That tool's a blessin'. Tomorrow I'll winnow the barley and store the grain in those barrels against the back wall. See?" He pointed to them.

"What's left?" I asked.

"We harvested the alfalfa at early buddin', too. Four tall haystacks stand next to the old bull pasture. The sayin' is true: many hands make light work. It's fragrant and green. Maggie-Moo and the four new cows lowed by the fence, so we threw them some, which they promptly grazed on. The horses love it, too."

After she cleaned her milking buckets and returned the cow to her pasture, Harriet stood by me and said, "The garden behind the house has produced tomatoes and basil all September. We already have thirty quarts of tomatoes put up, and we've bunched the basil and hung it in the kitchen to dry. After we're finished here, want to pick blackberries with me? The brambles are loaded. We've got to beat the cold weather. Ya know how unpredictable it can be in

November. One day it can be in the seventies and a few days later, get down below freezin' at night."

"That's true. Of course, I'll help." My mouth watered at the thought of the sweet berries I'd sample. "We'll bake a fresh blackberry pie for tonight, save a little to nibble on, and preserve the rest for winter. We'll harvest them for a couple of weeks, won't we? Afterward, we'll prune the spent canes from the brambles." Oatmeal with blackberries made a delicious breakfast. "I'd forgotten how much I loved living here. It's lots of work, but so satisfying. No wonder Pa chose this life over Boston."

Harriet put her hands on her hips. "Our parents were hard-workin' and determined, weren't they? To think, for a small filin' fee, the government *gave* them 160 acres of land to settle, build a home, and improve, thanks to the Homesteading Act. And, after only five years, they became the legal owners. I'm sorry your folks have passed on, Emeline. Really. But at least ya inherited their land." Her moist eyes twinkled.

I caught her hand and squeezed it. "That's alright, Harriet. I enjoy talking about them. Pa had taught me enough about the planting and harvesting of crops to make us self-sufficient. He said dairy cows produce more milk when fed some hay from our fields, as it's higher in nutrients than the pasture grasses. We used straw for bedding for the horses, dairy barn, and chicken coop, because it doesn't mold. We sold excess crops and composted manure." *Oh, thank you, Pa.*

When we finished, Huck said, "See ya gals later."

"Take care, Huck." Harriet waved goodbye.

We went to the garden to pick blackberries with four baskets, while Huck collected firewood with Dakota, pulling a cart through the forest.

"It's sure hot today, isn't it?" I asked as I tied a cotton scarf over my forehead and put on a straw hat. "Be careful. It's a prickly job." I popped two berries in my mouth. "Mm. But worth it." Thick brambles formed a long line on one side of the acre garden. Blueberry bushes and bare mounds where strawberries had grown lined the opposite side. They would bear fruit in the spring, along with newly planted strawberries. "Do you want to plant more strawberries for fall?"

"No, not this year. We have enough work on our hands." She stood and wiped her brow with her apron. "Don't forget, besides the tomatoes and basil, we also have to harvest the potatoes." She pointed to the field of leafy growth over about a third of the acre.

"Yes, then there's the forest. The apple trees near the edge are already ripe and falling off the trees. We haven't had the proper time to harvest as many apples as we could have. Some were ripe last month. And we'll pick up walnuts through October." I set down my full basket and regarded my stained hands. Standing tall, I arched my aching back and stretched my arms. "Whew! All besides milking three cows. Are you sure we don't need more help, Harriet? Remember, we also have your wedding dress to make and wood to split for winter. If one of us gets sick, we're sunk."

She laughed, and said, "Maybe. Huck is hard-workin', but I'm sure an extra hand would help, even if only for a few weeks."

"Remember, it was two men working the farm before: William and Logan. Sarah worked in the garden and in the house and handled all the customers' orders. Let's ask him tonight after supper," I said.

"Agreed." She carried her two baskets to the outdoor kitchen, and I followed with mine.

I pumped water into a bucket, and we washed the berries, eating a few now and then. The delicious fruit burst inside my mouth. While Harriet cooked a pie's worth of berries outside, I mixed up the dough inside and rolled out half of it before putting it in the pan. I rolled the other half out, too, but cut it into long strips to make a woven lattice top.

"Emeline, they're ready," she said as she brought in her pan of hot berries, water drained off.

I stirred in one and a quarter cup of sugar, four tablespoons of cornstarch, and one teaspoon each of cinnamon and nutmeg to them. "Now, let that cool for about fifteen minutes."

Harriet stirred the filling and took a deep breath. "Mm. Smells sweet and tart at the same time. My mouth is waterin'."

"What shall we make for supper? It's so hot today. How about some cheese from the icehouse on some of the bread we have, with a slice of pie?"

"Add tea or coffee, and you'll have it," she said. "Your teeth and tongue are purple, Emeline. Are mine?" She stuck out her tongue.

"Yes." We laughed.

When the filling had cooled, we filled the pie crust, topped it with the lattice dough, and sprinkled a tablespoon of sugar over the top. "Perfection," I said as I walked it outside to bake in the oven.

Huck returned with a wagonload of wood to split later. He tended to Dakota and the draft horses before he met us again. We were busy as bees with the milking of three cows. The days were shortening, we noticed, as suppertime arrived at twilight.

After supper, and our slice of pie, we brushed our teeth with baking soda to remove the blackberry stains. Then we relaxed on the porch, now lit by a lantern. A breeze blew, cooling us from a long, hot day. We rested in the wooden rockers, and I hummed a little song, since William wasn't there to play anything, and I missed it. Harriet was the first to approach the subject of extra help.

"Huck, Emeline and I were talkin' about all the things that still need to be done before our weddin' and winter. We both think it might be wise to hire another hand for extra help for a few weeks. Besides splittin' wood, we need to harvest the potatoes, apples, and walnuts, plus milk three cows twice daily. It's a busy time."

"You don't think we can handle it in three months? We can do it. Ask me again in a week or two if you haven't changed your minds, but I expect you will. You're panickin', that's all. It *is* a lot of work, but we have time. Trust me. Besides, money's tight."

Harriet stared at me, and I shrugged my shoulders. "Alright," I said. "I hope you're right, Huck." I raised my eyebrows toward Harriet.

With that, Huck said goodnight and rode his horse back to the Steiner's farmhouse. We went inside, too tired to work on her dress.

The next week, I visited Mark, the blacksmith. Dakota needed new shoes, and I hoped they would have time to shoe him during my shopping. Plus, I hadn't spoken with William since he left. Did he like his new job, or have time to help for a few weeks, possibly? Huck had said we might revisit the idea of extra help. William would be ideal, as he wouldn't need training.

Mark hammered a red-hot horseshoe on his anvil, while William removed shoes from a horse. What a hot and sweaty job this would be during summer! "Hello. Would you have time to shoe Dakota?"

Both men stopped and approached me. "Good day to you, Emeline. Sure, it's grand to see you again." William's smile gleamed.

Mark said, "We can after this one. Might be about two hours before Dakota's done. Do you have the time?"

"I'll make the time, thank you. I'll be shopping in the Pickwick Mercantile."

William waved and said, "He's a fine man, Andrew Pickwick is."

"Excellent." Mark said, returning to the fire to re-heat a horseshoe.

I stopped William from returning to the horse. "Might I have a moment?" I asked.

His smile returned. "Let me check." He turned and murmured to his boss, who nodded. William continued. "How have you been, Emeline?"

"Fine, thank you. But we miss you. How do you like this work? Are you happy here?"

"Aye, yes, I am, indeed. Have my room, Driftwood, regular hours during the day, and better pay. It's not as hot now, being September and all. But come December, it'll be a dream. Mark has become a kindred spirit, and we even visit the pub together for a pint on Fridays after work. I enjoy livin' in town."

"I'm glad for you, William. Truly. You'd better get back to work and I'll see you when I pick up Dakota." I could have guessed he'd be unavailable. Despite that, I was happy for him.

I greeted Audrey as she swept the floor. "Good morning, Mrs. Pickwick."

"Good morning, Emeline. What brings you to town?"

"We need a few staples: salt, sugar, and flour. I need a sack of each, please. By the way, has Harriet's catalog order arrived?"

"Yes, it has." She set a bundle wrapped in brown paper tied with cotton string on the counter. "Would you like to see it?"

"Let's." I covered my mouth.

She untied the string and opened the package. Inside lay the loveliest white trim. "What do you think?"

"Harriet will be in tears when she sees this. It's beautiful!"

She wrapped the package again and handed it to me. "Oh, you received another letter."

As she walked to retrieve it from the "O" slot in the post office, I asked, "Is Andrew here today?"

"He's meeting with the banker, Mr. Kingston."

"Oh, has the bank re-opened?"

"No, not yet. But Andrew and Mr. Kingston have been devising a plan to open again next week."

"Andrew's helping the banker?"

"He's a brilliant and shrewd business owner, as you, and now Mr. Kingston, know." She handed me the letter, which was from Jonathan.

"He certainly is." I grinned. "May I have a tall glass of lemonade, please?"

"Of course." I paid for it and the staples and sat down at a table with my packages. It would be some time before Dakota was ready, so I pulled the envelope from my pocket and opened it.

September 30, 1893

Dear Emeline,

This is a "good news" letter. As my "little sister", I thought you'd like to know that the Witherspoons have offered me a partnership. They realized they're getting on in years and needed a plan for the shop's future. Remember when you asked what my big dream was? This is it! Someday I will own the McFarland Trim Shop, but not too soon, I hope. There's still lots to learn.

And I've asked Ruth to marry me, and she's accepted my proposal. We plan to marry next September, 1894. The Witherspoons have extended an invitation for us to live here with them. It's a dream come true. Even my dad is pleased! Remember, he never thought I'd amount to anything unless I followed in his banker footsteps?

I hope this letter finds you well. Please write and let me know about the goings-on there in Kearney.

Always your "big brother",
Jonathan

Glad for Jonathan, I folded the paper, slipped it in my pocket, and giggled to myself. How quickly things changed. Someday soon, I'd write back, but not quite yet. Gus lay next to my chair, and I bent sideways to pet his head. "Such a handsome boy." He leapt up and barked.

The door to the mercantile opened, the door's bell tinkled, and Andrew walked in. Immediately, the terrier ran to him, tail wagging stiff and upright.

"Good boy, Gus." He gave him a rub and then noticed me. "Oh, hello, Emeline. Didn't see Dakota outside. I'm sorry it's been so long since I've visited, but I've been working with Mr. Kingston on the bank situation." He filled a glass with lemonade, then sat across from me.

"Can you share information, or is it confidential? Whatever it is, I'm impressed. So awed, in fact, I wonder what a guy like you sees in a girl like me." I stared at my hands in my lap, my cheeks and ears flushing.

Gently, he placed his hand under my chin and lifted it until our eyes met. He held my hands in his. "Oh, Emeline O'Connor. You have swept me away. Even though I'm managing the business side of your farm, my love for you has nothing to do with business. We could be poor as church mice, with no businesses at all, and I'd still love you. Nothing you'll ever do will change my feelings for you. Nothing. You'd never ever hurt me, nor would I you. You, Emeline, are my best friend, with whom I pray to spend the rest of my life."

"Really, Andrew?" I grinned demurely at him. "I'm enough for you?"

He smirked and winked at me. "More than enough, Em. You complete me. You bring dreams, fun, music, and life to my otherwise dull and pragmatic life."

I smiled. "And you keep my feet on the ground and my paths straight. You keep me from stumbling."

"See? Together, we're complete."

He was right. Even if I'd stayed in Indianapolis, Jonathan and I weren't a smart match, as we were both too similar. And, while I loved William's music, he would always be only a friend.

Andrew surprised me, and I admired and loved him for his honesty, hard-work, level-headedness, and passion. Yes, passion. I'd seen it on the road when he came to my defense against the drunken man, and later, when he asked if he could court me. Though he appeared cool, aloof, and in full control, his passion ran deep. I clung to the heart hanging from its chain around my neck. I couldn't love him more, nor wait to spend every minute together.

Back at home, Harriet was busy in the outside kitchen preparing dinner for us. "How were things in town?" she asked when I returned.

I held up the brown paper package and said, "Fabulous. Your package arrived! Come and see."

On the dining table, she untied the string and opened the paper. Collapsing in a chair, she held both hands to her face. "Oh, goodness!"

She picked up the end of the lace, then the appliqué. "Have you ever seen anythin' so delicate?" Tears rimmed her eyes and fell down her cheeks, as I expected.

"No, I haven't. Now, let's get started on that dress. Tonight, we'll read the instructions. I've already reviewed them, and some terms are new to me, so we'll need to understand them first."

After dinner, the afternoon flew by. Customers came by to purchase dairy products, eggs, and more. Harriet and I handled the orders near the house and barn, while Huck loaded wagons with alfalfa hay. Even though the bank was closed, people needed these items and had little money to pay, so we lowered our prices temporarily to assist.

Now, in the last week of September, we fell into a regular rhythm. The tomatoes and basil were about finished. For the next two months, we would harvest the remaining apples, potatoes, and walnuts. In November, we would have one more cutting, windrowing, and shucking of the alfalfa field this year. Though most of the work was doable with three people, we hired temporary field help for the final alfalfa harvest. Huck had been mostly right, but the heavy load took its toll on all of us. Exhausted, our patience wore thin, tempers flared, and we made complaints — a result of overwork. But, once we'd expressed our grievances, we buckled down to complete the work at hand.

Wedding Bells

Money was tight — our account barely in the black. Thanks to Huck's advice, we hadn't incurred the expense of an extra hand. William Kavanaugh's move to the blacksmith's turned out to be a blessing for both him and us, financially.

Harriet and I enjoyed the mid-October nights, windows open, and lanterns lit. We'd cut out the bodice of the dress and the skirt and basted it. With a few minor adjustments, it fit her perfectly. "Look at all those bugs on the screen, Emeline. Moths, mosquitoes, and all kinds of beetles. They're attracted to the lantern's light."

I couldn't answer with straight pins sticking out of my mouth. Once placed in the garment, I said, "I'm thankful for screens and have often thought about screening the whole front porch someday." I questioned our finances through the winter. Would I need to sell some of our assets, specifically my land? Selling off part of the forested part of the property would be the end of Pa and Ma's legacy.

It's the last thing I wanted to do. We *could* sell off some of our animals, but they wouldn't bring as much money as the land would, plus they produce our income. No, that makes no sense. And, in this economy, anything would likely sell for under its real value. Andrew was working behind the scenes with the banker. *Was it working?* Turning to Harriet, I said, "Tomorrow, I need to ride to the mercantile. Do you need anything?"

"No, thanks." Harriet folded three tucks in the top section of each sleeve, sewed them, and pressed them down. She regarded her work on the flat sleeve with huge bell shapes at the shoulder, for the puff, as well as three rows of basting around the bells for gathering later. "Beautiful. It was easy to make those three bands. Now we can sew the side seam of the sleeves, gather the puffs, and attach them to the bodice." She folded each sleeve, right sides together, and stitched them. "Satin is slippery to sew on, isn't it?"

"Yes, it can be tricky. But you're doing a fine job, Harriet." We worked until almost eleven, put everything away, and made our devotions. I re-read Luke 12, and the words spoken by Jesus rang through my mind like a loud, clanging bell.

> *"And seek not ye what ye shall eat, or what ye*
> *shall drink, neither be ye of doubtful mind.*
> *For all these things do the nations of the world seek after:*
> *and your Father knoweth that ye have need of these things.*
> *But rather seek ye the kingdom of God; and*
> *all these things shall be added unto you.*

The next morning, after milking, I saddled Dakota and headed to town and entered the Pickwick Mercantile. "Hello, Gus." His happy greeting warmed me, and I stroked his head. From the back of the store, Andrew emerged, broom in hand.

"Good morning, Em." He set down the broom, took my hand, and pulled out a chair at a table by the window. "You look lovely today. Would you like some coffee?"

"Yes, please. Do you have a few minutes to talk?" My eyes widened and searched his face. What should I do with my hands? I clasped them together in my lap.

"Sure. Not bad news, I hope." He prepared two cups of coffee, brought them over, and sat across from me. "Now, what's troubling you?"

"In my heart, I shouldn't be concerned because the Lord will take care of me — I mean, us. Can you please tell me what's happening with the bank? You've been keeping things on the quiet, and while I understand why, I need to know if it will re-open soon."

"You and everyone else in town." He leaned back with a grin and sipped smugly from his cup.

"Oh, Andrew, you're exasperating! Don't tease me now." Should I be angry or sad because he won't share? Tears of some sort welled up inside. "Can't you tell *me?*"

He stopped grinning. "I'm sorry, Emeline. I don't mean to be secretive with you. The *Courier-Tribune* will release the news to everyone tomorrow, so I can tell you all about it now. Just keep it under your hat 'til then."

"Do tell!" Elbows on the table, my chin rested on my clasped hands, as my eyes widened.

"Mr. Kingston and I approached several prominent business owners in town, and each of us has bought shares in the bank."

"Shares?"

"Yes. It means we've invested in it and are now part-owners. This income will give the bank the much-needed capital on its spreadsheet. Additionally, Mr. Kingston has written off a few bad debts."

"Oh, I understand. That's fantastic!"

"There's more, Em. Everyone who has money on deposit will have to sign an agreement."

"What kind?" I asked.

"It's a short-term contract. Every depositor must agree to receive only fifteen percent of their deposits immediately after re-opening, ten percent in thirty days thereafter, fifteen percent in sixty days, thirty percent in ninety days, and the balance in four months when the contract expires. What we need, more than anything, is to unite our community. We must build confidence and trust in each other, and in our one and only bank. Mr. Kingston's a bright man and bank president."

"Andrew. That's incredible. I'm so proud of you." I beamed and pressed his left hand with my right.

"Ha-ha! A team effort, I assure you. Please keep this to yourself until tomorrow, right?"

"Right. Thanks for sharing. Now I can rest easier. I thought I might need to sell part of my land." I angled toward the chair's corner, ready to stand.

"Hmm. You don't have to, yet. But honestly, it wouldn't hurt to keep it in mind, Em. You're not using all of it, anyway." He stood, still holding my hand, and walked me to the door.

"True." *But it represents Pa and Ma.*

"I enjoyed our visit, Em. Next week, I'll come visit the farm. All the bank restlessness should be over by then."

"I'll look forward to it." I squeezed his hand. "Enjoy your day."

"You, too."

October was one of my favorite months. I sat on the porch swing with a hot cup of coffee and surveyed the landscape. I loved the fall colors of the trees, the shorter days, and sleeping through cool nights. It was funny how the sounds changed with the seasons too: frogs in spring, crickets in summer, and locusts in late summer and fall. But, always, birds twittered and sang in the mornings. In fall and winter, we set seed and suet out for the birds. Our fully stocked larder, barn, icehouse, and root cellar would sustain us and our livestock throughout the winter. Mabel, our lovable St. Bernard, who'd doubled in size, spent an equal amount of time between us and the cows. She stretched out on the floor and watched over the property.

"Good morning, Emeline." Harriet joined me with her coffee.

"Morning, Harriet. Don't you love the fall?"

"Yes, I do. I think my favorite season is a toss-up between spring and fall. I can't wait until tonight when we can work on my dress. All we have left is the hand-sewin' of the appliqué."

"Yes, it will take us about a week to finish it completely. You'll make a beautiful bride. Shall we make the other plans? December 1st isn't far away. Have you or Huck already scheduled with the church and the pastor?"

"Of course, silly! Not much of a planner, are you? That was the first thing Huck did." She glanced at me and chuckled. "He wanted to make sure the time, place, and date were set. He's even asked William to play his fiddle for us at the reception."

"Pardon me." I returned her smile. "So, do you already have the invitations and guest list?"

"Yes, I do. I bought the paper from the Pickwicks, but still need to write them out by hand and deliver them. I'm not invitin' many, and a few, I'll mail to Westport. Will ya help me write them with your beautiful handwriting?"

"Of course. We can work on them right after milking today if you like. We're not hiding those from Huck, like the dress. Do you have a draft for it?"

Harriet rose and went into the house and returned with a slip of paper she'd written on. "Here's what I'd like it to say."

Now & Forever
Together with their parents
Harriet Steiner &
Henry (Huck) Malloy
Request the honor of your attendance
At their wedding on
Friday, December First
Eighteen Hundred Ninety-Three
At Twelve o'clock, Noon
303 South Grove St., Kearney, Missouri
Reception immediately following

"How many are on your list?"

"We're invitin' about twenty-five families. How does it look?"

"It's lovely. I wish we'd have thought to have it printed earlier. But handwriting will make it more personal."

"I didn't want to spend the money to print them. You know me."

"Right. We'll make them as beautiful as we can. If you like, we can use my sealing wax and maple leaf stamp to seal the envelopes."

"Thanks, but I've bought a stamp with an '**M**' on it. I'll use it for a lifetime since I'll soon be Harriet Malloy." She giggled and was clearly all atwitter about finally being married.

Huck arrived, and after giving Harriet a much-needed hug, we worked like a fine-tuned machine, milking three cows in as many hours, including clean-up.

Hungry, I said, "Harriet, would you start the bacon while I take care of the chickens and gather the eggs?"

"Certainly. I'll slice some bread too." Turning to Huck, she asked, "Will you help by settin' the table, please, Huck?"

"Of course." He smiled. It was his usual habit to help with breakfast. He loved to cook. It was fun watching them work together in the kitchen. They were a pair.

After breakfast, we took a break out front. We stood as Maude Ambrose drove up in her carriage. Mabel barked a few times until I hushed her to let her know Maude was an accepted visitor. "Hello! How have you been?" I asked.

"Fine, thank you, Emeline. Hello, Harriet, Huck." She climbed down and greeted Mabel with a pat on her head. Turning toward me, she said, "I came by with news. May we visit privately?"

"Sure. Let's go in the house." Facing Huck and Harriet, I said, "Excuse me, won't you?"

Inside, we sat at the kitchen table. "Would you like something to drink?"

"No, no, thank you. I've got very exciting news to share with you!"

"What's that?"

She held out her left hand and showed me a shiny ring with a single diamond set inside a gold band. "James Penn has asked me to marry him, and I've accepted. We've chosen a date: Saturday, April

24th next year. As you're aware, we dismiss school for the spring months to resume in the summer."

"How thrilling, Miss Ambrose. Congratulations! Perhaps, someday, when you have time, you can start a library for the community in your home, until the city grows enough to build one. But who will teach?"

"Indeed. Who?"

"I can't imagine."

"I've recommended *you* for the position, Emeline. You're smart, well-educated, and have substituted for me. You enjoy teaching, don't you?"

"Oh, yes, I do. But not for a career — not forever. Haven't I told you? Andrew Pickwick is currently courting me." I broke eye contact for a moment, while a smile crossed my face, and then looked up again. "Of course, I don't know if, or when, we might marry, yet."

"Would you consider it temporarily until we secure someone else?" Her breath caught.

I paused. "May I give you my answer in a week's time? I'd like to pray about it and discuss it with Andrew, Harriet, and Huck. It could mean hiring extra help for the farm, I believe."

"Potentially, yes. But you would be off during the busy spring season. We might find a replacement by summer, but possibly not until the 1894 winter term."

Speechless, more scenarios flew through my mind. Could things get any more complicated? Could the farm suffer more financial stress? Insecurity crept into my thoughts, but I shoved it down. I reminded myself that no good ever came from worry. "I'll decide soon, Miss Ambrose. Thank you for your confidence in me and for this invitation."

She sighed and said, "That's all I can ask — that you give it some thought. I believe you'd make a competent and compassionate teacher."

"When would you need me?"

"I can teach most of the 1893–4 winter term. You'd work with me for the last two weeks in February and take over through March. The summer term would start in June and run through August. If we search now, we might find a teacher by then, but we'll have to see. I'm sure we'll find someone by next December."

"I appreciate the offer, and I promise to give it urgent consideration." We rose and walked to the front door. After a hug, I said, "Thank you for coming by and congratulations, again."

"I'm excited! We'll talk soon." She climbed into her carriage and waved, her ring flashing in the sunlight.

With no idea how this would work, I had promised to think about it, so I would. Maude Ambrose had opened her home to me while the Coopers were still living here, but was this too much to bear?

The roots of my parents' farm ran *deep* within me. For so long, I'd identified with it, even when living elsewhere, though I'd tried to suppress it. Andrew rode in for a visit today, and I'd discuss the teaching post with him. While Huck and Harriet spread manure in the pasture, placing some in the compost heap, we chatted on the porch, he in one wooden rocker and I in another.

He surveyed the outbuildings and pasture toward the forest. "The fall colors are bright and beautiful this year because of all the rain we received this summer."

In the distance, a column of smoke rose in the air, and soon drifted away on the breeze. I took a deep breath. "Someone's burning wood already. We'll need to bring the stove back into the house soon. I'm happy you came today because I have something important to discuss with you."

"Oh?" He moved toward the front of his rocker, arms crossed over his knees.

I couldn't resist those beautiful, dark brown eyes. "Yes. Miss Ambrose and James Penn are engaged and plan to marry April 24th next year. She's asked me to take her place as a teacher — just until they find a new one. I don't see how I can afford to leave the farm, which would force us to spend even *more* money for help, in a time when we have little. I've been praying about it but haven't decided."

"Hmm. That *is* a tremendous commitment. Would you enjoy teaching, even if only for a short time?" His eyes scrutinized mine, unwavering.

"I love helping children, but I don't want to make it a career." Our eyes locked, I said, "Eventually, I want to marry."

His smile flashed like lightning across his face, and his eyes darted away briefly. "Um, yes. I remember."

I giggled at his pretense of disinterest. To relieve the awkwardness, I continued. "I'd like to help. It's just the money that's the problem."

Andrew said, "Remember what you said the other day in the store? You said you might have to resort to selling part of the forested acreage here? So, why not do it?"

"I'd forgotten about that. That *is* an option, though a painful one. If I did, how would I find a buyer?"

"Start with Mr. Kingston at the bank. If anyone's looking, they'd go through him, most likely. Although, the bank may not be secure enough to loan money on the property right now. But if someone has enough money to buy without borrowing, he would know that, too."

"I suppose we could try." In these times, I doubted there would be a buyer and, secretly, I hoped there wouldn't be. "If I write a note, will you give it to him to post, please?" I rose to get a pen, paper, and a book to write on. After I'd written the advertisement, I handed it to Andrew.

LAND FOR SALE

65 prime, undeveloped forested acres on rolling hills

Will sacrifice for $30 per acre.

Contact Mr. Kingston, President

Kearney Bank & Trust

He said, "But hold on a minute. Huck and Harriet must give their blessing on this too, remember? You're in a partnership."

"Right!" I'd always thought of it as my land, which it legally still is. But my partners must agree with any decision. I stood and ran down the steps and to the pasture's fence. "Harriet! Huck! May we speak with you, please?"

Huck shouted from the other side of the pasture. "Be right over."

Back on the porch, I sat and took the notice from Andrew's hand. In a few minutes, they gathered with us.

"Is something wrong?" Harriet asked. They stunk of manure.

I covered my nose with my hand for a moment. "Whew! You both have been hard at work, haven't you?" I knew it was a dirty job, and I appreciated it. I, too, would help them soon. "No. Nothing's wrong. Andrew and I have come up with a way that allows me to teach for Miss Ambrose for a while and still afford to hire two farmhands. Pa owned 160 acres, which is more than most people can settle. If we sell sixty-five acres of the woodland, we'll still have fifteen wooded acres for its wood, the orchard, the maple syrup, plus the eighty-acre farm. What do you think?" I asked Huck. He concerned me more than Harriet. *She* usually went along with all my ideas.

Huck's mind churned this idea over for a few minutes as he paced back and forth across the porch floor. Finally, he leaned against the porch rail and put his hands on his hips. "Andrew, do you like this idea?"

"Yes, I do. The land remains undeveloped. Do you think you'll ever want to expand further than 95 acres in your lifetime?"

"Doubtful. I'll agree with it. Harriet?"

"Fine with me," she said. "We're plenty busy with the land we work now. I can't imagine doin' any more or wantin' to."

"Perfect, it's settled then." I handed the paper back to Andrew.

"Fine. I'll inform you the minute I hear anything," he said.

After Andrew left, I prayed silently. *Lord, please, let it be your will.* To release anxiety, I flew through my chores, replacing all the old straw with new in the chicken coop and piling it onto the old cart. Dakota pulled it into the pasture where I worked with Huck and Harriet to finish piling manure, turning over piles, and incorporating the old straw which helped to aerate it. Tomorrow, I would give Miss Ambrose the news. She would be over the moon with relief and exhilaration.

Flickering Flame

Wrapped in a woolen shawl, I embraced a hot coffee cup and basked in the morning sun out front, though the air was crisp and smelled of coming rain. Gone were the colorful leaves from the deciduous trees, leaving behind woody skeletons, which poked their fingers skyward. Evergreen trees remained full, though darker, and pine cones littered the ground. More visible now, deer, birds, squirrels, and other wildlife moved through the forest and fields. November brought shorter days, much cooler weather, and an occasional warm day. Turning toward Harriet, I said, "I think I love the change of the seasons more than any one in particular."

"I still like spring and fall best, because winter's too cold and summer's too hot," she said.

"I've decided I like them all, for different reasons," I said.

By the time Huck came by, we had finished our coffees. "Morning, Huck! How are you today?" Harriet stood and smiled.

"Couldn't be better!" He rode his horse to the horse barn, took off the tack, and released him in the cow pasture. Mabel showed her devotion by following him the entire way.

After we'd finished with the first milking and breakfast, I said, "I have two appointments for young farmhands this morning at their family homes. Would you both like to join me?"

Harriet asked, "Who are they?"

"One is Oliver Parker. You remember him from school, don't you? His pa is Dr. Parker, and his ma's a seamstress."

"A seamstress?" Harriet's eyes brightened.

"Yes." I knew she wanted to ask her for advice on applying the appliqué to her dress.

"Who's the other?" Huck asked.

The other's another fellow who we knew in school, too, Jesse Jenkins. His parents own a cattle ranch near here. Bored with ranching, Jesse is quite bright and is eager to learn and loves fixing things. He has a bicycle! Have you seen them? It's a new thing around here, though Andrew and I saw some in Westport and Kansas City. His parents understand and have enough help, so they can spare him."

"I've seen those two-wheelers, though I've never ridden one. Looks like fun." Huck asked Harriet, "Want to tag along?"

"Try to stop me," she said.

"Ground rules. Before we go, we should discuss who's going to do the talking, plus our hours and rates of pay," I said.

Huck spoke up. "Since I've worked for a delivery company, I have a good idea how this should go. We'll talk with the fellas and get an idea of *why* they want the job and what they want down the road. We'll offer them a two-week trial period durin' which they're just paid a little. Then, if we decide to hire them, we'll offer them another rate of pay per hour for a period of, say, three months. Then, if they're pullin' their weight and doin' a good job, we'll give them a raise."

"That sounds reasonable, doesn't it, Harriet?" I asked. "What about the hours?"

"The hours would be from sunup to sundown. Field work durin' the week would depend on weather, so they'd have some time off then. Weekends, we would just do the milkin' and tend to the chickens. For the rest of those two days, they'd be free to go. Plus, we'd work around any special events."

"I'd like you to do the talking, Huck. You'll be the one working with them the most, right Harriet?"

"Right. Except we'd all do the milkin' together. And you'll be teachin' school sometimes."

We readied our carriage, and the three of us visited Jesse Jenkins first. Harriet and I stood by Huck while he asked his questions in front of their sprawling ranch home, twice the size of ours. "How old are ya and why are ya interested in workin' at a dairy farm, Jesse?"

"I'm fifteen and know everything about raising beef critters. Like to learn something new for a while. Earn some money. Someday, I hope to earn enough to open a bicycle shop in town and get off the farm. Like to fix things."

"Like to fix things, eh?" Huck pulled on his overall straps with his thumbs. "Are you mechanically inclined with machines, like the harvester?"

Jesse ran over to the side of the house and returned with his bicycle. "See this? It's lots more complicated than any harvester. Yeah, I can fix most anything. Come up with new ideas all the time."

"Do you think you'd give us two or three years? There's no sense trainin' someone who's plannin' to leave soon."

"Sure, I can. That's not too long. And I need time to earn enough money for my shop."

"In that case, do you want to try it for two weeks? You'll start at $.75 a day. If you like it and we like you, we'll hire you for $1.00 a day. After three months, when you've proved you're a hard and reliable worker, you'll earn a raise in pay to $1.30 per day. During harvest times, we pay $1.75 per day. What do you think?"

"I'm for it. I won't let you down."

"Fine. See you Monday mornin' at six o'clock, then?"

"Great!" Jesse waved at us as we climbed back into the carriage.

Next, we drove to Dr. Parker's, a red brick two-story home near Kearney's square. After tying up Dakota, we approached the open front door and knocked on its frame. Dr. Parker answered and smiled.

"Welcome. Come in, won't you? Have a seat in our parlor and I'll fetch Oliver for you." Harriet excused herself to ask Dr. Parker if she could speak with Mrs. Parker about sewing on appliqué. The sitting room wasn't terribly large, but a high ceiling made it seem so. Lace curtains hung over the long window to the street side, while a heavy braided rug covered most of the wood floor. On one wall, an upright piano stood in silent elegance. Several chairs of different styles lined the rest of the room, along with a few round side tables. Two hanging kerosene lamps with ivory colored glass shades hung from the ceiling, which could be drawn down when being lit. Andrew and I selected seats near the window and, shortly, we stood when a freckle-faced young man joined us.

"Hello. I'm Oliver. Do you remember me from school years ago?"

I spoke first. "Yes, Oliver, I do. You're only a year or two younger than me. You liked to give Miss Ambrose trouble, but we thought you were hilarious. How have you been?"

"Fine, thank you." He revealed an amiable smile.

With his short brown hair, he resembled Jesse Jenkins, except for his freckles and the set of his light blue eyes, which angled down at the outside corners. Both boys' smiles made dimples. Adorable.

"This is Huck," I said. "If you decide to work with us, you'll spend most of your time with him, so he'd like to ask you some questions."

"Howdy, Oliver," Huck said, as he shook his hand firmly, and we all sat down.

But Oliver moved his chair, so he sat across from us. "Howdy."

Huck began. "All right then. How old are you and why are you interested in workin' on a farm, especially a dairy farm?"

"I'm fifteen. Pa's a doctor, so you probably thought I'd be one too. But I'm not smart enough to go through medical school. Fooled around too much and never was very good at figures, readin', or writin'. I'm still not." He clutched his hands together in his lap and then glanced up. "But I love workin' with farm animals: horses, cows, goats, sheep, pigs, dogs, cats, whatever. Animals depend on you, and they don't judge. They love you no matter what."

"Right," Huck said. "So, after you work with us for a few years, then what? What's your dream?"

"Truthfully, I don't rightly know. But animals would have to be part of it. I'd like to be a veterinarian."

"Likely, your pa can help you achieve that dream," Huck said.

"I'd have to learn a lot more about readin', writin', and such. I don't know…"

I interrupted. "Miss Ambrose or I might tutor you in the evenings, Oliver, if you truly want to learn. Never think you can't. You can do it if you want it badly enough."

Oliver turned toward me. "Really? Maybe, then. We'll see." He beamed.

After Huck made him the same trial offer, Oliver agreed to the terms. "Fine. We look forward to workin' with you Monday mornin'. Please be prompt — by six o'clock." They shook on it and we made our farewells to Dr. Parker, who was reading in his library opposite the parlor. Then we collected Harriet from Mrs. Parker's sewing room and left.

Before we left town, we stopped by the Pickwick Mercantile to update Andrew on the latest developments. Pa's admonition had been true: *where there's a will, there's a way*. I treasured our relationship. Even though they'd gone to Heaven, I was grateful I could still feel their presence in my thoughts. They would be proud of how responsible I'd become. That, I was sure of.

For the next two weeks, we worked with our new helpers. Fortunately, they caught on quickly and agreed to the next stage of their employment: ninety days' probation at a higher rate. Now, if we sold those sixty-five acres, we'd have some breathing room. I prayed for peace about severing myself from this land. Oh, this economy! When would it recover?

Finally, we finished Harriet's wedding dress. It was intricate and luxurious: a masterpiece we would always remember creating together. A treasure. Someday, she'd pass it down to her daughter. The thought made me smile. After sending invitations, we received RSVPs. Now, to adorn the church for the ceremony. The wedding was tomorrow, Friday, December 1st, at noon.

Plenty of pine and evergreens grew in our forest. To decorate the church, Harriet, Huck, Andrew, and I cut small branches and wove them together with wire into beautiful garlands. We wrapped a long one around the pulpit, placed some over the piano, along with a candle, and tied others with white ribbons to decorate the end of every other pew along the center aisle. Mrs. Pickwick made some cuttings into a long, teardrop shaped bouquet for Harriet. She adorned it with pinecones, holly, cranberries, and a white ribbon bow with long tails. It was luxurious.

Ladies of the church graciously volunteered their time and talents for the reception to follow. They'd baked a lovely wedding cake and prepared a punch. We expected a modest turnout of twenty-five to thirty people in all.

Weather in the Midwest was always unpredictable, and Friday was no exception. A winter storm blew in overnight and drove temperatures down to 45°. Though the rain stopped, the wind blustered on, causing everyone to bundle up in their warmest coats, hats, gloves, and boots. Inside the church, the wood stove kept the room quite toasty, so guests hung their outer garments on coat racks in the foyer.

Unlike church, for the wedding ceremony, men and women sat together. They mingled, chatted, and laughed, while upstairs, Harriet and Huck readied themselves in separate chambers. Harriet chose me for her maid of honor, of course, while Huck chose Andrew for his best man. So, while courting, we'd stand next to the bride and groom at the altar. How common was this?

I finished putting a white comb made of mother-of-pearl in her hair, which was swept up on top of her head. I wore my best outfit, the black-and-white striped dress with Ma's cameo brooch at the neck, plaited my hair loosely down my back, and tied it off with a narrow white ribbon. "Harriet, you are a stunning bride."

"Thank you. You're beautiful, too." She held out a trembling hand. "Oh, Emeline, why am I so nervous?" Harriet asked.

"Ah, I'm guessing it's more anticipation than nervousness. You'll be fine, my friend. I'll be standing to your left, holding your bouquet of greenery. Don't fret." We heard a door close. "It's about that time. Huck and Andrew have gone downstairs."

Mary Dawson, a widow who'd offered to help coordinate activities, entered the room. "Are you ready, my dears?" she asked.

"Yes, ma'am, we are." Harriet said.

She escorted us down the stairs until we stood right outside the closed double doors to the sanctuary. Once the pianist began playing the 'Wedding March', Mrs. Dawson opened each door to its stop. She motioned for me to go first. After I arrived at the front, everyone stood for Harriet's grand entrance. Thrilled, my heart was in my throat, and I let a few tears fall, not wanting to dab at them in front of everyone.

Harriet beamed, her steps remained even, and her eyes never left Huck's. He grinned right along with her. He was dashing in a black dress coat, black brocade vest, and a white, high-collared, ruffled shirt. Andrew stood next to him, elegantly dressed in the same suit of clothes as Huck. Our eyes met, and we shared a wink and a smile.

When she reached her pa near the front, she, and the music, stopped and they continued together to the altar. The preacher asked, "Who gives this woman to be married to this man?" Her pa answered, "Her mother and I do." Harriet and her pa hugged, then he sat down. She handed me her bouquet, and Huck took her hand. They faced the preacher, and the ceremony began. He read some scripture, asked for any objections. They said their vows, exchanged rings, and the preacher announced them as Mr. and Mrs. Malloy. Finally, they sealed it with a kiss.

Everyone applauded and cheered for the new couple who hurried, hand in hand, to the back of the room to join the reception line with their parents, Andrew, and me. Of course, I returned the bouquet, which she promptly set aside so she could shake hands.

Next, the wedding party followed the guests to Congressional Hall, a room across from the sanctuary where the cake and punch awaited. Rows of tables and chairs lined the walls of the room, leaving the floor open for dancing later. The happy couple cut the cake, fed a bite to each other, and took their seats at the head table.

After Mrs. Dawson and other ladies from the church served the rest of us, guests made toasts. Then it was time for the couple's first dance. The pianist played 'Love's Old Sweet Song', and their graceful dance inspired the rest of us as they waltzed effortlessly around the dance floor. Had they practiced this? Afterward, William entertained us with his lively fiddle, and all but the oldest guests danced for another hour.

At departure time, Harriet threw her bouquet into a small group of eligible single ladies. I caught it! Well, to be honest, I had little competition, as most of the guests were married. The twosome donned their coats, hats, and gloves, and walked through a path cleared by the crowd. They had brought their carriage to the front of the church and waited for them. Everyone shouted congratulations, well wishes, God be with you, and more, as they rode away.

I knew in my heart that Harriet would always be my best childhood friend. But I didn't expect my heart to sink today, as if a balloon popped. Huck would be her best friend now. We'd still be close, but it would never be the same. Ever. Andrew came by my side, put his arm around my shoulders, and smiled down at me. I curbed tears and smiled back. I guessed change could be a good thing, after all.

Housing changed, of course. Huck and Harriet lived in my old farmhouse. Jesse and Oliver stayed at their homes and traveled each day to work. The Steiners moved from Westport back to their farmhouse and I moved my things back into Maude Ambrose's near the school.

One man, Mr. Nicholas Owen, expressed interest in our land for sale, but he had some other property to sell first. He toured it and was pursuing its purchase, but it could be some time. Hopefully, our money would hold out until then. We continued praying for the country's economic recovery.

It was January 1894, now, and cold weather set in. Students still came to school, though. Out of the entire year, winter was the best season for learning. Parents took turns bringing several children together in one carriage. If twenty were present, it was a full class.

Wind blew, snow drifted, and icicles hung from the rooftops, but inside the schoolhouse and individual homes, wood stoves kept everyone warm and toasty. Those who sat farther away from the stove kept their coats on. This month's work was split for me. Weekday mornings, I helped Miss Ambrose with chores and taught alongside her. In the late afternoons, I drove Dakota and the carriage to the farm to help with the second milking and check on everyone. Sundays, after church, I spent time with Andrew.

In the mercantile, we sat across from each other and drank cups of hot chocolate. "I miss seeing you, Andrew," I said one Sunday. Being with him was like breathing — natural. Did I *need* him or want him? Need. Want. Two very different things. No, I didn't need him. Satisfied with the person I'd grown to be, I didn't need him. But, yes, I *wanted* him. Badly. *He'd* become my best friend.

He held my hands in his. "Winter won't last long, Em. February and March will be the most difficult because you'll be teaching full time. I hope you won't have to visit the farm every day, like you are now. Enjoy your time with the children."

I sighed. "By then, Jesse and Oliver should be solid help, so they may not need me. I'll love helping students learn, but Sundays will be the highlight of my week." I watched the steam rise from my hot chocolate.

He pushed stray hairs behind my ear, placed the side of his hand under my chin, and gently tipped my face up to his, and released it. "Mine, too. I love you, Em."

Our eyes locked, and I smiled. Something deep passed between us, as if our souls touched each other. "I love you, too, Andrew."

We both let out a heavy sigh. We couldn't stop smiling at one another and spent the rest of the afternoon playing a couple of games of chess as Gus, our little fox terrier sentry, slept under our table. I enjoyed the game, but rarely won. At least he showed me where I could improve, and I was learning, albeit slowly. By spring, playing against me would hopefully be more challenging for him.

Land of Plenty

February was a cold, blustery month, but March approached. Miss Ambrose busied herself with wedding preparations, in addition to the making of her dress. She kindly prepared meals for both of us, too.

She'd stepped down from teaching, and now I held her title. I'd do my best, but teaching wasn't my dream. I prayed they would find a replacement soon, so I could return to the farm, though I would have to secure other living arrangements. Perhaps I'd live with Harriet's parents. I reminded myself to take one step at a time.

My first day began at seven o'clock in the morning, with my filling of the wood stove and stacking of more wood in front of the school. Five minutes before nine, I rang the bell outside, and then waited inside for the children. Bitterly cold, it made no sense for any of us to shiver in lines outside. As they arrived, they hung up their coats, placed their lunches on the shelf above, and quietly found their seats.

Of course, I reminded the more rambunctious children about the last part. Class began at nine o'clock, sharp.

Younger students sat in front, while the older settled in back. Our classroom held twenty desks, but attendance depended on the Morris family and varied from eleven to fifteen. Five families enrolled and the Morrises sent four school-aged children.

We first stood and pledged our allegiance to the flag. Then, we recited the Lord's Prayer. After one of the older children read a few verses from the Bible, we prayed and began our day of study. Morning lessons began with spelling, then handwriting, and finally arithmetic. We all enjoyed the lunch period, which was next, followed by recess. Unless the weather was bitterly cold and wet, we stepped outside for fresh air and play.

One child's behavior concerned me. Lately, Hattie had appeared sullen and quieter than usual. "Hattie, are you alright?"

She kept her eyes on her work and said unconvincingly, "Yes, Miss O'Connor. I'm fine."

One of the older children stoked the fire in the wood stove by filling it with more split wood, while I read a story aloud. Then, they recited short, memorized material in front of the class. Today, we studied the grammar rule: "i" before "e" except after "c", and all its exceptions. Advanced students worked on assigned seatwork, while I taught reading to the younger. When finished, they listened to the younger children read their lessons from the McGuffey Readers.

After reading, we studied science. Tomorrow it would be history instead. During the last period, we enjoyed music. We'd no instruments, so we sang a couple of songs and clapped along. George Morris played the harmonica when he was present, which added to the fun.

I looked forward to the weekend as much as the children because I met with Andrew after church. One Sunday, I asked him, "Are you familiar with the Reed family? Hattie Reed's in fifth grade, and I'm concerned about her. She's brooding about something. I'm sweet as you please, but she won't face me, and she completes the minimum of schoolwork."

"Hmm. Reed, Reed. I'm trying to remember them. Do they live way out south of the school?" He held Gus in his arms and rubbed the ears and head of the fox terrier pup.

"Yes. The Johnsons, who also live south, leave early to pick her up and bring her along with their children."

"I haven't seen the Reeds in a while. The last time I saw them was about a month ago, when Mr. Reed came in for supplies and food. I didn't see Mrs. Reed. Something wrong?"

"I don't know. Should I visit their house, or speak with Hattie first?"

"I'd start with the girl," Andrew said. "You're not aware of what's happening at home. If Mr. Reed comes by, I'll make inquiries of him."

"Thank you. That's what I'll do."

Monday after school, I pulled her aside and whispered to her. "Hattie, may I speak with you privately before you leave today?"

"I dunno, Miss O'Connor. Pa might get mad if I'm late. I must fix supper."

"Why? Doesn't your ma fix supper for you?"

She wiped away tears with her sleeve. "Ma's gone." She sat down and sobbed; her wall of defense broken.

"Oh, no. I'm sorry, dear. Let's talk, just for a few minutes. I'm sure the Johnsons won't mind waiting briefly."

"Alright." She glanced up at me for the first time since I'd been teaching and gave me a hug.

Pressing my head against hers, I recalled doing the same thing with Miss Ambrose after I'd lost Ma. Moreover, I'd been about her age. "Have a seat, please, while I speak to the Johnsons."

I returned and faced her from a desk chair across from hers. "Tell me about your ma, Hattie."

She sobbed into her hands until I passed her a handkerchief to use instead. "Sorry." She sniffed.

"It's alright. Will you tell me what happened?"

Twisting the cloth in her hands, she said, "Ma got sick — terribly sick. The doctor visited, but he couldn't help her. He told us to boil water before we drank it and to always wash our hands and faces after handling her, or anything she'd touched." She took a deep, trembling breath. "We didn't get sick, but she didn't get better. She died last month." Her moist eyes met mine.

"I'm sorry, Hattie. I understand, though. I lost both my ma and my pa. Coincidentally, I was about your age when I lost Ma. She died giving birth to my baby brother, who also died. The doctor couldn't get to them fast enough because he was busy with another birth. It devastated Pa and me for a long time. But I have good news to share with you."

"You do?"

"Yes. When I missed Ma, Miss Ambrose asked me to tell her stories about my favorite times with her — and then write them in a journal, too. Don't forget your ma, Hattie. Embrace her memory. She'll always be with you if you remember her. My parents are still with me, as a little voice in my mind. Your ma will be with you, too." I stood and walked to my desk, opened a drawer, and pulled out a blank journal, and the one I'd filled out on my journey to Boston. "Here." I handed the blank one to her. "Begin writing your favorite stories about her, and don't forget to pray, too. I wrote lots of stories about my parents in this book." I flipped through the pages of my filled journal to show her what I'd done.

"Thank you, Miss O'Connor." She rose and hugged me again.

"You're most welcome, dear. Best not keep the Johnsons or your pa waiting any longer. See you soon." At the door, she turned, smiled, and blew me a kiss. I returned it.

I regularly checked in with Huck and Harriet each evening after I'd finished grading and fine-tuning the lesson plans for the next day, except Sundays, of course. Oliver caught on to the dairy work with ease and soon, he'd finished his ninety-day probation period and earned more money. Jesse missed a couple of days of work because of drinking and carousing late into the night after work. Huck sat him down for a talkin'-to and suspended him for two weeks. Ever since, he'd been prompt, sober, and diligent. Leave it to Huck to pound business sense into the young man.

One February Saturday evening, after milking, all five of us visited around the table beneath the gas lamp, which hung from the ceiling. I asked Oliver, "Have you decided whether you want to be tutored yet?"

"Strange you should ask. The veterinarian in town said I could assist him in a few years if I boned up on book-learnin'. He says I must read and write because of medicines and books about animal care, and such. Plus, basic arithmetic is important. I understand some of it, but not well enough yet. I love workin' on this farm a lot. It's all I need, for now."

"I'm not pressuring you, but tell us if you ever decide it's something you want to do, Oliver."

"Sure will," he said.

"How about you, Jesse? How do you like working here?"

"I'm gettin' the hang of it. Workin' in the field, I already understood, of course. It's alright. Ya know I'm more interested in fixin' things, right? My favorite part is takin' care of the equipment and riggin'. And I love it when the iceman delivers, which isn't happenin' as much, now that winter is here."

Surprised, Huck asked, "Ya look forward to the ice delivery? Why? It's just a lot of unloadin' and stackin'.'"

"I like talkin' to the people. I'd love to chat with the customers when they pick up, but Harriet handles them all herself."

Harriet said, "Ordinarily, you're busy, Jesse. And it's kind of my bailiwick. I schedule our customers, which helps me prepare their order in advance. Then, of course, I handle the payment and record-keeping."

I remembered his dream. "You'll make an outstanding business owner someday, Jesse, if you keep your nose clean. Imagine: Jenkins Bicycle Shop." I lifted my eyes to the sky and waved my hand across, as if touching a sign.

"Jesse's Fix-It Shop." He corrected me. "Pa is the Jenkins Ranch, so I'll be informal and use my first name. And it won't be for bicycles alone. I'll fix anythin'."

I laughed. "I'm sure you will."

The last Saturday in February, Dakota and I walked through the advertised woodland part of my property to get away for a couple of hours. Sunny, and unseasonably warm, this was a notably pleasant walk, as I was completely alone to contemplate. Twigs snapped under my Morgan's hooves, squirrels scurried up trees, birds called each other and flew from tree to tree. I recalled spending time with Ma and Pa here and imagined what it must have been like to start from scratch, years ago. I hoped they would be as proud of me as I still am of them.

God is always good. He'd given me life, salvation, and direction from His words — and from helpful people. Amazing. He arranged the events in my life so I would become the person I am today, and I loved that person. He's given me joy and strength inside — even now, in this difficult time. Still reluctant about selling this acreage, somehow, I could let it go. This land had defined Pa and Ma, but I guessed it didn't need to define me any longer.

I dismounted and led Dakota around, as I stepped over fallen trees and around lichen-covered boulders. It would take arduous work by someone to clear this land for a home — or a farm. But its beauty made it worth the effort. Had Nicholas Owen sold his other property, yet, to buy these sixty-five acres? We'd need to close the sale soon to continue paying Jesse and Oliver. At least I'd a small teaching salary to contribute to our cause. Silently, I prayed, certain God would answer in His time.

Time flew, and March arrived. In a few weeks, school would dismiss for the spring planting season. In fact, most of the older students were already off preparing the fields, even though it was still freezing at times. The change of seasons in March resulted in unstable weather. From one year to the next, March could be spring-like, or frozen earth until April. Sometimes fierce winds, rain, snow, or ice increased.

One cool Sunday, Andrew and I met at the Pickwick Mercantile, per our custom after church. My chess game had improved. Today, I won a game. "My, you've developed strategy, Em," he said with a grin. "But I have news for you."

"News?" I asked. "Why did you wait until after our game to tell me? Is it good news?"

"It could be. Let me fetch us mugs of hot cider." He left and returned with the apple goodness, complete with cinnamon sticks.

Andrew and I met at the Pickwick Mercantile,
per our custom after church.

"Thank you, Andrew. Now, what's new?" I eagerly searched his face for a sign.

He leaned against his chair's back, raised his arms, and laced his fingers behind his head, like he always did when he held a secret. "Mr. Kingston has three applicants for the teaching position, potentially starting with this summer's term."

"Truly? Oh, that's sensational! Has Miss Ambrose heard?"

"Not yet. That's where you come in, since you live with her. Will you ask if she can meet with Mr. Kingston and each applicant two Saturdays from now?"

"Of course. Do you have any details about them?"

"I don't, but I remember one was from Kansas City, another from Cameron, and one from Liberty, Missouri. If Miss Ambrose could talk with Mr. Kingston tomorrow, that would be ideal, as he will need to write each of them to confirm the date and time."

"Consider it done. Oh, I'm so excited, Andrew."

He laughed. "I knew you would be."

He won the next game, probably because of my lack of concentration. Oh, well.

After completing the interviews, Minnie Clarke from Liberty won the position, which happily began with the summer term. At twenty-two, she was a pleasant and well-educated young woman who was ready to leave her parent's home. Minnie moved into the house by the school with me and Maude Ambrose.

On our first day together, we chatted over breakfast. I placed a plate of bacon and eggs in front of her and Miss Ambrose set a pitcher of milk on the table. "I'm so glad you've accepted this position. You won't be sorry. Kearney's a friendly town and you'll love the children. Do you plan to teach for quite a while?"

She sat and spread a cloth napkin over her lap. "Thank you, Emeline, for breakfast and the encouragement. I'm nervous, but excited, too. Yes, I'd like to teach for many years as I have no plans to settle down to married life soon. Above all, I love children and believe teaching is the best way of improving their chances for success."

"Exactly," said Miss Ambrose.

"I agree. But, as much as I enjoy it, I'm eager to turn this job over to you. Right now, I'm stretched thin between working here at the school and at the dairy."

"I imagine! I didn't realize." She poured milk into her glass and continued. "Let's finish eating and clean up so you can show me the ropes."

"I'll be busy getting ready for my wedding, so you won't see much of me," Miss Ambrose said.

Miss Clarke and I worked in tandem in the classroom during the last weeks of school. Afterward, I said, "You'll be a wonderful teacher, Minnie. The students love you and you've caught on to the routine. Now, you'll have a break to prepare for the summer term. I wish you well. Later, if you have questions, please, just ask me or Miss Ambrose, soon to be Mrs. Penn."

"I appreciate that offer, and I will. Thank you."

Finally, April arrived. Ah, spring rain, and plenty of it. If they hadn't already, farmers planted the seed early in April. Our farm was no exception. We sowed seeds in new fields of barley, oats, and alfalfa in rotation. Harriet and I also planted new potatoes and strawberries in the garden. We had tapped the sugar maple trees in March to drain their sap into buckets. In mid-April, we would boil down the sap to make our beloved maple syrup.

Of course, Maggie-Moo had calved late in March — a dark brown little heifer! In a couple of years, she would be another dairy cow. The Malloys named her Sarsaparilla, or Sassy, for short. Annabelle and Buttercup would calf sometime later this month. Mr. Cooper had left names of the bulls he'd used for breeding, so Huck tackled the job of arranging for our eligible cows to be bred: Maggie-Moo in about a month, and Annabelle and Buttercup in about two months. We'd wait another year before breeding Penny and Millie.

After paying Oliver and Jesse, we still struggled to make ends meet, and my reserves were nearly depleted. Fortunately, we'd received a modest income from the sale of farm goods and my small teaching salary. People loved our products, especially the dairy. If my land didn't sell soon, we'd have to lay them off.

We sold to individuals and the Pickwick Mercantile, of course. But Huck forged ahead with his idea for home delivery, which I'm sure came from his Westport experience. A people-person, Jesse made the perfect dairy deliveryman. Each morning, he relished delivering fresh ice-cold milk and other dairy products to homes, or businesses, who ordered the service in and around Kearney. Trustworthy and diligent, Jesse took payments and made records with no problem. This new endeavor provided Harriet with more time to churn butter, preserve food, bake bread, and garden, since fewer customers came to the house. People loved it, and our business grew. Hopefully, I wouldn't have to sell my precious land, after all.

Soon it was April 24th and Maude Ambrose's wedding day. The ceremony took place without a hitch. Radiant, she carried a bouquet of spring flowers: forsythia stems and greenery. She and James made a lovely, happy couple.

Since I no longer taught school, Andrew and I spent more time together. We either met in town at the mercantile, or at the farm. One day in May, as Huck, Harriet, and I emptied buckets of sap from the maple trees into a pail in the cart, Andrew appeared and asked if he could speak with me alone.

"Yes, of course," I said, turning to Harriet. "Will you excuse us for a while?"

She smiled, and said, "Sure."

We walked together, staying within their sight, and chatted about the store, the farm, the new teacher, and his ma. Then he said, "I have an important question to ask, Em."

We stopped under a fragrant, long-needled pine tree with low-hanging branches. "Certainly."

He held both of my hands in his, something I'd never tire of. "Would you consider taking on a new role — something other than dairy farming, teaching, or woodworking?"

I laughed. "Whatever would that be? That's all I know."

He swung my arms in and out now. "Work with me at the Pickwick Mercantile?"

"Full-time?"

"Yes. Full-time, for now."

I scanned his face. Was he serious, or was this more of his playful banter? "What do you mean, Andrew?"

He kneeled in front of me. "I'm not complete without you, Em, like a single glove without its match. You're my best friend in the world. Will you marry me? I love you deeply and always will." He pulled a gold engagement ring inset with a diamond from his pocket and held it up. It sparkled in the dappled sunlight.

Harriet squealed in the distance, but I ignored it. My hands clasped together under my chin, the heart of the necklace dangling between them. I didn't wait long to respond. "I love you, too. Yes, Andrew. I'd love to marry you and be your matching glove." I beamed. *Am I dreaming?*

He placed the ring on my finger. "A little loose, but we can get it adjusted in town." He stood and held me tight — closer than ever before. He trembled, as did I, and our hearts thrummed together. "Oh, Em, you've made me happier than a dog with two tails!" Sneaking a quick peek toward our 'chaperones', Andrew lifted my chin up with the side of his hand and kissed me softly. Somewhere deep inside, new sensations stirred. He stepped back and his smile flashed. "Could I be any more blessed? I have another surprise for you, too."

Breathless, my heart raced, my face flushed. "More? Andrew Pickwick, how could anything top this?"

"Impossible, clearly, but I believe you'll be pleased. Call it an early wedding present." He slipped a yellow paper out of his vest pocket and unfolded it for me to read.

PURCHASE AGREEMENT
65 acres of forested land from Emeline O'Connor,
legal owner of the property located south of
Kearney, Missouri for the sum of $1,950.00
Legal description: Lot #17, page 78 in the Record
of Deeds, originally settled and owned by her parents,
Tavis O'Connor and his wife, Kate O'Connor.
Seller:_______________________________________
Date:____
Buyer:______ Andrew K. Pickwick ______
Date:______ May 1st, 1893 ____________

"Andrew! Oh, Andrew!" Self-control gone, tears fell, and I sobbed into his chest as we held each other again. My eyes searched his, and I queried, "You want to build a home here with me and travel every day to the store?"

"Yes, absolutely. And I can't wait to pull the trigger. All you need to do is sign and date this form." He stepped back, and we stared at each other from arm's length. We both laughed, which helped release the built-up tension and heat of desire.

My voice quivered. "When? When shall we pull it?" I asked.

"We can plan for the house immediately after you sign. You pick the date for the wedding." We strolled, arm in arm, back toward the cart.

"Early November, after the harvest?"

"Perfect," he said.

Stronger than ever, I now looked forward to the glorious changes Andrew and I would experience together for the rest of our lives. Not to mention the added reward of living next door to the original farmstead and my friends. I could almost hear Ma and Pa cheering from heaven. *Thank you, Lord.*

Addendum

What I Learned While Researching

As a young student, I must admit history wasn't my favorite subject. I much preferred reading, writing, and science. Now I find myself fascinated by history — so much so, that I'm a historical fiction novelist. Who would have guessed?

What happened in 1893?

The late 19th century was a period of incredible changes, monetarily, politically, and technologically. Many books, articles, and videos have documented this pivotal time in America, which lasted until 1897. The shifts that occurred during this time would forever change our country.

Monetary Changes:

For years before, silver had been mined and used extensively in the monetary system. In 1890, the Sherman Silver Purchase Act was passed by Congress, which required the U.S. Treasury to purchase more silver: $4^1/_2$ million ounces each month. Unfortunately, this increased the demand for gold, in turn draining the nation's Treasury. By May of 1893, gold had reached the minimum allowed. People made runs on the banks to get what gold they could, and many banks closed temporarily or went under. Because gold was preferred, silver lost value. Silver mines closed, and farmers who provided food for mining towns went under. The people that suffered the most from this decision were those in the west and the south, especially miners and farmers.

Political Changes:

Opinions were split between individuals having control, versus the socialist/democratic view of the government coming to the aid of disadvantaged people, such as the unemployed — an average of 20% of the people. (Michigan had 43% unemployment, the highest rate.)

President McKinley took office in 1896 and the economy began to improve. He reinstated the gold standard for money and increased tariffs on foreign goods encouraging the American people to buy American products.

Technology:
Transportation:

Railroads:

Before railroads, people traveled by steamboat, horse, or by wagons pulled by horses or oxen. England was the first to experiment with the steam engine powering locomotives for profit. Soon, American cities took note and built rail lines to connect with river ports at first, and then more extensively, to other cities. During President Lincoln's term, the first transcontinental railroad ran clear across the country in only six days! In a few years, two more transcontinental railways emerged. Interestingly, there weren't as many railroads built in the south as in the north, which influenced the outcome of the Civil War.

Beginning in 1873, railroads began to have financial difficulties, which progressed until The Panic of 1893, when many were either bought up by larger ones, or bankrupt due to over-building and over-borrowing — especially those who borrowed foreign money. Additionally, the Pullman strike of 1894 caused lines west of Chicago to come to a screeching halt. This essentially was a labor union dispute which had a violent end in terms of damage, injuries, and deaths.

Bicycles:

Bicycles were the first rolling modes of transportation for people, other than horse-drawn vehicles. Popular in cities in 1890, by 1893, a few made it to people in small towns. Now, for the first time, individuals went places without a horse. Women especially enjoyed the freedom they felt when riding a bike. Fashion changed because of it, too. Instead of skirts, women wore bloomers.

During the Panic, their sales dropped, but soared again until cars took over in 1900. It would be a couple of decades before bicycles would enjoy another boom.

Automobiles:

Karl Benz (of Mercedes-Benz notoriety) had the first patent to build a car for sale in 1886. It had three wheels: two in the back, one in the front. No rear brakes. No fuel tank. These would be added later. It cost too much and took too long to make, so the average American couldn't buy one. That wouldn't happen until around 1900. Affordable, due to Ford's assembly line, the Model T became a popular car for the common man by 1908.

Utilities:

Indoor Plumbing:

Privies, or outhouses were still the norm in rural towns. But in the late 1800s, rural homes were able to heat water in coils behind a coal-burning stove, which could then be used for bathing, for example. Bathwater could now be drained through pipes to the outside.

Large cities, such as New York, Boston, and Chicago were among the first to have sewer systems and indoor plumbing. Rural areas, like Kearney, Missouri, wouldn't enjoy this luxury for everyone until the mid-1900s.

Electricity:

Most people in the 1890s used kerosene lamps or candles for lighting. Stoves were fueled with wood or coal, and kept the home warm, as well as cooked food. Stoves would either be moved outside during summer, or two stoves would be installed: one for inside (winter) and one for outside (summer).

But electricity made headway in New York and Chicago. Thomas Edison, with the DC current, started in New York. Tesla worked with Edison for six months for a salary of $25 per week but left to form his own company in New Jersey. Following Edison was Westinghouse, who developed the more economic AC current which traveled over long distances with less amperage and smaller wires. The three companies vied for electrifying the World's Fair in Chicago in 1893. Westinghouse won the honor.

Refrigeration:

Iceboxes kept food cold in all but the most rural homes by the 1890s. The ice industry continued to grow. Ice plants were not only found in large cities, but in smaller towns with the ability to ship ice by rail. Steam-driven ammonia compressors made the ice in cans. *Atmospheric condensers* were used to supply water for the ice, as quantities of river or well water were insufficient. (The precursor to today's air conditioner!)

Communication:

Telegraph/Telephone:

Telegraphs had been available for decades but remained expensive. Telephones gained a foothold in the large cities in the east but wouldn't be in rural homes until the early 1900s. The first phones in rural towns would be in a few locations, such as the general store, or the railroad depot. It wasn't unusual to have to travel to use the phone.

Mail:

Thanks to the railroads, the mail traveled quickly throughout the country, although during the Pullman Strike, it once again traveled by boat or horse to the west and south parts of the country.

In 1893, Rural Mail Carrier, Carl Frick, delivered the U.S. Mail by mule to the post office in the Arley Store in Kearney, Missouri, where residents picked it up until Rural Free Delivery around 1910. He rode a mule because he couldn't afford a horse. In this story, Emeline used the post office in the Pickwick Mercantile.

Print:

Of course, by this time, printing presses had printed many books, newspapers, catalogs, and magazines. Libraries were found in large cities, but small towns usually kept books for check-out at the school, church, general store, or perhaps someone's home. The general store typically sold copies of the local newspapers, the primary source of news.

Acknowledgements

This story began after the initial release of *A Journey*; however, renovating four houses replaced writing for two years. It took another year to complete it, including research, writing, and many edits.

I sincerely thank everyone instrumental in the successful completion of this novel.

Influencers:

Barbara Ellin Fox

Lura (Katy) Houk

Kristi Lefholz

Ella Anderson

Research Mentors:

Barbara Ellin Fox

William Rook

Mid-Continent Library
On-line Resources

Author Software & Resources:
Scrivener, AutoCrit, Atticus
Power Thesaurus
ProWritingAid
Book Brush

Critique Partners & Editor:
Louise Hare, The History Quill Group Coach
The History Quill (critique group)
Fija Callaghan

Illustrations: *Claudia Gadotti*
Audiobook Performance: *Ceci Garcia*
Cover & Interior Design: *Design for Writers*
Support and Encouragement:
My husband, Ed
My co-workers at Van's Fence

Kathy J Perry
Author, Speaker

As a young girl, I loved reading and writing. My favorite book when I was a middle-schooler was *Adventures of Perrine*. The historical, foreign setting attracted me. Most of all, I identified with Perrine and wanted to be like her: courageous, discerning, resourceful, and self-reliant. Written in the 1800s, it is no longer in print, but it inspired the writing of the Emeline series: *A Journey* and *Finding Strength (During the Panic of 1893)*.

A former teacher, my reason for writing is to provide today's youth with quality, relatable stories. I believe all stories, for good or bad, impact readers. We'll always value stories that illustrate moral character backed by biblical principles.

I'm currently "retired", but work part-time as an administrative assistant, while enjoying painting with watercolors, and baking. My husband of 42 years and I live north of the river in Kansas City, Missouri with our dog, Taz.

Claudia Gadotti

Illustrator

I was born and raised with one brother and two sisters in Trento, Italy. I always loved books, excelled in art, and wanted to be an illustrator someday. My parents did not want me to become an artist, but a nurse, so that's what I did for a while.

Eventually, I moved to London for a year to learn English, and then went to California. There I worked as an au pair before becoming a student at the Academy of Art University in San Francisco where I graduated with a BFA in art. My professional art career started from there.

I have enjoyed illustrating children's books for sixteen years now and I also teach art part-time in a primary school. I currently make my home with my husband and two dogs in New Zealand. We have lived here for nineteen years and love it.

Ceci Garcia

Narrator

Ceci Garcia is a born Kansan, now living in Florida. She has studied acting her whole life and is thrilled to be trusted to bring characters to life! Her passions include books, psychology, and crafting her own stories.